The latest volume in Reynolds' popular True-to-Life Series from Hamilton High is the ripped-from-the-headlines story of Eddie Barajas from Reynolds' novel *Shut Up*. Now seventeen, he is a senior at Hamilton High. When he impulsively paints over incendiary graffiti on one of the school's walls, he finds himself the target of a gang of white supremacists, who begin posting racist comments about him on social media (Eddie's mom is Mexican; his almost stepdad is black.) One example: "Enemy of free speech. Impure race. Defective." And then, after he stops one of their number from fleeing after a racially motivated incident, he is actually assaulted by a group of them, leaving him with a concussion and other serious injuries. Although he doesn't see his assailants, he recognizes the voice of one of them as being that of a boy in his yoga class at school. What will he choose to do: tell the police or take matters into his own hands? Reynolds does an excellent job of capturing the climate of bigotry and hatred that increasingly affects the lives of contemporary Americans in the wake of the 2016 election. Never didactic, her story is dramatic and compelling while her characters are fully realized and highly empathetic, especially Eddie and Rosie, the girl he meets and falls in love with. The combination of gentle love story and novel of gritty realism makes for a compelling read. The pull-no-punches novel is sure to excite discussion and -- excellent for both classroom use and independent reading -- it is a valuable addition to Reynold's excellent Hamilton High series.

—Michael Cart, *Booklist* columnist and reviewer

Reynolds' novel crackles with electric dialogue and vivid day-to-day details today's high school students will absolutely recognize as their own. The teens in *Eddie's Choice* anguish about not only life-choices but the expectations and pressures of family and friends. *Eddie's Choice* is a worthy successor to Reynolds' other prize-winning "True-to-Life from Hamilton High" novels.

—Daniel Acosta, author of *Iron River*

Another intense, true-to-life teen novel from Ms. Reynolds has Eddie Barajas, grown-up and in high school. Eddie is thrust in to doing the right thing when he encounters members of the white supremacist group and has to face a life-threatening situation. Reynolds once again does not hold back and the intense and real life of teenager life and difficult choices is brought to reality. The reader is rooting for Eddie as he deals with his past and sorts his way through his journey to his future. My students love these books and for many students it is the first set of novels they truly enjoyed and comprehended."

—Robert Huynh, English teacher, San Gabriel High School, Alhambra CA

After surviving a traumatic event when he was much younger, Hamilton High teen Eddie, is facing a new problem. Racial bulling and a group of white supremacists have affected the diverse students at school. Should Eddie leave it alone or stand up to the bullies and put a target on his back? Marilyn Reynolds writes what teens can relate to. She brings what is happening now in young people's lives and creates a page turning novel.

—Ramona Cheek, Teacher-librarian, Central High School, Fresno

In this stand-alone sequel to *Shut Up* where Eddie was a victim of sexual abuse as a young boy, Reynolds expertly shows Eddie's life as a teen experiencing his first love and learning what it means to be a true American.

— Dr. Joan F. Kaywell, Founder of the Ted Hipple Special Collection of Autographed YA & Tween Books

Right on target for Marilyn Reynolds: the continuation of Eddie's story from *Shut Up* delves into the thinking and reasoning progress of the teen mind.

—Andrea Catania-Stephenson, Teacher-librarian, El Camino Fundamental High School, Sacramento

It's often a challenge to find narratives that reflect the diversity of my young clients. Because I work in rural Eastern Washington, I have Hispanic clients, both teens and adults, who are especially concerned about some of the issues discussed in this book, including immigration policy and the white nationalist movement. Thank God for the Hamilton High Series! I'm grateful to have a book that explores issues of immigration policy and provides an opportunity for them to see people like themselves in a contemporary YA novel.
—Leesa Phaneuf, social worker, Walla Walla WA

The Complete True-to-Life Series

from Hamilton High

EDDIE'S CHOICE

Marilyn Reynolds

New Wind Publishing

SACRAMENTO, CALIFORNIA

New Wind Publishing

Copyright © 2019 by Marilyn Reynolds

Library of Congress Cataloging-in-Publication Data

Reynolds, Marilyn, 1935-

Eddie's Choice / Marilyn Reynolds

Summary: Senior Eddie Barajas stands up against white supremacists at his high school and becomes their target, triggering his old fears and new choices.

ISBN 978-1-929777-11-2

LCCN 2019905416

1. Teenagers—Fiction. 2.White supremacy movements—Fiction. 3.Bullying—Fiction. 4. High schools—Fiction. I. Title. II. Series: Reynolds, Marilyn. 1935- True-to-life series from Hamilton High

Cover design: Tannehill Designs

New Wind Publishing
Sacramento, California 95819
www.newwindpublishing.com

"Together, all things are possible."
—Cesar Chavez

To the young organizers and participants of the Global Climate Strike, the Parkland youth of #NeverAgain, the Gay Straight Alliance Networks, and to young people everywhere who work to heal our broken world.

Thank you to:

Katie McCleary and the Tuesday writers, Ed Cole, Susan Frazier, Kathy Les, Jasmine Shahbandi, and Julie Woodside.

Jan Haag and her loft writers.

Elizabeth Rosner and the Mendocino and Sea Ranch workshop participants.

Deborah Meltvedt and her students at Health Professions High School in her Medical Science class and Creative Writing Club, especially Lizeth, Alaiya, Angelica, Desyre, Blair, Lilliana, Sami, Gracie, and Diana.

Ramona Cheek, Teacher/Librarian, Central High School West, Fresno; Andrea Catania-Stephenson, Teacher/Librarian, El Camino Fundamental High School, Sacramento; Dr. Joan F. Kaywell, Founder of the Ted Hipple Special Collection of Autographed YA & Tween Books; for early readings, and for all they do on behalf of young readers of all levels and interests.

The 916 Ink writers at Walnutwood, especially Nick.

San Gabriel High School teachers, Cady Burkhart and Robert Huynh, and to their students for sharing their takes on life as they know it.

Maryam Jabari, Keith Atwater and Subei Reynolds Kyle for enlightening me in more ways than one.

Halima Smati of the Salam Islamic Center, and the participants in the center's leadership program, for their openness and willingness to share experiences and perceptions with me.

Dale Dodson, Kathy Harvey, Karen Kasaba, Beth Silverstein and Jeannie Ward, for invaluable help as readers, and for so much more.

CONTENTS

CHAPTER ONE

Treading Water

I turn into Brent's driveway and give a quick beep of the horn. Labor Day Sunday. Last beach day before we start our senior year at Hamilton High. Brent comes out with his rolled-up beach towel, his mom close behind. She comes to my side of the car.

"Hey, Mama B."

"Hi, Eddie," she says, handing sunscreen and a straw hat through the window. "Make sure that clown uses these, will you?"

I take the hat and sunscreen from her and put them on Brent's lap. "He won't listen to me. Maybe you should come with us?"

"Hmmm. Maybe," she says. We laugh.

Brent punches me in the arm. "Let's go!"

I've known Brent since kindergarten. We used to be at each other's houses a lot, back when we were still climbing trees and building Lego cities. I always had dinner at his house on pizza night, and when it was pizza night at our house, he had dinner with us.

Back then, we always sat next to each other in class, too—Brent Bruno, Eduardo Barajas, with no "B" names in between—so we knew each other pretty well.

Cameron's waiting in front of his house, so busy with his phone he doesn't even look up until I give him a loud blast of the horn.

Brent and I are kind of average looking. We probably weigh about the same, somewhere in the low 150s. We were the same height in the fourth grade, and we're the same height now, except then we were 4'3" and now we're 5'9". I'm a little darker. His hair's curlier. But, you know, pretty average. My mom, Max, says I can't possibly be average looking because of my sparkling eyes and my "manly physique." She goes overboard with that "manly physique" stuff though. I mean, yeah, I work out some and do the strength building kind of yoga, so I'm a little bit buff. Nothing special, though, except to a mom.

Cameron's tall, probably six feet, and skinny, light hair with a face full of freckles and zits. And he dresses funny, always a long-sleeved white shirt with a tie, like he's a 1950s TV dad, except his tie is always loose, and his sleeves are rolled up. And he wears Tough Skin Jeans. Tough Skins! The kind nobody over the age of eight would be caught dead wearing! But the thing is, Cameron's always got a bunch of girls hanging around him. Popular girls, too, like the whole Hamilton High cheer team. I don't get it. Brent thinks it's because Cameron plays drums. He says girls like drummers. Maybe so. Brent's got those four sisters, so he knows about girls.

I pull into the Gato Gas station at the edge of town. Cash only. Windshield cleaner and paper towel bins are always empty. The little window on the pump with the rolling dials that show how much gas you're getting and how much money it's costing is so scratched up you can't read any of the numbers. But it's cheap.

Cameron and Brent go inside to pay for gas. That's the deal. My car. Their gas.

While they're paying and pumping, I pull *The Autobiography of Malcolm X* from under the seat and find my place. William, my sort of stepdad, loaned the book to me. I usually like his books. It's about a black guy who was a straight A student in junior high school. He was crazy smart, and he wanted to be a lawyer, but after some white teacher told him practicing law wasn't a "realistic goal for a nigger," he dropped out. How screwed up is that?

I was about halfway through ninth grade when William and his daughter, Imani, AKA the pest, moved in with us. She was in kindergarten then, and she always pestered me to watch "Frozen" with her, and to be Kristoff to her Anna. That, or I'd barely get off my bike in the driveway and she'd come running out, both arms lifted, yelling, "Swing me! Swing me!"

Anyways, the first thing William did after he got Imani's room set up with her "Frozen" bedspread, and posters, and her giant stuffed Sven pillow, was to add another section of bookshelves under the dining room window, next to Max's, where she had all of her books carefully arranged.

So I should tell you why me and my brother call our mom Max. It's from a long time ago when we were both still little. I was probably about four, so Mario was around twelve. We'd been complaining, me mostly, but Mario, too, about how our mom was never around like other moms—Brent's mom, or Mario's friend Walker's mom. I hated daycare and that she didn't bring cupcakes on my birthday. Mario hated that he had to walk me home from daycare at 4:30 every day and stay with me 'til Max got home from work. On what I guess was a seriously whiny day, Max sat us in our triangle at the kitchen table and said, "Let's get this straight." Max is famous for her "Let's get this straight" talks. At least she's famous for them with me and Mario.

On that day, after one whine too many, it was "Let's get this straight. I'm sorry I got you guys such a minimum dad. I wish he'd been the kind of dad who took care of you, who took care of us of all. He wasn't a good dad to you, Mario. I know you still remember some of that. And he wasn't *any* kind of dad to you, Eddie. Ever. He was just the sperm donor for you."

I didn't know what she meant by sperm donor back then, but Max never talked down to us. She went over her whole schedule, Macy's, and the National Guard to make enough money to support us, Dental Assistant school so pretty soon she could get a better job that paid more.

"See, it's because he was such a minimum dad that I've got to be a maximum mom."

And from then on, we called her Max. But back to the bookshelves.

William's shelves are the same height, but they don't exactly match. Max's are made of oak, a light tan, and William's are Ikea-black.

It wasn't planned that way or anything, but it's kind of symbolic how Max-the-Mexican has brown bookshelves that hold a lot of brown people stories—stuff by Sandra Cisneros and Gary Soto, and about Cesar Chavez and Dolores Huerta. And William-the-African-American has black bookshelves with a lot of black people stories, like about Martin Luther King and Booker T. Washington, and a book we read in 9th grade English, *I Know Why the Caged Bird Sings*, plus this book I'm reading right now, *The Autobiography of Malcolm X.*

Not long after William and Imani moved in, Brent came over to play video games. He looked at the tan shelves and read a few titles, and the black shelves and read a few titles, and said, "Where're the white shelves?"

William called out from the other room, "The white shelves are in your classrooms, and your library, and every other damned place in this country!"

"Just asking," Brent called back.

William laughed. "Just sayin'."

* * * * *

Tank filled and back on the 210, I switch the radio to 105.2, classic rock. Our compromise station. If Cameron had his way, it would be the jazz station. Brent? Hip-hop. Me? Probably pop-rock with a bit of Latin.

Triple digit heat and the air is heavy with L. A. basin smog so the beach is the place to be. But traffic is bumper to bumper on the 605, the freeway we'd take to the beach, so I stay on the 210.

"Traffic sucks," I say. "Let's go to the lake."

"That's cool," Cameron says. "There's always a lot of fierce girls at Arrowhead."

Instead of going on to Arrowhead, I take the turn off to Lake Gregory. Closer and probably not as crowded.

"Not Gregory," Cameron groans. "Too many rug rats."

"Driver's choice," I say.

At the lake we strip down to our trunks, grab our towels, lock our phones in the car, run to the shore, plunge into the cold mountain water, and race to the dock. Cameron gets there first, then me, then Brent. That's how it's been since we were freshmen, like 99% of the time. Cameron's always the fastest—fastest out of the car, fastest to the dock, fastest out of class, fastest to the lunch table. Maybe longer legs have something to do with it, but it's like he's always in a hurry, always has to be first in line, always has to be first to get wherever he's going. He just got his license three months ago, and he's already had two speeding tickets.

On the dock and shaking water from my hair, I see these four girls sitting near the ladder, watching. I dive back in and swim farther out to a buoy. When I look back, I see that Cameron's already got the girls looking at him like he's a god or something. Like I said, I don't get it. Cameron's so skinny you can barely see him when he stands sideways. And there's the zits. But the girls hang around him like he's Justin Bieber or something.

I duck underwater to cool off, and when I come up, I see this girl swimming toward the buoy, about five feet away. She takes another stroke and reaches for the buoy. I move over to make room for her. Awkward.

"Hi," she says.

"Hi," I say, letting go of the buoy and treading water.

"You don't remember me, do you?"

I give her a closer look. I guess I've seen her around school, but remember? "No." I'm not too good at this talking to girls shit.

"I'm Rosie. Fourth grade. Ms. Summers' class."

I tread water.

"Oh, yeah," I say. "You've changed."

She laughs. "I hope so!"

I tread water.

"I remember those funny cat pictures you used to draw, and your jokes. It's like you always had a joke, and you were so funny, Ms. Summers never got mad at you."

I still tread water.

"Know any jokes?" she asks.

"Just, you know, little kid jokes."

"Tell me a little kid joke. I've got a little sister who loves little kid jokes."

I tread water.

The thing is, I *do* know a lot of little kid jokes because of Imani. We have a deal that if I tell her a joke, she has to not mention anything about "Frozen" for thirty minutes.

"Come on."

"Yeah, so, well…Why does the elephant bring toilet paper to the party?"

"I don't know…why?"

"No, you have to guess."

"Ummmm. Because toilet paper was on sale?'

"Noooo. Because he was a party pooper."

Rosie laughs like, I don't know, like I've turned into that Bo Burnham comedian guy or something. Her laugh gets me laughing so hard I have to grab the buoy to stay up.

Brent dives from the dock and comes up in front of our buoy, wiping water from his eyes.

"Man, I could hear you laughing all the way from the dock! What's so funny?"

"Hard to say," I tell him, my laughter fading into the water.

"Try me," he says. "What's so funny."

He looks from me to Rosie, whose laughter has also faded...but her smile hasn't. I'm noticing she's got a great smile.

"You had to be here," I tell him.

"I *am* here."

"But you *weren't*."

"Okay," Rosie says, "Why does the elephant bring toilet..."

"NOOOO! Not the old party pooper elephant joke!"

Brent lunges at me, pushing my shoulders down. I sink under the buoy. Come up on the other side. Brent lunges again, and again I go under. This time when I come up, Rosie's swimming in the direction of the dock, already halfway there. I don't know a lot about girls, but I do know they get bored when guys start messing around.

Brent reaches for the other side of the buoy.

"Why was she out here talking to you?"

"I don't know. She said she remembered me from Palm Ave. Fourth grade."

"I went to Palm Ave. She never talks to me."

"Maybe she doesn't remember you. She remembers me because I was funny."

"I was funny at Palm Avenue in the fourth grade. I was funnier than you. Besides, you were barely even in fourth grade at Palm. You were supposed to be master of ceremony for that Harvest Festival thing, and you didn't even show up for it. You didn't show up again until the ninth grade, so how can she remember you and not me?"

"Maybe I'm just memorable."

"Your hand's memorable. Everybody remembers Captain Hook. Maybe if I had a creepy Captain Hook hand, she'd remember me."

"Doubt it," I say, sinking under water and surfacing right before I get to the dock. We're like that, Cameron and Brent and I, always raggin' on each other. That's what friends do. Guys, anyways. Brent's "Blockhead." He's one of the smartest guys I know. He even did that Academic Decathlon thing last year. Except he could never take a math question. He can count to 100, add two and two, and say his times tables up to the fives. That's about it. And get this: Brent's dad wants him to be an *engineer*, like he is.

Cameron is "Zitter," for obvious reasons. I'm "Captain Hook", or mostly just "Hook". On my right hand, I've got a thumb, two grown together stubs for my index finger and my middle finger, and just a glob of flesh where my fourth finger and pinkie would attach, if I had a fourth finger and a pinky. I came out that way. Not a problem. I can do anything anyone else can. Well, I didn't take piano lessons, but I'm okay. My hand's a mark of distinction. People who don't remember my name say: "that kid with the hand." Which is stupid because all the kids have hands, but everyone knows they're talking about me when they say "that kid with the hand."

I start up the ladder to the dock. Too many people. I mostly like people one or two at a time. Three's about my limit. I slide back into the water and swim to shore.

* * * * *

Later, when I see Rosie walk to the drink stand, I go scoot in behind her. I don't want a drink—I just want to stand near her. I know it sounds crazy, but something happened out there at the buoy. At least, that's how it felt to me.

We get drinks and go to a shady place beside the stand. I take a long swallow of lemonade and try to think of something to say.

"Did you get the classes you want?" I ask. What a dork! All of a sudden, I'm asking questions like your grandma would ask?

Rosie doesn't seem to mind though. "Yeah. but I don't have much choice. Between having to take AP English and

History, French IV and AP Calculus, and staying with Peer Communications and Choir, plus playing soccer, my program's set. How about you? Did you get the classes you want?"

"I got the two I want. I don't want any of the rest of them. I'm not much of a school boy."

"Why not? You were like the smartest kid in Mrs. Summer's class. You were a school boy then."

"Yeah. Well, that was back before they gave kids homework." I take another long swallow of lemonade.

"Well, so, what are the two classes you wanted to get?"

"WriteLight and Yoga."

"Zero period and 6th period?"

"Yeah."

"What do you have in between?"

"Dunno. I've got whatever it says on my program card. I'll look Tuesday morning."

Rosie gives me a raised eyebrow look.

I focus on my lemonade. Is it my turn to talk? It was easier when we were in the water, like treading water made it okay to be quiet.

Rosie looks back toward where her friends are sitting. "I think Fiona's ready to leave. I should go." She tosses her soda bottle into the recycle bin and walks back to her friends.

"Bye," I call after her. At least I know to say that.

She turns and flashes her toothpaste ad smile at me. "Bye."

* * * * *

Hot sun, cold water, gritty sand, stop-and-go traffic. I zone out in the white noise that is Brent and Cameron worrying about AP classes, and college essays, and applications. I'm watching the road ahead, but it's Rosie's smile I'm seeing.

It's after seven by the time we take the off-ramp toward Hamilton Heights. Turning onto Main Street, on the way to Cameron's, I see crowds of people a few blocks down, in front of City Hall.

At the next block, there's a barrier with two guys in fluorescent vests, waving their flashlights to move traffic off of Main Street and onto 2nd. Closer now, and barely moving, we see cops all over the place, some in riot gear. Some are on horses. There's a crowd of people in front of City Hall with signs that say stuff like "Justice for Devon Parker," and "Equality for ALL," and "Black Lives Matter," and other stuff I can't read from here. Then there's a barrier of cops between the Black Lives Matter group and another bunch of demonstrators with tiki torches and clubs, and signs that say "White Lives Matter," and "America for Americans," and "P8RIOTS," and some with swastikas.

"I wouldn't want to get in the way of one of those horses," Brent says. "They're huge!"

Traffic's picked up again, and the crowd's soon out of sight.

"I don't get that Black Lives Matter shit," Cameron says. "Like, doesn't everybody's life matter?

"Devon Parker's didn't matter," I say. "Or Michael Brown's or Tamir Rice's or Stephon Clark's, or a ton of others."

"From what I saw on TV, the cop shot that Michael Brown guy in self-defense."

"Really?" I say.

"Well, he'd stolen stuff from a store, like those cigarillo things."

"Not a death penalty offense," I say.

"William's got you brainwashed," Cameron says.

"More like brain expanded," I say.

"Somebody's got to get your brain expanded," Brent says with a laugh. "With the amount of work you do at school, it won't happen at Hamilton High."

We all laugh at that. Smoothing the waters is one of Brent's talents, maybe because there are so many people in his family to get along with.

When I get home, Max is at the kitchen table, staring into her laptop.

"I thought this was game night," I say.

Max is glued to her computer, her phone face up, showing an unanswered text to William.

"Where's William?"

She turns the computer screen toward me. City hall. Torches, horses, riot gear, signs . . . oh shit. William. Black Lives Matter. I sit next to Max and watch the screen, following the ribbon across the bottom, "Live news report from Hamilton Heights. White nationalist groups chanting racist slogans and hurling rocks threaten peaceful Black Lives Matter demonstration."

Max turns to me. "Look at that bunch of P8RIOT guys with their clubs and torches! It's like the Make America Great bunch is drawing all of the racists and haters out from whatever rocks they've been hiding under."

Max's frown is tight, and deep. Like her whole face is frowning—like the frowns she brought back from Iraq. "It's all good guys versus bad guys," she says, "and anyone who's an immigrant, or Muslim, or doesn't look like the guys in the MAGA hats is a bad guy. Fear and hate. It worries me."

On the screen, there're more guys with torches now, yelling, throwing stuff—I'm not sure what—toward the Black Lives Matter demonstrators, who are throwing stuff back. More police, with dogs, trying to keep the groups separated.

"Will you get Imani to bed?" Max says, not looking away from the computer screen.

"Sure."

All I want is a hot shower and to fall into bed, but I know Imani's bedtime routine as well as anyone, and Max'll stay glued to the news until she hears from William.

I stand in the hall and call to Imani, "You want strawberry or lavender?"

"Lavender," she says, not turning around.

I start the water in the bathtub, pour lavender bubble bath powder directly under the stream of water and watch it foam up. While the tub fills, I get Imani's PJs from her top dresser drawer, set them on a stool at the end of the bathtub, squeeze toothpaste onto her "Frozen" toothbrush, and shut the water off.

"Bath's ready," I tell her.

"I want to see the rest of this!"

"Nope. It's already way past your bedtime," I say, shutting off the TV.

"No fair!"

"Go on. Get your bath before the water gets cold."

She pouts.

"If you get your bath and are all ready for bed in twenty minutes, I've got a joke for you."

"A bear joke?"

"Some joke," I tell her.

I stretch out on the couch, thinking about Rosie, and about the start of my senior year, and Black Lives Matter, and Rosie, and...

"Joke!" startles me fully awake.

"In bed," I say.

Once she's all snuggled down in bed, I ask her, "Why aren't Teddy Bears ever hungry?"

"Why?"

I wait for the guess.

"Because Mama Bear always feeds them?"

"No, because they're always stuffed."

"Not a very good joke," she says.

"The best I could do," I tell her. I gesture toward her bookshelves.

"Daddy's going to read to me," she says.

"Well, he's not home right now. What book do you want?"

"I want my Daddy!" she says, sniffling. "I'm scared."

"Do you want me to read to you or not?"

She shakes her head. I turn on her nightlight and switch the ceiling light off. "Goodnight, then," I say.

I'm in the bathroom, so ready for a shower, when Imani calls, "Eddie! I'm scared!" I wait, hoping to hear Max on her way to Imani's room. "Eddie!"

I go back to her room.

"I want my Daddy. I'm scared."

"Try counting sheep," I tell her.

"Stay with me," she says.

I take my shoes off and lie down next to her, on top of the covers, feeling her hand in mine as I drift—or more like plunge—into sleep.

Sometime after midnight, William's weight on the other side of the bed wakens me. He's looking down at Imani. "Thanks, Eddie," he whispers.

As I walk toward the door, I see William lean his face down beside Imani's.

"Daddy?"

"I'm here, Baby."

I fall into my own bed, showerless, and dream of treading water.

CHAPTER TWO

What Eddie Knows

Tuesday morning, I jostle my way through the metal detectors and head out to the quad. Walking past the Tech building, I see a new piece of graffiti shit: "Kill Raghead Muslim Terrorists," slapped up with a black permanent marker. So much for the back-to-school email reminder that "Hamilton High is a Hate-free Environment." It pisses me off, the haters who want to get rid of everyone who's not white.

Underneath the Muslim hate, underlined twice, it says "14 Words." I don't know what that means, but I'm pretty sure it's more hate shit.

At the quad, there are six lunch tables lined up with office people and aides behind them, handing out programs and first-day information.

I join Brent in the A-D line. He looks all anxious and worried.

"How's it going?"

He shakes his head. "I told my dad I don't *want* to be an engineer! Like I've been telling him at least once a month for the past four years! And he tells me, 'Stick with it. You've got a great opportunity here!' like he's been telling me for the past *eight* years."

Phong wanders over from the I-L line carrying his program packet. Phong Liu.

"Did you take WriteLight again this year?"

I nod.

"Cool! Maybe you can turn Simba into a vampire. He can help Vernon."

I laugh. "Simba's a vegetarian, except for mice."

"Yeah, but if he eats a vampire mouse, then he'll be a vampire cat."

Phong cracks me up. He's got this thing for a cowardly vampire—Vernon the Cowardly Vampire. He's always doodling pictures of him. Vernon looks a lot like that guy Edward in the vampire movies, except Edward has these wicked teeth and Vernon has tiny baby teeth.

Me, I doodle pictures of Simba the cat, who is strong and brave. He's my doodling specialty—has been since I was a little kid and obsessed with "The Lion King." I even named my kitten Simba because I wanted him to grow into a lion. What can I say? I was a kid. Simba grew into a regular cat, like the one I'm drawing now.

"Later," Phong says as I reach the front of the line.

Ms. Cordano, one of the office ladies, hands me my packet. As I step aside to wait for Brent, I notice Rosie about halfway back and wander over. She points to the bulky envelope I have tucked under my arm.

"What classes do you have?"

"I haven't looked yet."

She laughs. "Then, look!"

I take my program out and read the list of classes to her as she inches along in line. "WriteLight. World History. I like history," I tell her. "I probably won't do the homework, but class discussion will be okay."

Rosie's looking at me like maybe I'm from another planet or something.

"Environmental Ecology. I don't even know what that is," I tell her, "but I've heard it's easy and it'll meet the science requirement. 20th Century American Lit. That might be okay. I might read some of those books…"

Finally at the front of the line, Rosie gets her packet and rips it open. She skims her program information and waves it in the air.

"Brianna!!" she yells to a girl standing over by the fence.

The girl runs over to Rosie. "You got it?"

"Yes!"

"Me, too!"

Rosie throws her arms around Brianna, and they jump around, laughing and hugging and doing that squealing girl thing. "We got it!" Rosie says. "We got it!"

"Come on!" Brianna grabs Rosie by the hand and moves back toward the other girls.

"In a sec," Rosie says, turning back to me. "So, American Lit and what else?" she says, her smile still all glowing.

Brianna looks from Rosie to me and back to Rosie. "I'll see you at the assembly, then," Brianna says, and goes back to the others.

"What else have you got?" Rosie asks.

"What have *you* got that you're so happy about?"

She shows me her program, pointing to sixth period, Tuesday and Thursday. R.O.P. Music Therapy. She says it's some "consortium" with students chosen from all of the schools in the county—super hard to get into. But if you do get in, it's almost certain you can get into this highly competitive Music Therapy program at University of the Foothills. "I've wanted to be a music therapist since I first learned about it in seventh grade and UOF has this great program. I love music and I love helping people, so it'll be perfect...What're your other classes?" she asks.

"Earth Science, Life Skills, Yoga, Business Math."

"Business Math? Not Calculus?"

"I'm not going to college. I don't need calculus. Besides, I'm learning the painting business with my sort of stepdad. Business Math will be good to know."

"Painting?"

"Yeah. House painting. Office painting. Buildings. You know."

Rosie stands looking at me for too long. Too serious. I'd like to be treading water.

"But...I remember how smart you were back in the 4th grade. Why aren't you going to college?"

"I guess I'm smart enough to know I don't want to go to college."

"Well, okay, speaking of 4th grade, know any more of those little kid jokes?" She laughs, like even asking is a joke.

It's a relief to get off the no-college subject, so I tell her, "Here's the one I told Imani yesterday afternoon so she'd stop telling me every detail of "Frozen" for about the millionth time. I told her the joke in exchange for some quiet time."

"Oh, my gosh. My little sister is constantly talking about 'Frozen.' She watches it practically every day when she gets home from school, and then she tells me all about it, like she did the day before, and the day before that."

"Try buying some quiet time with a joke."

"Zoe can't possibly be quiet for an hour."

"Start with half an hour."

"What's the joke you used for your stepsister?"

"My sort of stepsister."

"Okay, so what's the joke you used for your *sort of* stepsister?"

"It might not work for your sister."

"C'mon!"

"Okay. Why are elephants smarter than chickens?"

"Why?"

"You have to guess."

"Because they have bigger brains?"

"No."

"Why?"

"Think about it. They have to be smarter, because have you ever heard of Kentucky Fried Elephant?"

Rosie laughs and laughs. It's kind of musical and tinkly, but hearty at the same time. I love her laugh. She's a great audience for dumb, corny jokes. She probably wouldn't ever like me, like for a boyfriend, but...?

It's a minimum day schedule. We check in at classes, get our textbooks and whatever else teachers hand out on the first day, reading lists, schedule of assignments, that stuff. There's a note on my program card from Mr. Kaiser, the senior counselor: "See me at 12:30."

I go to his office after 6th period when what I most want to do is go to lunch. I text Brent. Me: *Stuck in Kaiser's office.*

Brent: *I'm starving. Frowning face, triple taco emojis*

Me: *Go ahead. I'll catch up.*

Brent: *Just hurry.*

Me: *Thumbs up.*

Brent: *Say yes and nod your head to everything.*

Me: *Okay emoji*

I've already had five texts from Brent, all saying "hurry!" and three texts from Cameron saying "starving" by the time Kaiser calls me into his office. He takes my folder from the "permanent records" file cabinet next to his desk and opens it.

"What classes are you taking?" he asks.

I hand my program card to him. He frowns. Shakes his head. Turns the open folder to face me. There's my whole high school history, neatly recorded grades next to every class I've taken, in consecutive order, semester by semester. I know what comes next. It's the old "not living up to your potential" talk that I got from my freshman counselor, and sophomore counselor, and junior counselor. It always comes within a week or two of when school starts in September, and again a week or two before school gets out in June. Usually though, they don't give me the talk on the very first day of school. This first day thing totally gets in the way of my back-to-school lunch tradition with Brent and Cameron.

Mr. Kaiser points to numbers in a box at the top of my transcript. "Look at these test scores, Eddie. Some of your college-bound friends would be thrilled with such test scores."

I shrug.

"And look at this!" he says, pointing to another section. "All through high school, you've taken the easiest classes you can get by with and your grades are mediocre at best. And this?" He pushes my program card back to me. "This is a joke! WriteLight, and Yoga," he sneers, then lets out a long sigh. "You've got such potential! And you're squandering it. Why?"

I shrug.

Another long sigh. "What're you going to be doing next year, after all of your friends are off to college, working their butts off to make something of themselves? You gonna be sitting around wasting your excellent brain on video games?"

"I don't play video games," I say, which is mostly true.

"People in your class are going to be doctors, and educators, and musicians, and business administrators, and tech experts. What are *you* going to be?"

I hate that "what are you going to be?" question.

"I already *am*." I tell him. "I've *been* from the day I was born."

Long pause. Slow head shake. "Okay then, how *will* you be wasting your brain while all of your friends are growing theirs in college? What will *you* be doing?"

"I'll be working with my stepdad in his painting business."

Kaiser shakes his head sadly again, like painting houses is work for losers or something. It pisses me off. I bet William's read twice as many books in his life as this college graduate guy has. William drives a year-old Lexus. Kaiser drives an old beat-up Prius. So, I don't know where he gets off thinking college is so much better than going straight to work at a job I like. After another long sigh, Kaiser puts my records back in the file folder and pushes it aside.

"Okay. I give up. Waste it if you want to. It's your life," he says.

"Right. I *know* that."

Cameron and Brent are waiting by my car when I get to the parking lot. "Starving!" Brent says.

"Double starving," Cameron says.

Our first day of school lunch is always at the Taqueria. It's close to 1:30 by the time we get there, and the lunch crowd's mostly gone by now. Much earlier and there'd be a line out to the sidewalk. We order at the counter and take a table toward the back. I hear the cook and one of the busboy guys in the kitchen, arguing in Spanish about the best way to cook a goat. Rotisserie over a fire pit, one says. The other says it's got to be grilled.

Except for a few (maybe more than a few) swear words, and words for family—*abuela, abuelo, tia, tio, gracias, de nada*—I don't speak much Spanish. I understand almost everything, though. While I was living in Redville with Tia Josie and Tio Hector, they'd always slip back and forth between Spanish and English, and Spanish was the playground language when I was going to school up there. I took Spanish in the ninth grade to check off the foreign language requirement for high school graduation, but that was a different kind of Spanish.

Cameron looks back toward the kitchen. "I'm weak with hunger," he says, slumping down in his chair.

"Calculus is going to be a bitch," Brent says. "It'd be a bitch with anyone, but I've got that asshole Epstein."

Epstein has a reputation for being one of the toughest and meanest teachers on campus. Brent's frowning so hard his eyebrows practically meet in the middle. "God, I dread that class."

"Know what you mean," Cameron says. "Fourth year French is gonna kill me."

The goat cooking expert brings our order to us. I've got three grilled fish tacos, refried beans, and a salad. Cameron's got carnitas and a double order of refried beans, with a double order of cheese on top. Brent's got the super burrito. Really, I think it's got every single thing on the menu all rolled up in a giant flour tortilla, then slathered in red sauce and cheese.

Cameron looks at my tacos. "Fish? Grilled?" he says.

That's something else we rag on each other about. What we eat.

I nod toward his carnitas. "Pig? In lard?"

Brent cuts into his too-big-to-put-in-your-mouth burrito and takes a giant forkful, but he's staring off into space like he doesn't even hear us.

"Why not give yourself a break?" I say. "Take Business Math instead of calculus. It'd be an easy change—same period as Epstein's calculus. I could help you."

He gives me a long, serious look. "Then, could I come live with you when my dad kicks me out?"

Cameron groans. "High school's supposed to be the best years of our lives, but I already know I'm going to hate senior year. What if I've already lived the best years of my life? That sucks."

"Yeah, I know this is going to be the *worst* year of my life, ever," Brent says.

"Take Yoga. It'd help you de-stress," I tell them.

"Just looking at Yoga Joe stresses me out. I couldn't sit through fifty minutes of him every day," Brent says, shaking his head. "Hey, but you know that book that was on our summer reading list? *Into the Wild*? I've been thinking maybe that Chris McCandless guy had the right idea. Get away from all the pressures of school and parents, live in the natural world."

"That's ridiculous," Cameron says. "You don't even like to go camping. Besides, the guy died out there. Starved to death. No burritos."

"Yeah, well I'd take more stuff with me, and warmer clothes . . ."

That's weird. I read the same book and no way did it sound like anything I would ever even think about doing. I know Brent feels stressed with the whole math thing, but into the wild? Really?

CHAPTER THREE

Smart Enough

Monday morning, second week of school, I'm waiting at the door when Miss May, loaded with books and notebooks, and a big tote bag full of I don't know what, comes swishing down the hall in one of those loose-fitting kind of dress things she always wears. And it's always swishing because she's always in a hurry. She's tall, with super close-cropped hair, like that Danai somebody in "Black Panther."

Her name's May Tucker, but she tells people to call her Miss May. Says she doesn't want to be formal. I don't think it's about being formal. I think she doesn't want some smart ass calling her Miss Fucker.

I've been her aide since the middle of my sophomore year, so over two years now. Being an aide in two classes makes me sound like a suck-up, but that's not how it is. Except for WriteLight, which is zero period, and Yoga, which is 6th period, I slide by.

Miss May shoves her stuff at me, unlocks the classroom door, and swishes inside. Her sleeves are rolled up to her elbows. I've never seen her sleeves unrolled. Unrolled. Is that even a word?

When I started the WriteLight class back when I was a sophomore, I thought maybe she was pregnant because of how she always wore the same kind of loose dress-thingy, but in lots of different colors. One day, Jessica, this girl with an annoying, baby kind of voice and a too sweet smile, said, "Miss May? Some of us are wondering, like, when's your little baby due?"

Miss May grabbed a long string of beads from the prompt basket and tied it tightly enough around her bunched up dress to show a waist about the size of Imani's and, matching Jessica's too sweet voice and smile, said, "My little baby's due sometime between ten years from now and never. How about your little baby?"

That got a big laugh from everyone but Jessica, who turned bright red. Her smile turned upside down, like maybe she was going to cry. At first, I thought, "That's what you get for asking such a stupid question," but then I felt kind of sorry for Jessica. I mean, she only asked out loud what a lot of us had been wondering about. Maybe Miss May felt sorry for her too, because a few minutes before the end of the period she told Jessica, in front of us all, that today wasn't the first time anyone asked, "When's your baby due?" She guessed maybe she invited such questions because of the way she dressed, but she was all about comfort and convenience. Let people think whatever.

But back to now. Miss May says, "Just dump that stuff on my desk. We'll sort it out later."

I have a regular aide routine for Miss May. First, I clean all the tables. The transportation department uses this room at night for school bus training classes and they're a bunch of slobs. They bring in hamburgers, fries, pizza, Big Gulps, cans of Red Bull and sodas, you name it; if it's junk food, it's part of learning to drive a school bus. And they never bother to throw their trash away, much less wipe up their spills.

After the tables, I unlock the supply cabinets and get out the pens, pencils, composition books, and snack stuff. We never used to lock anything up, but when the transportation department started using the room, things started to go missing. At first, it was pens and markers, a little bit at a time. Then we noticed the supply of composition books was dwindling. And a stapler went missing.

The morning Miss May discovered the huge canister of ground coffee she'd opened days before was nearly empty, that was it. From then on, it was lockdown. It turns out, school bus drivers can't be trusted.

So now the coffee maker is doing its thing. Water's come to a boil in the electric tea kettle. Tea bags, sugar, creamer, napkins, plastic spoons, all there. The box of bottled water is also on the coffee/tea table. Bananas, oranges, and protein bars fill a basket next to the coffee maker. Miss May says it's hard to write if you're hungry.

Mr. Taggerty, the music teacher, comes in and pours himself a cup of coffee. Miss May and Taggerty have what May calls an "I'll scratch your back, you scratch mine" arrangement. He gets his morning coffee, and she gets to use the copy machine that's in the choir room next door.

"Did you hear Agent Orange last night? About the Mexican criminals and rapists and drug lords at the border?" Taggerty asks Miss M. "How is that not racist?"

"Shhhh," she says, nodding in my direction.

"I know!" he says. "But how is he even a candidate??"

Miss May takes Taggerty by the arm and leads him out to the hall. There's some rule about teachers not talking about politics in school, but Taggerty's not the only one who can't help himself. It seems like a lot of teachers are just as worried as Max and William are about the coming election.

* * * * *

6:55. Five minutes before the zero-period bell. I step out into the hall to see if I can "happen" to catch Rosie on her way to choir. I get a glimpse of long, shiny, dark brown hair and cut through the crowd to meet her. If Rosie's hair were a paint sample, it would be Roasted Chestnut, Glossy.

"Hey, Rosie."

"Hey, Eddie," she says, flashing her Polar White smile. "Zoe loved your smart elephant joke."

"Zoe?"

"My little sister."

"Oh, yeah. Did it buy you quiet time?"

"I'll try that trick with the next joke..."

With the beginning of the annoyingly loud BUZZZZ of the tardy bell, we both rush to our classrooms. I slide into my seat as the last ZZZZ goes silent. I'm a master at sliding into my seat at the last nanosecond.

Phong's already in the desk next to me, his sketch pad out on the desk. While Miss May gives the general set-up of the class, Phong flips from one sketch to another, showing me new ideas for "Vernon the Cowardly Vampire." We both pretty much know the writing routine by heart. We write to prompts. Even though we're getting English credit, we don't mess with grammar, punctuation, spelling, or making every paragraph start with a topic sentence. There aren't any heavy, assigned topics, like analyze the symbolism in *The Scarlet Letter*, or "In a five-paragraph essay, explore the character development of Scout in *To Kill a Mockingbird.*" It's called WriteLight because we have a light-hearted attitude about writing.

Sometimes people write about heavy stuff though, like their dad beats them up or their mom's always drunk or something, but that's when the other part of "Light" comes in. Like it's shedding light on something that's been in the dark. WriteLight's the official name but we mostly just call it "Write."

The first week or so, the only people who read what they write are kids from last year's class. But after that, almost everyone reads their stuff. Miss May writes, too, and reads her work. She says we're all in it together.

Today, the prompt is to write about a place where you, or your character, feel safe. I think about where I feel safe—home, my car, this classroom, with family in Redville. But I end up writing about Simba, who feels safe on Pride Rock, where he can look out over the whole expanse of land, and rivers, and creatures of all shapes and sizes. I made it sound better than that, but you get the idea.

When it's Phong's turn to read, he starts off with how Vernon the Cowardly Vampire feels...that's as far as he gets when kids who were in this class last year start clapping. Everyone loves Vernon the Cowardly Vampire.

Phong starts over, "Vernon the Cowardly Vampire feels safe at the crowded Vegan Co-op meetings, where there's no pressure for him to refill his blood supply."

One girl reads a story about a mom who's addicted to oxycontin. It's supposed to be fiction, but she cries when she reads it, so I'm pretty sure it's her own story only with names changed. We talk about what's strong, or what will stay with us. What will stay with me is the image of the little brother trying to get his mom to wake up while the big sister is calling 911.

Back when I was a freshman, when I first took WriteLight, I never wanted to read my stuff out loud in class. First off, I'm a quiet kind of guy, and second, I didn't think it was any good. But Miss May kept pushing me. Not demanding exactly, but she kept at it. She did that with another kid, too, this girl, Felicia.

After weeks and weeks of inviting me to read and me disinviting myself, Miss May asked me to stay after. By this time, everyone in the class but me and Felicia were reading their stuff, and I was afraid maybe May was going to kick me out of the class. Really, I liked WriteLight better than any of my other classes except Yoga, which was pretty much tied with WriteLight for best class. The rest of my classes were tied for worst place.

Anyways, Miss May was cool and funny, and I liked hearing what other kids had written. So, I stayed after, dreading whatever was going to happen. Probably some demand that I either start reading my stuff or get out.

Instead, Miss May took a paper from her folder and said, "This is a good piece, Eddie. Do you mind if I read it out loud? I won't use your name."

I was happy not to be getting kicked out, but still...

"I've got five other pieces that I want to read anonymously, so it won't be like your paper's the only one...It's funny. We can always use a laugh."

I nodded. And she read my paper and Felicia's and some others the next day. Mine was about my dog, Buddy. I got Buddy back when things were hard for me, when shit kept coming back to me. I was so messed up, I even had to see a shrink for a while. But the good part was that the shrink thought a dog could help me not be so anxious and scared. I liked that idea. I'd never had a dog before. Dr. Cranston, the shrink, said it would be a specially trained dog. A comfort dog.

Buddy was a year old when we got him, so I guess he's eight years old now. Besides flecks of grey on his head, his muzzle is totally grey. Max says he's 72 in dog years, but I don't like to think about him getting old. And he still runs around like he did when he was a pup.

My story was about how Buddy wrote a letter to his mother. It started, "Dear Bitch Mom." He thanked her for bringing him up right and for teaching him to cock his ears so his rescue humans would think he was cute. When May read it, everyone burst out laughing. They asked her to read it again. And they laughed even harder the next time. So, okay, I started reading my stuff. At first, I only read the funny stuff, about Buddy, and Simba the Cat, but then, gradually, I started reading the serious stuff, too. I almost always read now. We have this "mutually-supportive-writers-total-confidentiality" rule in here so it's okay to get serious when I want to.

I zone out through the next three classes and make my way to the quad. Brent's at the usual table. I sit across from him, unpacking my lunch, as Cameron brings his junk food tray to the table and slides in next to Brent. He looks at Brent's tray that's holding an almost empty bottle of soda and about two bites left of a po-boy sandwich.

"You get here early?" Cameron says.

"Calculus was cancelled."

"Why don't you look happier?" I ask.

"It was cancelled because someone put a big swastika up on the white board with a black permanent marker."

"Who?" I say.

"Don't know. Some cretins."

"You sure it wasn't you, Blockhead? A good way to get out of class?" Cameron says.

"Not even funny," Brent says.

"Why? What do you care? You hate the guy!" Cameron says.

"I hate him because he's an asshole calculus teacher. I don't hate him because he's a Jew."

"Whatever," Cameron laughs. "At least you didn't have to go to class."

Brent dumps his trash and takes his tray to the cart. I open my container of leftover brown rice with broccoli and cheese, add a packet of soy sauce, and stir it all together. An apple, organic, whole wheat pita chips, celery smeared with peanut butter and a can of lemon-lime sparkling water make up the rest of my lunch.

Cameron takes a look, makes a gagging sound, then shoves a handful of greasy french fries into his mouth. I take a pose and flex my twice-as-big-as-Cameron's biceps.

* * * * *

There's no Yoga today so I could leave early, but I wait around until after 6th period, hoping to "accidentally" meet up with Rosie when she gets out of soccer practice. The timing is right because I practically run into her as she's walking out of the gym. As soon as I see her, I blurt out, "Want a ride?"

Not too smooth. Like I probably should have said "Hi," or "How was practice?" or *something* first. But Rosie smiles at me like whatever I've said is just fine.

"My mom's picking me up," she says. "Thanks, though."

I walk with her a little ways, even though it's in the opposite direction of my car in the student lot.

"How were your classes?" she asks.

"Okay. How were yours?"

"Good, except I've already got a ton of homework."

"That sucks. I don't have any homework. At least none that I'll do."

She pauses, then, "I still don't get why you're not going to college. I don't know anyone else who's not going to college."

"Maybe I'm a maverick."

"See, that's what I mean. 'Maverick.' That's one of the words on the SAT word list and you don't even have to study to know how to use it."

"I know some four syllable words, too," I tell her. "Like 'prerogative', as in it's my prerogative not to go to college."

She laughs, then waves toward a car pulling up to the curb. "My mom. Gotta go." She smiles her sparkle smile. "Thanks for the offer of a ride though!"

"Anytime," I call after her.

* * * * *

As I drive to the job, I think about Rosie. Her smile, her hair, her laugh. It seems like maybe she could like me. Could she? And I think about the college/no college choice. Am I being lazy? Taking the easy way out? I know that's what most people think.

I park in front of a shabby looking house in a mostly nice neighborhood in Alhambra. I get my paint clothes from the trunk, go around to the back where I know the door won't be locked, call out to William that I'm here, go into the bathroom and change clothes.

Two thirty-ish men, married, moved into the house a few weeks ago. Wesley, the guy who does most of the talking, said they got the place for way below market value because, in Wesley's words, "It's a poster child for run down." They want the whole place painted, inside and out, so we'll be working here for a while.

This past Saturday I scraped and sanded and spackled the walls in the master bedroom, and now William's priming them. Today, my job's to prep the walls and woodwork in the second bedroom. I get another ladder from the truck and put it in a corner of the bedroom. I like working. Lifting, moving stuff around, climbing up and down the ladder, using my strength to scrape and sand the rough spots. I like making money, having enough to pay for my car and insurance and not have to ask for anything from Max. And I like seeing the transformation. "Transformation." Another four-syllable word. This place will be totally transformed by the time we're through with it.

I don't care what anybody else thinks. I know this is the right choice.

CHAPTER FOUR

The Handshake Test

Even though this is the fourth week of school, it's the first day of Yoga because Yoga Joe's been away on a retreat.

"Eight mats," Joe says as I walk through the door to the small weight room across from the main gym. I get out the mats and put them in two rows of four each. We won't be using the straps or blocks today.

As kids enter, Joe says, "Shoes off. Take a seat on a mat."

Rosie's hella stressed about getting into the right college, and writing her essay, and getting recommendations, and filling out applications, and getting all A's. Yoga would for sure help her de-stress, but it's the same time as that special music therapy class she's so psyched about.

I'm glad I don't have to be all stressed out about school. My cousin Vincent's a lawyer and he keeps trying to talk me into going to college and becoming a lawyer. He says I'm smart and I could do good work in the world. Right now, he's working 24-7 with people who are scared of being deported, mostly farmworkers who live up around Redville. I know what he does is important, and I hate to disappoint him, but no, I'm not changing my mind about working in the painting business. I like that every job's different. You get to know a lot of different kinds of people—rich people and not so rich, business and shop owners, decorators and builders. No job is the same so it's never boring.

Last summer, William and I spent over two weeks painting the "great room" at a mansion up in San Marino. I'd never seen such a place in my whole life. The woman who owned the house was super picky but so's William, so it worked out. The colors? Rocky River for the walls and Quietude for the trim. That cracked me up. At first, I thought why not just say light greyish green and dark greyish green? But now I get how even a little lighter shade or a little darker shade of any color can make a big difference in the total look of a room. So besides Rocky River, there has to be a Brook Green, and a Morning Zen, etc., etc.

But back to yoga. Mr. Lee, Joe Lee, isn't like a lot of yoga guys—all skinny and Gumby-looking. Joe's got hard-as-rock bulging biceps and a definite six-pack. On his upper right arm, he has a tattoo of a rose and a broken chain. I can always tell if Joe's worried or annoyed because that's when he rubs his tattoo.

He says he used to have a gang tattoo across the back of his neck, but he paid big bucks to have it removed. He says he kept the rose and chain, though, to remind him of his prison days, and that the chains of the past can be broken, and that there's beauty in life if you open your eyes to it.

Joe isn't a regular Hamilton High teacher. He does this yoga class as some kind of special deal. He sits in front, legs crossed, palms upwards on his knees, and starts the group today the way he starts every new group.

"I'm Joe Lee, been practicing yoga for the past nine years—started in prison so it would look good to the parole board. Turns out, it changed my life and, trust me, mine was a life that needed changing.

"Okay. Loud enough that we can all hear: your name, grade in school, have you ever before, even once, done yoga, and, if you're comfortable telling us, why you're taking Yoga. We'll start with you," Joe says, nodding to the girl on the left in the front row.

"Um...Maricella Foster?" she says, like it's a question. Like maybe there's a right or wrong answer to "What's your name?"

"Okay, Maricella. And...?"

Her face turns pink.

"And…grade in school, yoga experience, and why you're taking yoga."

"Junior. Elective credit. It fit my schedule."

"Yoga experience?"

"Once. On YouTube."

"Okay, thanks, Maricella."

Next, it's Alice Stevens, and another girl, and then Joe nods at a guy sitting off by himself in the back. "Name?"

"Jason Paulson. 11th. Assigned." Everyone turns to look at Jason. He's got this surprising high, squeaky voice that sounds like it could be coming from an excited Miss Piggy on an old Sesame Street show.

"Okay," Joe says. "Have you ever done yoga before?"

Jason gives Joe a stony look and shakes his head.

Sometimes the assigned kids *really* don't want to take yoga. And they can be a pain in the butt. Especially the anger management guys—it's always guys. Why aren't there ever any girls in anger management? I'm sure there's plenty of anger to go around. I bet Jason's an anger management guy. More like anger mismanagement judging by the look on his face and the way he's all slumped down.

When it's my turn, I say, "Eddie Barajas. Senior. Stress reduction."

That was my short, fit-for-class introduction version. I don't say I'm an aide 'cause it gives people the wrong impression. The too-long-for-a-class-none-of-their-business-introduction would be that I started taking yoga back when I lived in Redville when I was nine, or maybe ten. I'd been through some bad shit, and so had my mom. Her bad shit was when she was in Iraq, in the National Guard. My bad shit was here in Hamilton Heights. So, we were both seeing a shrink. Not the same one, but at the same time. So, this therapist woman told Max about some research project that showed that yoga could help people with post-traumatic stress.

Max was pretty much ready to try anything to get rid of the nightmares that were so terrible she was afraid to go to sleep. The only yoga place with that kind of specialty was down in Fresno, about thirty miles from Redville. That was back when Max never wanted to be alone, so I said okay, I'd go with her. Really, I didn't see how twisting my body into a pretzel would do anything but make me feel even more weird than I already felt, but it turned out it did help. Not only Max, but me, too. That's how I started a yoga practice. That's what they call it when you do yoga a lot—a practice. I guess bad shit never goes completely away, but you can do stuff to zap its power.

When we moved back to Hamilton Heights, right before I started high school, I wanted to find a place like the one in Fresno because by that time, I knew yoga helped me stay cool and calm. I tried classes at the Y, and one through Parks and Recreation, and a "Hot Yoga" place. None of them felt right. I was about ready to give up when I found Joe Lee's tiny studio in a converted garage only a few blocks from where we live. It's a good fit. When the school's yoga class isn't in session, I practice at Joe's studio two or three times a week. I can't afford to pay for his classes, so instead of money, I pay by doing work for him. Like, just yesterday, I went to his home studio and opened the windows, vacuumed and dusted like he texted me to do—said he didn't want to come home to a stale studio.

Twice a week, Joe goes to a place in L.A. where he leads a series of classes. On those days, I walk his dog, Peppy, after school and again before bedtime.

I've already told you how buff and tough looking Joe is. You'd think he'd have a Pit Bull, or a Rottweiler, or some other big, scary dog. But Peppy is this dainty little poodle, white, and she prances around like she's afraid of getting her feet dirty. I used to think you could tell a lot about a person by what kind of dog they have, but Joe and Peppy blew any of those ideas out of my head. My dog, Buddy, is a yellow lab. Some people might think I'm not a yellow lab kind of guy, either. If yellow labs could talk, they'd be non-stop talkers.

Anyways, I walk Peppy, and clean the studio, and sometimes do other odd jobs for Joe in payment for classes. Between that, and working with William, and taking care of the pest one night a week, I've got a pretty busy schedule. Everybody I know has a busy schedule, but I'm the only one who's not all stressed out about my busy-ness.

But back to the now. That's a good thing for people with bad shit to do. Stay in the now. After introductions, Joe outlines the regular routine, from taking a mat and getting centered when we get to class, to leaving with a final Namaste. He says there are probably hundreds of interpretations of "Namaste," but our Namaste is "The spirit within me honors the spirit within you." He asks me to demonstrate with him.

Joe is still seated cross-legged in front of the group. About half of us, me included, are also cross-legged; the rest are however else they can get comfortable. Joe faces me, hands in prayer position, head half bowed. I mirror his position. "Namaste," he says.

"Namaste," I return.

He goes on to say that the Namaste routine is not required. He likes it because it's important for us to remember that each and every one of us has a pure spirit within us. But if it's against somebody's other religious practice, or if it feels phony, it's okay to skip it.

After the basics, we go into a smaller room where we sit in plastic chairs that have those attached half desk things, and Joe sets up an "Introduction to Yoga" video. I take my sketch pad and charcoal pencils from my backpack because I've seen this video enough times to have it memorized, and I'll need to doodle.

Joe told me he had to look at more than thirty videos before he could find one that included an equal number of men and women. He didn't want a video that made it seem like yoga was a wimpy, girly thing. But no one could look at Joe in the "warrior pose" and think yoga is wimpy.

The video defines yoga as a method for mental, physical, and spiritual health. It covers breathing techniques, a few basic poses, and something about quieting the mind. I'm quieting my mind by drawing Simba in basic yoga poses.

Jason is sitting next to me, barely glancing at the video. Instead he keeps looking at my hand, sideways, like I won't notice. I stop shading in Simba's grinning face long enough to glance over at Jason. He looks back at the video for a few seconds, then it's back to my hand. I think he's new to Hamilton High. I don't remember ever seeing him around before, and if he'd been around, my hand would be old news to him. He's kind of skinny. Not as skinny as Cameron. More like normal skinny, with a haircut so short it's hard to tell what color his hair is.

I make a few changes to Simba's mouth and eyes, and shift his expression from a happy grin to one that's mean and evil. Jason isn't even looking at the cat. Just my hand. I set my pencil down and hold my half-hand right in front of his eyes.

"Want a good look?"

He shoots *his* hand, middle finger up, in front of my face.

"Fuck you!" he says, and walks out of the room, slamming the door behind him.

I go back to doodling. That wasn't exactly a yoga thing. We were definitely not honoring the pure spirit within each other. Oh well.

I don't know why I let him get to me. I'm pretty used to all kinds of responses to my hand. I should be. I've had it all my life. When I shake hands with someone I've just met, that's kind of a test. Like some guys—it's usually guys who shake hands, mostly older guys, too—but if they reach out and grip my hand like it's any old hand, they pass. But if they barely touch my hand and pull back like maybe they're going to catch creepy hand from me, well, let's say I know we're not going to be best friends. I'm pretty sure Jason and I won't be best friends, either.

For a while, back when I was a little kid, I was self-conscious about my hand, but the thing is, I'm wicked good at drawing. In elementary school, once other kids saw what my hand could do, no one cared what it looked like.

When the video's over, Joe says it's okay to leave, we don't have to wait for the bell. I grab the disinfectant wipes from the supply closet and start wiping the mats. Joe's watching me. Like does he think I've forgotten the clean-up routine over the summer?

"What was that about?" he asks.

"What?" I say, moving to the next mat.

"Don't play dumb with me, Eddie." Sometimes it seems like Joe's eyes can see into your soul. "Well?" he says.

"You mean Jason?"

"Yes! I mean Jason! Isn't it a bit unusual for one yoga student to flip another one off and yell the 'F' word?"

"I guess."

"And isn't it unusual for a yoga student to storm out of the room halfway through class?"

I nod.

"And?"

"That Jason guy hella irritates me."

"And…?"

"He kept looking at my hand," I say, holding my hand out. "And then I gave him a good close-up. That's all."

"And?"

"And I guess it pissed him off."

"Good guess, Eddie."

Next mat. I concentrate on spraying the disinfectant, being sure I get the corners clean.

"Eddie? What would have been a better way to handle that?"

I stop wiping. Look up at Joe. "Yeah. Okay. Deep breath. Get centered."

"Right. That's what I'm going to do right now," he says, walking toward his office. "That's what you be better be able to do tomorrow."

CHAPTER FIVE

Surprise Package

I don't know how it happened—it all just…happened. Rosie has zero period madrigals, I have zero period WriteLight, we're just down the hall from each other. By the time of the Harvest Festival, we were with each other a lot. I started getting to zero period a few minutes early every day, hoping to see her before she went to choir. And then I noticed I wasn't the only one going out of my way to just happen to meet up in the hall. And then, one day Rosie came in all upset. Her mom had promised her the car, then ended up needing it herself. Rosie didn't know how she was going to get from school to Sofia's in time for extra practice on this song they're working on.

"I can chauffeur you," I said.

She laughed. "See what I mean, Eddie? Another SAT word."

So, I took Rosie to Sofia's that day, and home the next, and then pretty soon almost every day, her mom only dropped her off in the mornings and I took her home. I liked hanging around with Rosie, and I started seriously liking her. But then I got scared.

Sophomore year, I had this girlfriend, Diana. We had a pretty good time for two or three months, but then things got too intense for me. I know it's usually the other way around—the guy wants to do more stuff, sex stuff, and the girl backs away. But Diana kept pushing for more, and I didn't want more. After we broke up, I got worried. Like maybe the bad shit I'd been through as a kid messed me up for normal sex. Well…I guess I'll just stop hinting and say it.

Back when I was nine and Mario was seventeen, Max was sent off to Iraq with the National Guard, and Mario and I went to live with our aunt. And then our aunt's boyfriend, Denton, started...it's hard even to write, but...he started molesting me. Sex stuff. When Mario found out, he took my mom's car, which was up on blocks and off limits, and we drove two hundred miles up to our aunt and uncle's place in Redville. So, after the bad shit sex stuff, I guess you can see that I might be worried about having regular normal sex. And when I didn't want to do everything Diana wanted, well, I went back to the shrink for a tune-up.

This guy is not the kind of psychologist who has you talking forever about old stuff. I mean, yeah, we talked about some old stuff, but mainly he gave me ideas and exercises to help make things better. I won't go into detail about the exercises because that's all too personal. But after a month of seeing the psychologist and practicing the exercises, I ended up feeling like I was just a normal guy who'd been with a girl who was too pushy for him.

But back to now. Me and Rosie are at the big Harvest Festival, and it's like still being little kids. Riding the Ferris wheel, eating pumpkin spice cookies, throwing baseballs at the leaded bowling pin things that seem never, ever, to fall down. We wander over to the pumpkin tent to check out the winners from the pumpkin carving contest.

I point to the pumpkin with the white third place ribbon pinned to it. "That's Imani's," I tell Rosie.

"Really? Imani carved that?"

"Well, maybe it's mostly William's pumpkin, but the pest poked out the eye holes."

"Mom told Zoe if she was going to put her name on a carved pumpkin for the contest, she had to do all the work herself."

"Look at this," I say, pointing to the blue ribbon. "No way was that done by anyone under twelve."

"It's a great pumpkin, though, with its evil smile and that small haunted house carved into its cheek...Mom should have let me help Zoe," Rosie says, pointing to Zoe's pumpkin. It could have been a winner if they'd handed out booby prizes.

We decide to get some kind of consolation prize for Zoe, for honesty. I don't have much money left and neither does Rosie, so we choose the easy ping-pong toss into the goldfish bowl. We win two of them.

"You can have one for Imani," Rosie tells me.

"For what? The cheater prize? Take both of them. One of them will probably be dead by morning anyways."

Around ten or so, some guys line up at the booth with the leaded bowling pins. I think some of them were those guys carrying the P8RIOTS signs at the Black Lives Matter demonstration last month, but I couldn't say for sure. They're wearing Make America Great hats, and their tough guy camo jackets with American flag patches on their sleeves. One of them yells, "Hillary!" hella loud and throws the ball with all his might at the bowling pin pyramid. He misses, and the next guy to throw yells out, "Ragheads!", rears back and heaves the ball. This one hits, and the top pin falls over. Two older guys with orange Harvest Festival vests go over and say something to the camo jackets. Rosie gives me a nudge.

"Look. Isn't that Jason? The guy from your yoga class?" she asks, nodding in the direction of the pin-ball throw.

I take a closer look.

"Yeah, that's Jason," I say. "Figures. Puffed up 'Patriot' guys slinging hate at leaded pins. They so piss me off."

Rosie says, "Somebody draped slices of raw bacon through the handle of Sofia's locker last week. Fatima's, too."

"Bacon?"

"You know. Pork? Pork is forbidden to Muslims. Unclean," she says.

"Oh, yeah. I guess I heard that."

"It totally freaked them out. I pulled the bacon off while Brianna got soapy paper towels from the restroom. We washed it all off, but it was *soooo* gross. I love bacon, but handling those slimy pieces?? I won't be hungry for bacon for a long time."

"So did Squeaky Voice Jason do that?"

"I don't know. Somebody said they saw two guys in camo jackets rushing away."

Pooling the last of our money, we get a soda to share, then leave. I drive us a little ways up the Angeles Crest Highway and park in a turnout where we can get a clear view of the stars. We're mostly just talking. Like, what else can you do when your girlfriend's balancing two occupied fish bowls on her lap?

Right in the middle of trying to find the North Star, Rosie yells, "I'm late! I've got to call home before my parents freak out!"

She's balancing the fish bowls and poking around in this canvas bag thing that she carried her little sister's carved pumpkin in—the booby prize-winning pumpkin.

"Here, let me hold the fish for you."

I take the bowls, careful not to spill the water, and Rosie dives into the bag with both hands. I don't know what all she's got in there, but it's still pretty full even without the pumpkin. Finally, she gets frustrated and dumps everything out on her lap. And yes, the phone shows up, but so does a six-pack condom package. She quick grabs it and stuffs it back into the bag, and even though it's a pretty dark night, I swear I could read a book by the glow of her face right now.

"I...it's not mine...I mean...it's not...my mom... Ohhhhhhh, it's so embarrassing!"

And I start laughing. I hand Rosie the bowls so I can reach into my back pocket. I pull out a condom package, though mine's a different brand.

"My mom, too." I tell Rosie, between gasps of laughter. "I've never even ever used one, but my mom..."

And then Rosie starts laughing, too. And we laugh until we can't anymore, and then we tell our stories. It turns out, both of our moms got pregnant in their teens. Rosie's mom was only sixteen when she had her. My mom was seventeen when she had my brother. Practically since pre-school, each of our moms has been preaching at us not to follow their same paths. They both say they wouldn't have it any other way for them, because they love the kids they got so much, but it was really hard, and stupid, and on and on. I swear my mom was sneaking condoms into my pockets by the time I was thirteen. Rosie says it was twelve for her: in her purse, in her backpack, sometimes in that little plastic zip thing that comes in notebooks.

"Embarrassing! Girl Scouts! A condom dropped out of my little heart shaped backpack when I was on a Girl Scout hike!"

Later, as I'm driving us down the winding road from the Flats, I say to Rosie, "Maybe we should start using those gifts from our moms sometime." I hold my breath, waiting for what she might say. Then, right when I think she might not ever talk to me again, in a voice so soft I can hardly hear her, she says, "Maybe."

I like talking in the car at night, while I'm driving. First of all, you don't have to look straight at each other. And second, the darkness makes everything seem more private, safer.

The first time she let me borrow her car to take a girl out, Max gave me one of her "Let's get this straight" talks. "You always walk a girl to her door. You don't just reach across, push her door open, and tell her good-bye like she's some hitchhiker you picked up. You get out of the car, go around and open her door for her, and walk her to the door of her house."

She even had me practice with her. And then, because she'd told me not to treat the girl like a hitchhiker, I got another long "Let's get this straight" Max talk about how I'd better never, ever, pick up a hitchhiker. If I did, I'd be grounded for life, never get to use her car again, and on and on.

But back to now. I walk around to Rosie's side of the car and open the door for her. Usually Rosie's out of the car before I get to her side. "I'm not helpless!" she'd said the first time I tried to follow Max's rules. Tonight, though, she has to wait because she's juggling two fish bowls and the big canvas bag. So, I open the door for her and take the fish bowls. We're almost to the front porch when Rosie stops suddenly. "Oh wait!" she says. "I've got to get my French book from Tilly."

"Who's Tilly?"

She laughs. "Tilly the Trailer. We take her on a family road trip every summer, but the rest of the time she stays at the side of the garage."

"But…your book?"

"Yeah, so I usually study in Tilly where it's quiet and there aren't any interruptions."

Rosie turns and walks toward the driveway. I follow, balancing the fish bowls. "Oh, here," she says, taking the bowls from me and setting them on the back step. "I'll get them before I go into the house."

I walk along beside her, down the driveway to the garage, then around to the side of the garage.

"See?"

I'd guess the trailer's about twelve feet long, but my guesses aren't always accurate. It's rounded at both ends and it's on blocks, to save the tires, I guess.

Rosie opens the door, steps inside, and turns on a sort of lantern. "Battery operated," she says. "Come in, but duck!"

I step inside and look around. "Cool!"

Everything's tiny, except for me and Rosie. There's a tiny kitchen at one end. At the other end is a sort of U-shaped bench with cushions on it. There's a tiny table, covered with books and papers, in the middle of the U. Rosie's laptop sits on the cushion that's under the tiny window.

"My own private study," Rosie says, pulling her French book from the pile.

We're standing so close I can smell her hair. I turn to her, pull her close. She leans into me, tips her head to meet my lips. I grip her butt, pull her closer against my hardness. For a second, she leans into me, then pulls back.

"I've got to go," she whispers, her arms on my shoulders, her eyes holding mine.

I kiss her again, wanting more. She steps away, gets her book, and opens the door. Everything's within arms' reach in Tilly.

"Oh, the light," she says, switching the lantern off.

We walk to her back door, kiss again, and again, until she turns the doorknob and steps inside.

There are no traffic sounds now, only the faint sounds of my footsteps as I walk to my car. A light breeze barely stirs the leaves of the aspen near the edge of the driveway. I breathe in the quiet of the night, still feeling the warmth of Rosie's body against mine. Filled with the sweetness of life.

* * * * *

Eight years ago. Max'd only been back from Iraq for a couple of weeks, and every night she'd have screaming, sweating, crying nightmares, like she was back in Iraq—gunfire, road bombs going off, buddies being blown to bits. And me? Any blue trucks that reminded me of the pervert's truck sent me running back home at top speed where I'd lock myself in the bathroom and brush my teeth so hard my gums bled.

On the way home after my second session, I was doodling around on my sketch pad when Max said, "Look. Do you think that's another coffee place they're building on that corner?"

"Can't look," I told her, turning to a fresh page.

"What?"

"Can't look. I'm practicing trigger avoidance."

"What does that mean?"

"Dr. P. asked me about triggers, like all the things that remind me of…Denton. And what he did. He said if I knew the triggers, I could learn how to avoid them. If I don't look out the window, I won't see any blue trucks."

By the time we got back to Tia Josie's and Tio Hector's, I'd filled a sketch pad with Simbas—all tough, muscle cat

Simbas who'd never be bossed around by some bigger cat per-vert. I hadn't looked out the window even once.

Max picked me up after school the next day and took me to my favorite ice cream place, The Big Scoop. On the way over there, I filled in color and detail on the drawings from the day before. It turned out it was easy not to look out the window.

At The Big Scoop, I went for a hot fudge sundae, with a sliced, not split, banana. No nuts. No cherry. Hot fudge served on the side in a separate container, double whipped cream. Max got a one dip vanilla cone. After a few minutes of quiet ice cream eating, Max said, "I've been thinking about how you're not looking out the window because you might see something that could trigger a panic attack."

"I hate panic attacks," I told her.

"Me, too," Max said.

More silent tastes of ice cream. Then she said, "On the way over here, I saw a red-tailed hawk spread its wings and take off from its perch on a telephone pole. And then I noticed the first buds on trees in the almond orchards. And I saw the clear blue sky and white fluffy clouds, and I thought about what you were missing by not looking out the window."

Max licked the dripping ice cream from her cone. I spooned out the perfect balance of banana, chocolate ice cream, and whipped cream, and let it melt together in my mouth. Then Max talked about how we'd each been caught, helpless, in places where we'd had no control. We'd each had different kinds of hurt—different, but nasty hurts that would take time to recover from.

"Here's the thing, though," she said. "We can always be on the lookout for triggers, afraid that something will pull us back to the past, worried about the next panic attack or the next nightmare. Or we can choose to stay in the now, being on the lookout for the sweetness of life. I don't want us to miss the sweetness of life. Do you know what I mean?"

"Like I missed the hawk and blossoms 'cause I wasn't looking out the window?"

"Right. We get to decide what to look for."

Then it was on to all that was good in our lives, the sweetness of ice cream and of Tia Josie's cookies, the inherent goodness of people. She named every good person she knew, which went on for a long, long time. As Max's words washed over me, I thought about the one hella bad person I'd known in my whole life, and the hundreds of other good people. Max talked about the beauty of the earth. The sea, the sky, the mountains, the beautiful lettuce and grapes that grew there in the Central Valley. Crops that would soon be feeding the whole country.

"It's up to us to choose, Eddie. Do we focus on the pain of the past, or do we focus on the sweetness of now?"

On the way home from The Big Scoop, I looked out the window, watching for hawks and noticing the whiteness of the clouds against the bright blue sky. And I decided right then not to let fear of the sight of a blue pick-up truck keep me from seeing the good stuff.

Later in the week, Max took Mario for ice cream and gave him the sweetness of life talk, too. Since then, every now and then, Max and I—Mario, too, if he's in town—we go for ice cream and tell each other about our sweetness of life moments. But tonight's sweetness of life moment with Rosie, that won't be ice cream talk. That moment I'll hold safe within my private heart.

CHAPTER SIX

You Betcha

The cornhole game is already set up on the front lawn when I get to Brent's. " 'Bout time you showed up," he says.

Cameron tosses a beanbag toward the hole in the middle of the board. Not only does the beanbag not go into the hole, it doesn't even land on the board. "You suck!" I yell at him.

"Yeah. Okay. Let's see what you can do, Hook."

"I can do more with this hook than you can do with both of your hands!"

Cameron laughs. "We'll see, won't we?"

Brent's got a sheet of rules in one hand and one of those heavy-duty metal measuring tapes in the other—like the tape William uses to measure rooms with. "This has to be regulation," he says, pulling out a few inches of the tape and handing the end to me. He walks toward the farthest board, the tape measure unrolling along with him, and motions me toward the closer board. "Twenty-seven feet. It has to be 27 feet from one end of the board to the other."

Cameron groans. "Let's just play. I'll whip your asses no matter how many feet apart the boards are."

"Dude! I've got to practice on a regulation court! When I play my dad, he'll have everything measured down to the millimeter," Brent says.

Brent and his dad don't have much to do with each other. Brent's dad is this hotshot bridge engineer who, after three girls, wanted that like-father-like-son thing with Brent, which included the engineer thing. That doesn't work too well for a guy who got skipped over when the math brains were handed out. Brent's oldest sister, Britney, is already finishing a degree in structural engineering at Cal Tech. Seems like that would be enough to satisfy Mr. Bruno, but I guess it's a dad/son thing. I wouldn't know about that.

It's weird, but it's like Brent's parents have this love of BR or something. His dad is Brad Bruno. His mom is Brenda. The rest of the Brunos are the sisters, Britney, Brook, and Bridget, and then there's Brent.

Brent and his dad mostly get along by staying out of each other's way. But sometimes they get into this thing where they bet on stuff. Like whether or not it's going to rain, or how high is Mt. Wilson, or who will be the first one to spot a dog on some road trip. Anything. They don't bet money. They bet "services." Like, I remember a time back in the third grade, I was at their house for dinner. It was pizza night. Bridget asked if we liked our teacher, Mrs. Calahan, the same teacher she'd had two years earlier.

"She's okay," Brent said. "Except she likes Eddie better than me."

Bridget laughed. "I like Eddie better than you. Everyone likes Eddie better than you."

"Yeah? Well, I like Eddie better than you, too!" Brent said.

I just sat, munching pizza, trying to be likable. Mr. Bruno said, "Mrs. Calahan? Is that the blonde one who plays the piano?"

Bridget nodded her head but Brent said, "Black hair. Mrs. Calahan has black hair."

"The teacher all of the girls had? In that room where the walls are mostly whiteboards? That Mrs. Calahan? She doesn't have black hair," Brent's dad said.

"Does too," Brent said, picking bits of tomatoes off of his pizza.

Mr. Bruno looked at Brent like he was crazy. "Mrs. Calahan. Third grade? She does not have black hair!"

"Betcha," Brent said.

"You're on, Buddy. What're the stakes?"

"You take me and Eddie for a day at Disneyland."

"Whoa. That's a big bet! What're you gonna do for me when you lose?"

Brent didn't know what to say to that, because he didn't plan on losing. He thought for a long time. "Maybe Eddie and me wash your car every Saturday for a month?"

"How about every Saturday for a year? You and Eddie wash, wipe down, leave no streaks. Clean the inside, too. Inside of the windows, vacuum, leave it looking like it's right off the showroom floor."

Mr. Bruno was a fanatic about his car—a little red Lamborghini that he bought with some bridge-building bonus money.

Brent's mom turned to me. "Don't let them drag you into this," she said. I didn't care, though. I knew Brent would win. I was already thinking about which rides I wanted to go on first. Maybe Space Mountain.

The next morning, I watched as Brent led his dad into the classroom. Mr. Bruno did one of those cartoon double-takes when he saw our teacher.

She said, "Oh, Mr. Bruno. It's nice to see you. How are those three sweet girls of yours?"

"Mrs. Calahan?" He stared at her, his mouth half open. She laughed.

"Some people don't even recognize me with this black hair," she said. "I'm going to be Maria in 'West Side Story' at the Community Theatre. I'm too old for the role, and too blonde. I couldn't get younger, but at least I could get black hair."

"Is it a wig?" Mr. Bruno asked, looking for some out on a technicality, I guess.

"No! A wig would be too hard to manage—all of that dancing and running around. Hot, too. No, I had it dyed. I may even keep it this way. Like it?"

"I like it!" Brent said, pulling his dad toward the door.

Besides being a stickler for math, Mr. Bruno also prided himself on playing by the rules, and once a bet was made, there was no backing out. So, he kept his end of the bargain and took us to Disneyland. One of the best days ever!

Brent and his dad have probably made hundreds of bets since then, and Brent probably hasn't won more than two or three. But he's determined to win this one. High stakes! If Brent beats his dad in cornhole, in what they're calling a tournament, he doesn't have to do the summer math camp thing. If he loses, he not only has to go to math camp, he has to work with a math tutor for the whole rest of senior year.

Brent's dad went to some big, important engineering and science college back east somewhere. Maine, or Montana, or Massachusetts, or Michigan, one of those M states. And cornhole was like their main school sport. I've heard of colleges with Frisbee teams, and skateboarding teams, but cornhole? Here's the thing, though. Brent's dad was a college cornhole star, and I don't think Brent's ever in his life beaten his dad at the game.

* * * * *

Brent and I play first, with Cameron as the ref. He's supposed to be watching to be sure that we don't step past the platform when we pitch. If that happens, the throw doesn't count, and Brent will want every throw to count so he's got to practice staying in the boundary. But Cameron's so busy texting, we could step ten feet out of the box and he wouldn't notice.

I take the first throw with a red beanbag, give it an easy lob, and it drops straight into the hole—doesn't even touch the sides. Brent takes the next toss. It hits the edge of the platform and bounces off. "Shit."

My next throw lands on the platform and rests inches from the hole.

Brent's blue bag lands a few inches from mine, slides, and pushes mine into the hole. "Fuck!"

Cameron looks up, sees my two red beanbags on the grass under the hole. "Hey, Blockhead! I know a cute math tutor. If you're going to be spending all year with a math tutor, might as well be a cute one."

"Up yours, Quinn!"

Cameron laughs, turns back to his phone.

By mid-afternoon we're all starving. Out of seven games, I've won three, Brent and Cameron each won two. But it was the last two that Brent won, so maybe with enough practice...

"Sonic's?" Brent asks.

"Nah. That's crap food. Let's go to the taqueria," I say.

"Sonic's is crap and the taqueria isn't?" Cameron says.

Brent turns to Cameron. "Let's do McDonald's. Salad for Eddie, crap for us?"

I dangle my keys in front of them, letting them know it doesn't matter where they want to go. I'm driving, and the car goes wherever I take it.

"Goin' to lunch," Brent yells in the general direction of the kitchen. The kitchen door opens, and his mom yells back at him, "What about the lawn??"

"After lunch!"

"It better be done by the time your dad gets home!"

* * * * *

The taqueria's so crowded we go down a block to the McDonald's drive thru line. We order at the window, crap for them, salad for me, like Brent said. At the window, I pass the food over to Cameron and drive away.

"No eating in my car!" I say to Cameron as he reaches into the bag for a french fry.

"I'm starving!"

"You're also a slob."

Brent laughs. "You're as bad as my dad is about his car."

"Yeah, well, I hate when my car smells like McDonald's."

At Dodsworth Park, we find a table in the shade and tear into our lunches. For the first few minutes, we're dedicated to eating, then Brent says, "We've got time for another practice tournament before I have to mow the lawn."

"Not me," I say. "I've got to meet William on the job at 2:00."

"Thought you had the day off, Dude," Cameron says.

"Nope. The only reason I got the morning off was because Max and William are over on the east side, registering voters."

"Can't people register for themselves?" Brent asks.

"I guess not everyone has a way to get to a place to register, and some people might have trouble filling out the forms."

"Why the east side?" Cameron says.

I shrug. "Maybe because that's where a lot of people who might have trouble voting live?"

Brent says, "I hope they'll be registering voters again next Saturday. All day, next Saturday. I need all of the cornhole practice I can get. Zitter screws around too much for it to seem like a real tournament."

"I'm a multi-tasker," Cameron says, grinning. "While you two were in such a serious competition, I got a time to meet Nora at her place, where her parents won't be, and I arranged to borrow thirty bucks from my dad and another thirty from my grandma, and I got two John Wicks on Fortnite. All that, plus I nearly won the second cornhole!"

"If losing by seven points counts as nearly winning," Brent says.

CHAPTER SEVEN

Irritable Teacher Day

Usually when I leave for zero period, no one else is up. This morning, though, Max and William are at the kitchen table, drinking coffee. Empty greasy popcorn bowls are on the counter.

Max shakes her head. "He won," she says, pointing to the front page of the morning *Times* with election results plastered across the headlines.

"Yeah—looked like he was in when I went to bed last night."

"We kept hoping things would change."

William stares into his coffee cup.

"At least California didn't go for him," Max says.

William looks up. "Doesn't matter. He'll still be president in California."

When I get to school, Miss May's searching frantically through a pile of papers.

"Hey," I say, grabbing a stack of paper towels and the vinegar/water spray bottle for the tables. Between cleaning the yoga mats in the afternoon and the tables in the morning, I'm beginning to think the job high school is preparing me for is to be a school custodian. Which, if I didn't already know I was going to be a painting contractor, might not be a bad thing. Mr. Manchester seems like a pretty happy guy. Happier than most of the teachers, if you ask me.

Papers are flying around May's desk.

"Looking for something?" I ask, expecting a laugh.

"No, Eddie," she says, all sarcastic, "I'm working on putting together a band with the sounds of flying paper providing major harmonies."

"Sorr—eeee."

She stops long enough to look at me. Lets out a long, deep sigh.

"Help me find that Appleman poem. You know, we read it last year. It was one of your favorites…oh…something something puddin' and pie?"

"The Karma poem?"

"Yeah. That one."

I pull *Good Poems* off the shelf, check the index, turn to page 132, and show Miss May.

"Oh, good! Take this to the choir room and make twenty copies."

In the choir room Taggerty sits at the desk in his office, tapping out a one-fingered text.

"Okay to use the copier?" I ask.

He pauses, looks over his little half glasses, nods his head. "She owes me paper," he says, then goes back to texting.

I wonder if this is Irritable Teacher Day? Like there are teacher conference days, and department meeting days, and now they've got Irritable Teacher Day? I'll have to wait until 2nd period to see. It's always an irritable day for Crandall, my first period teacher. But 2nd period? If Ms. Cortez is irritable in Life Skills, I'll know it's an official irritable day.

Between clearing a paper jam and reloading the machine, it's almost class time when I finish copying the poem, and a few kids are straggling into the choir room. I leave slowly, hoping Rosie will be the next one through the door. She's not, but at least I'll get to see her after school. I like that I always take her home now.

Miss May is on her phone when I get back to the classroom.

"I can't believe it, either," she says. "After eight years of such an intelligent, well-spoken leader and then we get this racist…"

She notices me putting the copies on her desk and stops abruptly.

"I've got to go now," she says, and stashes her phone in one of her giant pockets.

By the time the tardy bell rings, kids are loading up on stuff from the snack table, getting coffee or tea or hot chocolate, and taking it to their table. Unlike most of the other classes with individual student desks arranged in rows, we sit facing each other at big, oblong tables that are arranged in a horseshoe. I mark attendance in Miss May's roll book, then take my seat next to Phong. Usually Consuelo's on my other side, but she's not here today. Neither are Maryam and Sarah, the two quiet girls who wear those head scarves.

We always start class with a "read-around" of a poem or some other short bit of writing. Today it's the poem May had me copy. "'O Karma, Dharma, Pudding and Pie' by Philip Appleman," she reads.

We go around the table, each of us reading a line. I like this poem because it rhymes and because it's funny. I don't care much about the poems that are all like the beauty of the sky and the sea, with big words like "rhapsody" and "confluence" and no rhymes.

When we finish the read-around, Miss May reads the poem through. I'd like to show you the whole poem, but that's against some kind of copyright law, so I'll try to explain. The poet is asking for strength and wisdom, and to be a good person, and then it shifts to the poet wanting to give the gods advice on how to make the world a better place. Turn the bad people into good people, and have the good people be nice. It ends with "and before our world goes over the brink/teach the believers how to think."

May pauses, then reads the last lines again. "Wouldn't that be nice? Or, better yet, teach the *voters* how to think...Never mind, I didn't say that...Write whatever comes to mind. Whatever you want."

I write about Buddy, who is trustworthy, loyal, helpful and kind, but doesn't have great abs. Even though I write for laughs, it's all true about Buddy. When it's my turn to read, everyone laughs at my last two lines, "It's true Buddy's not got great abs/ but they're better than those on most other labs."

It's all about positive feedback in here, and what kids say is that they saw the dog's personality. They liked the thump, thump sound of his tail.

Phong wrote about his cowardly vampire—nothing to do with the poem we read. He usually writes about vampires. He says he's working on a trilogy.

When it's Miss May's turn to read, she does what she almost never does: she skips her turn. "Revision time," she says, handing back typed copies of papers we've chosen that we might want to have published in this year's WriteLight book. "Use your revision guidelines."

Phong passes one of his vampire pieces to me, and I pass a Simba story to him. Vernon the Cowardly Vampire, who faints at the sight of blood, always makes me laugh. I mark a place where he's used the same word, "cowardly", only two sentences apart.

"This Simba is one bad-ass cat," he says to me. He's bracketed a paragraph and written "More details."

"Yeah, Vampire Vernon is a total wuss," I say. "But, hey! What if they met each other?"

Phong gets this big smile. "Yeah! Maybe Vernon could hire Simba as a bodyguard. That'd show that bully Viceroy Vampire!"

We're going on about the Vernon/Simba partnership, laughing about the possibilities, when Miss May tells us we're disturbing our fellow writers.

"We're being creative," Phong says.

"Well, create more quietly," she says.

It's hard, though, to stop laughing once you get started, and now everything is funnier and funnier. Luckily, the bell rings before we've totally pissed May off.

It for sure is Irritable Teacher Day. Second period, Life Skills. Ms. Cortez is not, as usual, standing at the door, smiling, greeting everyone by name as they come into class. Today she's sitting at her desk, not looking at anyone. The first thing I notice after I sit down is "No Talking!" written on the whiteboard in big red letters. Below that is, "Chapter Six, Banking and Credit Costs, read and answer odd numbered questions. Even numbers for extra credit."

Whenever we start a new chapter, Ms. Cortez always has a personal story to tell us to "show relevance." "Relevance" is like her favorite word. With the "Taxes and Insurance" chapter she told about how she realized she was paying way too much insurance for full coverage on her old car. It wouldn't be worth it to pay for any body repair if it got messed up in a car crash. Then she told a story about someone who lost his business because he got sued for an accident that was his fault and he didn't have any liability insurance.

"The moral of this story is to be sure you've got enough liability insurance and not too much collision," she'd said. Really, I guess that was relevant because after that chapter I took a closer look at my car insurance and changed a few things, which ended up saving me about $600 a year.

Before today, she always started us with a story. I flip to Chapter Six and skim through it. Really? She expects us to read twenty-one pages and answer fifteen questions in 50 minutes?

Danny, the guy who has to be told everything at least ten times before it sinks in, has his hand up. Ms. Cortez glances his way and points to the board.

"But Miss, I don't get…"

She gets up, underlines "No Talking" twice, adds an exclamation mark, sits back down, opens her roll book, and starts silently taking roll.

The guy who sits next to me, Nick, says a little too loud, "What's with her today? She on the rag or something?"

"Well, duh!" Jane leans across me to whisper to Nick. "Remember that story she told us about how her parents never learned English even though they'd been here a long time? It was that personal finance unit. Remember? How that car salesman took advantage of them because they couldn't read the contract? How if we can't understand a contract, don't sign it until someone you trust looks it over?"

"What's that got to do with 'No Talking'?" Nick says.

"Her parents. They didn't learn English. What if they never became citizens?"

I push my desk back to get out of the middle.

Nick gives her a blank look. I know what she's talking about. I don't pay a lot of attention to politics, but I know the guy who just won the election has been spouting off for months about sending all of the criminals back to Mexico, and by "criminals" he means anyone who doesn't have papers.

I've heard stories about how scary it was for Tia Josie and Tio Hector until they got papers. They came on some kind of temporary work permit back in the 70s. I think it was the 70s. Then, because life was so much better here than what they'd left behind in Mexico, they stayed. They had Victor, bought a small farm. Tio Hector had a good job with one of the growers, but it took them a few years to get the papers they needed to stay here legally. They could have lost everything if they'd been deported before they could get legal. Now, with all the talk about deportation that was thrown around during the campaign, I bet there are plenty of people like Tia Josie and Tio Hector used to be—scared. Maybe Ms. Cortez is scared for her parents.

Jane keeps talking. Nick still has that blank look. I find Chapter Six again and flip to the page with the questions we have to answer. No need to read the whole thing. I finish most of the questions before the end of the period. This stuff is way boring, though, without Cortez's stories. I'm wondering if this is going to be Irritable Teacher Day for Mr. Lowe, in English, but it turns out he's the same old, not happy, not mad, boring guy.

We've finished American poetry, and now we're on to an American novel. Lowe has us come one at a time to his desk where he writes the number of a book next to our name in his roll book, hands us a copy of *The Grapes of Wrath*, and tells us he wants to see it with a cover tomorrow. John Steinbeck. It may not be boring. Not all assigned books are boring.

Back in the 8th grade, in Redville, we read *The Red Pony*, by Steinbeck. I don't know why I liked it so much because all four of the stories in the book were sad. Maybe I liked it because it showed how a ten-year-old boy thought. I was more than ten in the 8th grade, but I could still relate to how the boy thought and how he had to balance that with the way the adults around him thought.

To tell the truth, I'm tired of *The Autobiography of Malcolm X*. I liked it a lot at first. It was amazing what that guy experienced—when he was six his dad was killed, probably by white racists, though that was never proven. When he was thirteen, his mom had some mental breakdown and he and his brothers and sisters were all sent to different foster care families. Malcolm pretty much took care of himself any way he could from the time he was fourteen on. He was in prison by the time he was twenty. That's where he joined the Nation of Islam and then became a leader. That's pretty interesting, but then he goes on and on about black supremacy, and the importance of keeping black and white Americans separate, and the blue-eyed white devils, and it got tiresome. I know Malcolm X is a hero to William, but so is Martin Luther King, and they didn't exactly stand for the same things. Ready for a change of reading material, I'll put William's book back in the black bookshelf and start *The Grapes of Wrath* this evening.

Brent and Cameron already have our favorite table under the big oak tree, lunch trays full of what they call food. Third period they both have classes near the lunch court. My class is clear at the other end of campus. If it weren't for Brent and Cameron, I'd probably be eating my lunch standing up most of the time. Not today, though. It's not so crowded today. I slide onto the bench and unpack my lunch. I take sliced tomatoes and lettuce out of a baggie and add them to my sandwich.

"Epstein was so on the rag last period!" Brent says.

"I think today is an official Irritable Teacher Day," I tell them.

"I guess. I mean, Epstein? He's always on the rag but you can measure how pissed he is by his spray level. Today was as high as I've ever seen it. He even managed to spray when he said 'Calculus' this morning. I feel sorry for the kids who sit in the front row. 'Solution' even caught some kids in the third row back!"

"Can we talk about something besides Epstein's spray while I'm eating lunch?" I ask.

"I was supporting your 'Irritable Teacher Day' hypothesis," Brent says.

Meghan waves at Cameron from the cute-girls table. Cameron smiles and waves back. I guess Cameron's got a thing with Meghan now. I don't know what happened to Nora. Maybe she's only his girlfriend when her parents aren't home.

"Hey, Brent, do you want to go out with me and Meghan Friday night?" Cameron asks.

Brent looks at Cameron as if he's suddenly lost the capacity to understand English.

"We could double date. Me and Meghan and you and Brianna. You know. Brianna Kaufman. She's friends with Meghan."

"Brianna?"

"Yeah, she said she'd go with you. Probably 'cause she doesn't know you yet."

"Ha. Ha. Very funny."

"Listen, Meghan's dad won't let her go out alone with a guy, but if she double dates it's okay."

"What's she look like?" Brent asks.

"She's cute. You'll like her. C'mon, you're always whining about not having a girlfriend."

"No. I'm always whining about not having Adele for a girlfriend."

"Brianna's cuter than Adele," Cameron says.

"Doubt it," Brent says, then turns to me. "You know Brianna?"

"Yeah. She and Rosie are good friends."

"And?"

"She's not as cute as Rosie but she's cuter than Meghan," I tell him.

"That's cold, Hook!" Cameron says, throwing his empty, wadded up french fries bag at me.

"Okay for me to tell her you're on for Friday night?" Cameron asks.

"I don't know. What're you doing?"

"Maybe go to a movie."

Brent's quiet for a minute, then suddenly he gets this big grin. "I know! We can play cornhole!"

Cameron groans. "Is that all you can think about? Practicing cornhole?"

"My ticket to freedom from tutoring, freedom from math camp? Yep, that's all I can think about, getting good enough to beat my dad."

"I don't know," Cameron says. "Maybe Artie from History would do it."

"Maybe," Brent says, like he's got the upper hand.

Cameron's quiet for a while, then he says, "How many games?"

"Five," Brent says.

"How about two?"

"Can't have an even number. One team's got to win."

"Okay then, one?"

"Three. Take it or leave it," Brent says. Then, "Why don't you and Rosie come over, too?"

"Yeah, you should," Cameron says.

"Maybe. I'll check with Rosie."

I finish my strawberry/coconut protein drink and carry my trash and recycle stuff over to the bins. I know how this is going to turn out. Brent will hang out with Brianna. He'll think she's okay, but they'll never go out again because Brent's been crushing on Adele since ninth grade and no one can measure up to his Adele fantasy. Maybe I'm wrong about that, though. Maybe he'll get real with Brianna.

CHAPTER EIGHT

A Different Wednesday

The first Wednesday of every month I leave Yoga a little early so I can be there when Imani gets home from school. Joe's cool with it. I've been doing that for the past two years. William usually gets Imani from school and takes her back to wherever he's working. She does her homework, and sometimes William lets her paint a little section of a wall. On first Wednesdays, though, he and Max always go to some veterans' support thing. They go to help other vets who are having a hard time, but I think it probably helps them, too. William's big on supporting vets. Whenever we get behind with work and William has to hire extra help, it's always a vet.

It's okay, staying with the pest on first Wednesdays. Her BFF, Olivia, comes over to play, and they're always so busy pretending to be Anna and Elsa, I don't even have to come up with a joke to get them to leave me alone.

Olivia's mom, Carla, and Max have been good friends ever since Max started working for Dr. White. Carla does the front desk stuff, Max is the dental hygienist. That's how they met. Then, when Imani and William moved in with us, Imani didn't know any other kids at her school or in the neighborhood so Max invited Olivia to come play, and they both loved "Frozen." They've been best friends since they were five, and they still love "Frozen." Max and Carla took them to see "Moana" and "Finding Dory" and a bunch of other movies, but they stay obsessed with "Frozen."

This first Wednesday, things are different. I've only been home for about five minutes, long enough to take a swig of orange juice from the fridge, toss my backpack on my bed, and wrestle around with Buddy, when Imani comes barreling through the door, wailing, and runs straight to her room where she throws herself across the bed, face down.

"What's wrong?"

She sobs.

"Are you hurt?"

More sobs.

I sit on her bed next to her. "C'mon, Imani. What's wrong?"

"Olivia didn't..." short little gasps... "come..." gasp, gasp... "to school today! And she was supposed to come play 'Frozen' with..." gasp... "me. Like she always does!"

"Do you want to watch 'Frozen' on the big TV?"

"No! I want..." gasp... "Olivia to play Anna and Elsa with me. Like she's supposed to!"

"Well, maybe she stayed home 'cause she's sick. I bet she'll come home with you next time."

"But...today..."

"Hey! I've got an idea. Why don't you call her? If she's feeling better, we can go get her and bring her back to play with you."

Imani sits up and rubs her eyes.

"You know her number?" I ask.

She goes to her dresser, pulls out the bottom drawer, takes a little pink notebook from it, and turns to a page that's labeled "contacts." On the first three lines are numbers for William, Max, and me. They're in William's writing. I know his writing because sometimes he leaves notes for me in case I get to a job before he does.

Below the first three names, in careful eight-year-old printing, beside a big pink heart, is "Olivia" and her number. I hand Imani my phone, and she taps in the numbers. She waits a moment or two, then, "May I please speak to Olivia?"

William's a stickler for good phone manners, and I guess it's worked with Imani.

"Olivia?...Can you come over?...Eddie and I can come get you...Why not? ...But it's Wednesday...Really?"

Imani hands my phone back to me. "She can't come over."

"Is she sick?"

"She has to stay with her family. All of her family have to stay together."

It looks like she's about to start crying again so I ask if she wants to play Legos. She rubs her eyes and nods her head. I carry the giant Lego bin out to the living room.

I actually like building Lego things with her. I mean, I'm seventeen, I guess I should have outgrown Legos, but I haven't. And Imani likes when I build things with her. Max and William like it, too, when me and Imani are being nice to each other. "The bliss of domestic tranquility," is what Max always says when Imani and I are on the floor with the Legos.

Imani starts building a house. I start a super car. That's what we do, except sometimes she insists on building an ice castle. I'm thinking maybe Rosie and I'll play cornhole with Cameron and Brent and those other girls. It might be fun. And I'm wondering about going over to Rosie's after I walk Peppy, and Buddy, and maybe we'll hang out in Tilly the Trailer? Probably not, though. Weeknights are nothing but homework and studying for Rosie.

"I want a chimney on my house," Imani says.

"Well...build one."

"I did. But it doesn't fit." She shows me the chimney she built, which is as big as the house she's built.

"Okay. The house either needs to be bigger, or the chimney needs to be smaller." We poke around in the Legos to find better pieces.

Max calls to say they're bringing lasagna from Dimitri's. That's the place where Max and Mario and I used to always go before Iraq and running away to Josie and Hector's. And it's still there, with Dimitri and his family still running it. And it's the best.

"Any special requests besides the lasagna?" Max asks

"Double garlic bread," I say. "Imani? Special request?"

She shakes her head, not looking up from her house-expanding project. I add to my super car, then text Rosie: *See u later?*

We're still trying to get the chimney to fit the roof of the house when Max and William come in carrying two big Dimitri bags.

"Ah! Domestic tranquility!" Max calls out.

Imani runs to William and holds on. "Hey," he says, looking down at her. He sets his Dimitri bag on the counter and kisses her head. "Whasup?" He lifts her up, places her on one of the kitchen chairs, and bends down to eye level. "Whasup?" he says again.

"Olivia didn't come play 'Frozen' with me. Like she always does. Like she's s'posed to," Imani says, starting to cry all over again, then gasping out the story of how Olivia wasn't at school, didn't come to our house like she's *supposed* to, and she wouldn't even come over when we were going to go get her. And her whole family had to stay together. And it's not fair!

"Ummm," Max says. "Carla wasn't at work today, either."

William gives Max a look, like they know some secret or something. He says to Imani, "Well, go wash your face now, and come back for lasagna. You'll probably get to see Olivia at school tomorrow."

Imani drags herself to the bathroom like her shoes are made of cement. Max gets her phone from the counter charger and takes it into the living room. Parts of Max's end of the phone conversation drift into the kitchen while William and I empty the Dimitri bags, open cartons, unwrap garlic bread and put it all out on the table.

"I know...Yes, it's awful...Oh...I didn't know that...But you can't keep the kids out of school...I know...Oh, Carla..."

Now it sounds like Max could cry, except she won't. She doesn't.

It's a quiet dinner.

This is one of Joe's late-night classes in L.A., so after dinner, I go over to his place, take his extra key from the fake rock, and let myself in. Peppy jumps up and down, turns in circles, then sits right in front of me, waiting. I grab her leash from the hook by the door, fasten it to her collar, and we're out of there. Peppy lives up to her name. She rushes to the front gate, sniffs, scratches at the latch until I open it. Then it's out to the tree in the neighbor's yard, sniffing, circling, running back to me, then bouncing back to the tree. Really, she bounces, not like Buddy, who mostly shuffles along, slow and relaxed.

I've heard people refer to the houses in our neighborhood as California Ranch. None of the lots is big enough for horses or cows or any ranch stuff. William says California Ranch is mainly single story with a long, low roofline. It's funny about William. He knows a lot about architectural styles. We'll pull up to some big painting job in Pasadena, and he'll say, "Monterey Revival," or "Mediterranean," "Spanish Colonial," or "Craftsman." Well, that one's easy. Even I recognize "Craftsman," lots of wood, simple lines, lots of windows...Well, I guess that's not much of a description, but I know one when I see it.

Anyway, in our neighborhood the houses are almost all single story, usually three bedrooms, two baths, with attached garages. It sounds boring, but I like to notice how the yards are planted. Ever since the drought, a lot of people have dug out their lawns and put in native plants that don't take as much water. Lots of lavender and sage and poppies and rocks. Lots of native rocks.

We're coming up to the Husong's yard, still with a lawn and Peppy's favorite place to stop for a pee. Sure enough, she tugs at her leash to change direction and angles onto their lawn. Mrs. Husong told me once that she didn't care if Peppy peed on her lawn because she was such a delicate little thing, not big enough to turn a patch of lawn yellow. But she didn't want Buddy emptying his copious load of urine on her lawn. That's what she said, "copious load of urine."

While we circle around the neighborhood, I'm thinking about the day. How worried Max and William seem. And so many irritable teachers! And then I think about Ms. Cortez, and Olivia staying at home, and I guess it's because of the way the election turned out.

Back at Joe's, I check to be sure Peppy has water, give her a quick ear-rub, and go out the kitchen door into the garage/studio. Most people bring their own mats, so there are only two that need to be wiped down, rolled up, and put away. I vacuum the carpet, dust the Buddha in the corner, rub his belly for luck, straighten papers, wipe the desk in the corner by the door, lock up, put the key back in its rock, and leave.

Buddy's waiting by the door, thumping his tail, when I get home. I grab his leash and take him in the opposite direction of where I walked Peppy. For a while, I tried walking both dogs together, wanting to save time. But I spent so much time untangling their leashes that it took about as long walking them together as it did separately. And untangling's not fun so I ended that trial pretty fast. Besides, walking's good thinking time. On this round, I'm thinking about Rosie again, wishing she'd answer my text. Thinking about how intent Brent is on winning the cornhole bet, thinking about the job I'll be working on with William after school tomorrow. While William's painting a master bedroom, I'll be painting someone's wrought iron patio furniture, unless it rains.

By the time I get home, Imani's in bed, Max has gone out for groceries, and William's in his recliner, watching "Game of Thrones." I watch with him for a little while. I like dragons and ancient kinds of armor, but I haven't been watching it much lately, and I don't have a clue about what's happening.

Walking back toward my room, William calls after me, "Don't forget the black spray paint for tomorrow's job."

"Already in the car," I tell him.

I sit at my desk in my ergonomic, rolling, adjustable desk chair, doodling Simba/Vampire sketches. I love my chair. Last summer, we were working in one of those giant houses, painting the lady's home office. I mentioned to William that I liked her desk chair. I didn't even know she heard me, but on the day we finished, she wrote a check for William and she rolled the chair out to me. "A bonus," she said, smiling. Really, I was speechless. Well, by now you know I'm often speechless. But "thank you" didn't seem like enough. That's what I said, though, after being speechless, "Thank you, thank you, thank you."

"You're welcome," she said. "I've got a new chair on order—a better fit for the new color scheme."

So that's why I have such a top-quality, ergonomically designed chair. Max says my chair and William's recliner are the best pieces of furniture in the house.

I check my text messages even though I've been listening for that ding since 4:00 this afternoon. No message. I call.

"Hey, Eddie," she says.

"Hey, Rosie. Did you get my texts?"

"Yeah, sorry. I've been working on my college application essay, and I'm just so stressed!"

"I can come rub your back," I say, all hopeful.

It's like she hasn't even heard me. She says the application guidelines say a successful essay is based on your own unique experiences, world view, way of thinking, and personal style.

"I mean, seriously??" she says, her voice all high and choked. "My world view? My way of thinking? I don't have a clue!"

I know not to tell her she worries too much because that irritates her. But she does worry too much. It seems like everyone I know is all stressed out about college applications and what to emphasize in their essays, and where to apply, and will they get financial aid, and...and...and. I'm glad it's not my thing.

"Let's talk about something else," Rosie says.

"Yeah, okay. You know how Brianna and Meghan hang out together sometimes?"

"Yeah. They're both on Student Council."

"So, Cameron's set Brent up with her. Meghan can't go out alone with a guy, but she can double date so Brent and Brianna are getting together with them."

Rosie busts out laughing.

"What?" I ask.

"You know, Brent Bruno, Brianna?"

"Oh...the 'BR' thing!" Now I'm laughing, too.

"It'll be perfect. It's meant to be," Rosie says. Another bout of laughter. It's good to hear Rosie laugh.

"So, do you want to hang out with them Friday night?"

"Doing what?" Rosie asks.

"Well..."

"Doing what?"

"Playing cornhole?"

"Cornhole???"

"Yeah. You know. You throw beanbags at a board with a hole in it—try to get the beanbag into the hole."

"Well...okay. But first we have to stop by that fancy toy store I've been telling you about. I need to figure out what I'm getting Zoe for her birthday."

"Sure, that's fine."

We decide on a time, talk a little more about Rosie's application anxiety, my Irritable Teacher Day observations, how Zoe was all upset when she came home from school, too. Something about some mean kids saying bad things or something. Then it's back to Brianna and Brent.

"I hope they like each other," Rosie says. "Brianna's been pretty sad in the guy department ever since she broke up with Christopher."

"Why's she sad if she's the one who broke up with him?"

"She says she feels like she's the only senior who doesn't have a special person in her life, especially now that you and I are together."

After we hang up, I see by my phone that we've talked for twenty-one minutes. I never talk with *anyone* for twenty-one minutes, but it's easy with Rosie.

CHAPTER NINE

And You Eat Health Food?

Fuck! It's the first thing I see as I speed into the empty student parking lot. Halfway across the outside wall of the music building, in big black letters:
Out Jews!
Out Mexicans!
Out Niggers!
Out Moslums!
Keep America White!

I screech to a stop near the scrawled hate, grab the spray paint from my trunk, and start spraying over the words. The idiot who did this can't even spell Muslims! Cretin! Whoever wrote this shit has the brains of an earthworm! I stand back for a better look, give the near empty spray paint can a quick shake, and fill in a spot I missed.

"Barajas!" I turn to see Marcus, the security guy, sprinting toward me. "You working on a suspension??"

I point to the giant "Welcome to Hamilton High" sign that's painted on the front of the administration building.

"I don't think we want an 'unwelcome' sign," I tell him. "Did you see that shit I just painted over?"

"Yeah, I saw it. That's why I started down here . . . It's nasty stuff, but it's not up to you to mess with it." He nods toward the paint can. "I'll take that," he says.

I hand him the can. It's almost empty now, anyways.

"You should have left this to the custodians. That's their job."

Marcus is a big, buffed up black guy who some kids say did prison time. I don't know about that. I don't think they do, either. I know it's best not to get Marcus mad, though, so I don't say what I think about how slow the custodians are to clean up graffiti.

"I'm letting you off this time, but any more paint can antics and it'll be a suspension. Defacing is defacing, whatever the reason." Marcus says, walking over to where kids are getting off the early bus.

I'm glad they're not seeing that white supremacist shit. And except for the sick, the pretend-to-be-sick, and whoever's been suspended, all the rest of the 3,127 Hamilton High student body will be here in another 20 minutes and they won't see that crap, either. I don't care what Marcus thinks, I'm glad I painted out the hate. I move my car to a marked parking space, get my backpack, and jog to WriteLight.

Miss May is rushing around, pulling coffee and snacks from locked cabinets emptying oranges out of her big tote bag.

"Where've you been?" she asks, not looking up.

I grab the cleaner and paper towels. "Sorry. I had an errand," I say, cleaning the table closest to me.

"At 6:30 in the morning?"

"Yeah, well, you know, some things can't wait," I tell her.

She pauses to look at me. "Like getting the writing room set up for zero period?" she says, all sarcastic.

She'll get over it. I'm almost never absent or late, and besides, if Miss May had seen that graffiti out there this morning, she'd have covered it up herself.

Even though I'm late getting started, I still have time to slip out and meet Rosie in the hall before she goes to class. I put my arm around her and give her a quick peck on the cheek. She leans into me, nuzzles her head against my shoulder.

"I'm so tired," she says. "I was up until two this morning finishing the 'Macbeth' assignment."

"Maybe you can sleep in class," I say. "It's not that hard."

She gives me one of her affectionate pokes in the arm, then there's the bell, and we rush off to our classes.

Lunchtime. Brent and Cameron, as usual, already have a table in the quad. I open a plastic container and show them my spinach and kale salad, expecting some smartass remark. But Cameron hands his phone across to me. Instagram. A picture of me in front of the painted over graffiti, handing my paint can to Marcus. Caption: Get spics outta my country. #pepe #StopWhiteGenocide #P8RIOTS.

I dump a small can of chicken and a packet of ranch dressing onto my salad, and mix it up. Cameron takes his phone from me, goes to Twitter, and hands it back. #P8RIOTS. Same picture with a black swastika over it.

Brent's got his phone out now. "Facebook, too," he says.

I give Cameron's phone back and find the Facebook post on my own phone. It's a crude drawing of a brown guy. Whoever did it isn't good at drawing hands, but he (probably he and not she) was good enough that he could draw five stick fingers on one hand and a thumb and a blob for the other. There's a red prohibit symbol over the brown guy and "Enemy of Free Speech. Impure Race. Defective" in the comment box.

I sit staring at the post. Whoever wrote it can spell better than the "artist" from this morning's crap.

"What'd you do that for?" Brent says.

"Do what?" I ask.

"You shouldn't have painted over that stuff!" Brent says. "Whatever it said, it didn't mean shit."

"Yes. It did. It exactly meant shit."

"But c'mon, Nature Boy," Cameron says. "You eat health food, but you piss off the Patriots? That is definitely not healthy!"

"Hate's not healthy," I say.

"What's it to you? You're not a Muslim," Cameron says.

"Barajas. Remember me? Your friend? Eduardo Barajas?"

"Yeah. But you're not really Mexican…I mean…not illegal or anything."

"Well, they don't make distinctions about what kind of Mexican I am. None of this stuff is saying 'Oh, never mind. He's legal. We take it all back.'"

Brent gets up, dumps his trash, and carries his tray to the counter. He comes back with another Coke and sits opposite me.

"But man, you know. Those guys can be brutal. Fuck! Remember what they did to that gay guy last year? He ended up with broken ribs and a smashed-in face! He was in the hospital for over a week! And he hadn't even done anything."

"I don't know how they got away with that," Cameron says. "Everyone knew who did it."

"He wouldn't testify," Brent says.

The warning bell rings, and we go our separate ways. World History: Film day. That's good. I can zone out. Text ding. From Rosie, the picture of the stick figure guy with the blobby hand.

Rosie: *u ok?*

Me: *thumbs up emoji*

The thing is, I don't care what anybody posts about me. If I'm good with my friends, I'm good.

Yoga's down to a routine now. In the beginning, everyone was all stiff and awkward, but now it's just grab a mat and start stretching as soon they get into the room. Even the skinny girl with the greasy hair. Right away, she starts going through stretches and postures like there's no one else around—way different from the first few weeks.

The only one who *doesn't* start stretching is that squeaky-voiced Jason guy. Still sits way in the back of the room. And when Joe tells him to bring his mat closer to the rest of the group, he drags his mat about two inches. And he does the most minimum possible for any of the postures. If he's in here for anger management, I don't think it's working. He always looks pissed. Today he looks *really* pissed. And he wears that camo jacket all through the class. It's got to be hard to do yoga wearing a heavy camo jacket.

I've just put the last of the mats and blocks away when Joe motions me into his office.

"I'm supposed to meet Rosie, like five minutes ago," I tell him.

"I'll make it quick," he says. "I saw those Snapchat and Twitter posts. You know what I'm talking about?"

I nod. "No big," I tell him.

He rubs his tattoo. "Yeah, big. Hockney's scheduled an emergency faculty meeting for about right now. Friday afternoon. You know how much teachers want to stick around school on a Friday afternoon?? That's how big a deal it is."

"Why? Those guys are just a bunch of losers. They don't scare me."

"You might want to rethink that," Joe says. "I know their kind from the prison skinheads. They're vicious."

"Those guys aren't *skinheads*," I say.

"Same thing. Whites only in America. Get rid of everyone else." Joe stands and grabs his jacket. We walk out together. "Watch your back," he says, as I turn in the direction of the gym.

Rosie's on a bench by the tennis courts, her notebook open on her lap.

"Sorry I'm late," I tell her.

She smiles her bright smile. "It's okay. I need all the time I can get to study for tomorrow's calculus test."

We walk to the office to pick up my spray paint, then back to the choir room so she can get her music folder. She'll be singing a solo at the winter concert, and Sofia's going to accompany her. "Accompany." Maybe another SAT word?

By the time we get to the choir room, clear on the other side of campus from the gym, and then back to the parking lot, my car's practically alone and . . .

"FUCK!" I run to the car to be sure I'm seeing what I don't want to see. "FUCK!"

Rosie comes rushing up. "What's wrong?" I point to the front tire. Flat as a pancake. So are the other three. "Oh, my gosh! You got four flat tires all at once?"

I run my hand around the front tire wall, then the back. "Slashed. They were slashed."

"Oh, my gosh! That's horrible! Who would do that?"

I shrug.

"I bet it's whoever's been posting all of that stuff about you."

"Maybe."

"What're you going to do? My mom should be home by now. I can call her to come get us."

"No. I need to call Triple A. But, shit! All four tires! They're not that old, either." I stand staring at my tires, as if maybe that'll pump them up again.

Rosie takes her phone from the special phone pocket in her backpack and calls her mom. Ever since the embarrassing canvas bag dump, Rosie keeps her phone in a special place so she always knows where it is. Me? It's like: is my phone in my backpack? My jacket pocket? My car? I check my jacket pockets, then my jeans pockets, then the outer pocket of my backpack where I finally find it buried at the bottom, under binders and *The Grapes of Wrath* and my dirty lunch containers.

I call Triple A, then text William to tell him I probably can't get to the job this afternoon. Then I text Max to see if she can swing by to get me on her way home from work.

Max texts back: *all ok?*

Me: *4 flats. calling aaa.*

Another text ding. Max: *Where r u?*

Me: *HH parking lot*

Max: *Be there by 5*

Me: *k*

Rosie moves close beside me and slips her arm around my waist. "My mom'll be here in a few minutes—sure we can't take you anywhere?"

"Triple A should be here soon."

I lean into her, knowing now that she for sure likes me.

Rosie's mom pulls up beside us in her bright red Honda, lowers her window, and sticks her head out. "Hey, Eddie. What happened?"

"Somebody slashed my tires," I say.

"That's terrible! Who did it?"

"Not sure," I tell her.

Rosie and I'd only been hanging around together for a couple of weeks when her parents said it was time for them to meet me. Awkward! It turned out not to be too bad, though. We met for dinner at JJ's, a kind of hamburger place that's lots better than McDonald's. It was cool that we met there instead of them picking me up and all of us going together in the family car. That would have been double awkward.

Rosie's mom and dad are cool. They weren't all like, what do you plan to major in in college? Or, what's your favorite subject in school? One of the first things Ms. Coulter asked after the glad-to-meet-yous were over was: what did I like to read? I told her straight out I usually didn't read assigned books, but that I liked true stories about real people, and some historical fiction and regular fiction. Mrs. Coulter's a librarian at the alternative school, and pretty soon she was sending books my way, always with sticky notes that said something like "You might like this. Take your time."

Rosie gives me a quick kiss and, after shoving about twenty mostly hardcover books to the side, climbs into the backseat. I've never seen Mrs. Coulter's car without a bunch of books in the backseat. I guess it's a librarian thing. Zoe is in the passenger seat, licking what's left of a chocolate chip cookie dough ice cream cone. I know it's chocolate chip cookie dough because that's the only kind of ice cream Zoe ever eats.

"What're you reading, Eddie?"

"*The Grapes of Wrath.*"

Rosie leans forward and sticks her head in that space between the two front seats. "Mom…"

"Like it?"

"Just started it."

"MOM…"

Ms. Coulter turns to look at Rosie. "I know. You've got to get to Sofia's."She turns back toward me. "Isn't that required reading?" she laughs.

"I'm giving it a try, anyways."

Rosie's doing that eye-roll thing.

"Okay. Okay," her mom says, giving me a wave as they drive off.

I get into my car. Not that I'm going anywhere, but I'm tired of standing there, watching my tires stay flat. I take *The Grapes of Wrath* from my backpack and settle in to read.

I've just finished the part where Joad, the hitchhiker, tells the truck driver that he got out of prison after seven years 'cause he killed a guy when I see Max turn into the parking lot. She pulls up beside me on the passenger side, gets out of her car, and into mine.

"Triple A should be here pretty soon," I tell her.

"How'd this happen?"

I shrug.

"No idea? Not even a guess?"

I shrug again.

"Talk to me, Eddie. Talk to me."

That's Max. Whenever anything, I mean *anything* goes wrong, she pushes me to talk about it. But the thing is, back when I was nine, after that guy molested me, I stopped talking for a while. Like for weeks. Not one single word. So, Max gets worried and pushy when I go silent. I understand where she's coming from, but it still bugs me. Sometimes I just don't feel like talking.

CHAPTER TEN

WWCCD?

Between waiting for Triple A to come, then waiting for their flatbed truck to come, and for the car to get loaded onto the truck and taken to the tire place, then filling out the paperwork, etc., etc., it's nearly nine o'clock by the time we get home. Buddy runs a circle around me, then around Max, then around me again. It's his happy greeting.

"Hey, Buddy," I say, leaning down to ruffle his big, grey-flecked, yellow head.

"There's leftover pizza in the fridge," William calls to us from the living room where he and Imani are watching "Frozen" for about the thousandth time. "And salad."

When William and Imani moved in, Max said with more people in the house, we had to be better organized. Max and William both work full time, sometimes more, and, according to Max, it's easy to get sloppy with home stuff—food, cleaning, clutter. So, she and William share the cooking—Max cooks Monday and Tuesday, William, Wednesday and Thursday. Friday's usually takeout, which is why I'm eating pizza right now. Saturday and Sunday? Depends on what else is going on.

Before William and Imani moved in, we had a family meeting. It wasn't like all of a sudden Imani and I would have two parents to deal with. If I needed permission to do something, or if I got in trouble at school, that would be between me and Max, like always. And William would be doing all of the parent stuff with Imani, like always. I was happy to hear that 'cause I had this friend up in Redville whose mom's boyfriend moved in with them, and all of a sudden the guy was telling the kid what he could and couldn't do and acting like the big boss. That's not how it is here, though.

Imani started calling Max "Mommy" about half-an-hour after they moved in, but William's still the guy who's in charge of all things Imani. Max takes Imani shopping for clothes sometimes, and once in a while, they bake cookies together, but that's about it for the mom stuff.

On the chest in Imani's room there's a framed picture of her and her mom and William. She's probably about two in the picture, in a white frilly dress with a sparkly silver headband holding back her thick, black, frizzy hair. They're probably at some park. The mom and William are sitting close together on the grass, with trees in the background. William's got his arm around the mom. Imani's standing between them leaning into William. She and her mom are a Bristol Chocolate color. William's a darker Natural Bark. They look happy in the picture. Imani says her mom went to heaven a long time ago, but I don't know any of the details.

When I hear "Some People Are Worth Melting For," I know "Frozen's" nearly over. Moments later, William comes into the kitchen and kisses Max on the forehead. He's about six inches taller than Max, so her forehead is an easy reach.

"We tried to wait for you, but Imani was starving."

Max reaches into the refrigerator to get the leftovers. I reach past her, snag the O.J., and take a long swig from the bottle.

She gives me the look.

"C'mon, Max. I'm the only one who ever drinks out of this."

"Because everyone else in the house is afraid they'll get your cooties," she says.

William hands me a glass. I pour juice into it for the sake of domestic tranquility.

My dad split before I was even born, and I got over wanting a replacement dad a long time ago. But I like that there's another guy in the house. And that he's teaching me the painting business. Also, that he treats Max good.

Max and I finish the pizza and salad while William sits at the table with us, nursing a beer. Between bites, Max fills him in on the tire mess.

"Who would do that?" he says to me.

I give the same answer I gave Max. A shrug.

"You're telling me someone wandered into that jam-packed student parking lot, carrying what had to be a pretty heavy-duty knife, and happened to get the urge to slash four tires as they just happened to be near your car? I don't think so, Eddie. There was a reason. What was it?"

I focus on the last three crumbs of pizza crust.

"Eddie?" Max says.

I don't want to go into it, have it turn into a bigger deal than it already is.

"We need to file a police report," Max says.

"No way. I'm not filing a police report!"

"Well then, I am," Max says.

"Max! No! It's my car. No police report."

There's another one of those long looks. "Eddie. I don't want to fight you on this, but you know, officially that's my car, and I'm filing a report."

"That sucks! I paid for the car with my own work money. Insurance, too. It's not your car!"

"Whose name is on the registration?"

So, we go to the computer and file a police report.

* * * * *

It's nearly midnight. I'm in bed, leaning back against the headboard, playing Fortnite, when Max, in her funky clown pajamas and her beat-up slippers, comes in and sits on the bed next to me.

"Eddie...stop for a minute. Look at me."

I look up.

"I hate fighting with you, pulling rank so to speak, but..."

"I hate it, too," I tell her.

"Remember when I was in Iraq, in the hospital, and I didn't even tell you and Mario my leg was all torn apart—kept emailing that everything was fine—loved the macaroni and cheese you guys sent? And you and Mario had run away to Redville, and Mario was trying to save you from that awful mess with Denton, and Carmen was trying to get Mario arrested, and you guys kept emailing me that everything was fine? Remember?"

"Yeah, sure."

"We didn't want to worry each other? Remember?"

I nod.

"And we decided we had to level with each other, no matter what. That we didn't want to have that kind of meaningless everything-is-fine relationship?

"Yeah."

"And we worked everything out together?"

"Yeah."

"And part of working it out was that you started to talk again?"

"Yeah."

"Talk to me, Eddie."

"I don't want it to be a big deal."

"Well, it is. Somebody slashed all four of your tires. That's a big deal!"

Max is propped up on her elbow, watching, waiting, the frown marks she brought home from Iraq deepening, like they always do when she's worried.

I do five deep centering breaths, like I learned in yoga a long time ago. Five more. "So. Okay. I don't know for sure who did it, but I think it's because I covered over something someone had written on a wall at school."

"Like what?"

So, I tell her the whole story, the hate sign, the black spray paint I had with me, how I wiped out that Nazi anti-Muslim, Mexican, Jew, nigger shit before hardly anyone got to school.

"And...?"

"And that's it."

"Who wrote it in the first place?"

"I don't know."

Which is true. I don't exactly know, even though I'm like 99.99% sure it was those Patriot guys.

"You must have some idea."

I shrug. The last thing I want is for Max to go all law and order again and fill in more blanks on the police report.

"Well...okay," she says, leaning in to kiss my cheek. "Stop with the games and get some sleep." She stands up, stretches and walks toward the door, then stops and looks back at me. "I'm proud of you, Eddie. Worried, but proud."

"Well...you know. What would Cesar Chavez do?"

She smiles and shakes her head. "Sometimes I'm almost sorry we ever taught you to ask that question."

"Yeah, me too," I say. "But it's too late now."

I hear Max telling William about the history of my WWCCD bracelet, and it takes me back to that little kid time, back when I was ten or so, during our Redville years.

A lot of the kids in my class wore these bracelets with the letters "WWJD" on them: "What Would Jesus Do?" I wanted one. I mean I *really* wanted one. It was a time I was looking for answers and it seemed like the WWJD kids had a lot of answers. I begged Max to get one for me but she wouldn't—said I didn't know anything about what Jesus would do so the bracelet would be like a lie. I complained to Mario that I needed a WWJD bracelet and that Max was being unreasonable. I complained to my cousin Vincent, and his daughter, Hannah, and his wife, Jordan, and my aunt and uncle, and I guess to everyone else in Redville because I really, really wanted one of those bracelets.

Then, one evening, Vincent came over to help Max fill out a complicated Army disability request form. He's a lawyer so Vincent is the go-to guy for stuff like that. Max's leg had healed by then, but her right leg ended up being about an inch shorter than the left and that was messing her back up.

Anyways, Mario and I were in the living room watching "The Simpsons" when Victor came in. He held up one of those bracelets, dangled it in the air. He gave me a big smile. "Want it?" he said.

I jumped up and grabbed it, threw my arms around his waist, and gave him a giant hug. He tied the bracelet on my wrist and it was then that I noticed it wasn't WWJD. It was WWCCD. What?? I just stared at it, fighting tears.

Vincent took hold of my wrist and pointed to each letter. "What. Would. Cesar. Chavez. Do. That's the question."

I knew who Cesar Chavez was. Everybody in Redville knew who Cesar Chavez was. He's the guy who started the farmworkers union. Tio Hector and Tia Josie marched with him when Vincent was still a baby in a stroller. They laugh that Vincent's first sentence was "Si Se Puede." (Yes, it can be done). That's what the farmworkers chanted when they marched and demonstrated for fair pay and better working conditions. So yeah, I knew who the guy was, but I wanted to know what Jesus would do, like those kids at my school with the real bracelets. I untied the bracelet and handed it back to Vincent. Max jumped up from her chair and practically flew across the room, bad leg and all. She took the bracelet from Vincent and tied it to my wrist so tight I thought my hand would drop off, my good hand, and she marched me into the bedroom for one of her "let's get this straight" talks.

After that, our bedtime reading turned from Harry Potter to Cesar Chavez biographies and stories about "the movement." And Max started taking us to church every Sunday so we'd learn something about Jesus. Whenever Mario or I had a problem or a complaint, the question would be WWCCD? WWJD? After months of what Max and Vincent referred to as my education in the real world, I stopped always wearing shirts with sleeves long enough to hide the WWCCD bracelet. I guess you could say I chose CC over Jesus. I mean Jesus is holy and all that, but it's clearer to me what CC would do than what J would do.

I wonder, what *would* CC have done about the hate graffiti? Organize a group? Lead a strike? March? Boycott? That's what he led the farmworkers to do back in the day. I don't have a clue what he'd be up to these days, but for sure, he wouldn't have liked that hate crap, 'cause he was big on equality and respect for everybody.

* * * * *

So, Rosie and I missed the Friday night triple date cornhole thing because I was dealing with slashed tires, but Cameron texted early this morning saying Brent finally has a girlfriend because Brianna likes him now. Brent texts to set up another cornhole practice. He's so obsessed with cornhole he forgot I have to work today. We'll be back at that place in Alhambra, painting the living room walls a Wabi-Sabi Versatile Green with glossy Soft Focus Warm White baseboards.

After work, once I'm cleaned up and have convinced Max to let me borrow her car, I head over to Rosie's. She's in Tilly the Trailer where she's been working on college applications and studying for a test on *Macbeth*. Tilly's table is strewn with college booklets and application forms, and Shakespeare, and orange rinds and peanut shells. Oranges and peanuts, the key to academic success, according to Rosie.

"I bet you haven't even looked at your phone today," she says.

"This morning I got texts from Cameron and Brent, but I only pay attention if it's your special ring. Besides, William's got a thing about not looking at our phones during work hours."

"Well, you should look at this," Rosie says, handing me her phone.

Instagram, with a big X over a stick figure of a guy and a caption that says "Cleanse the Bloodline." I know the guy is supposed to be me because it's another one of the stick figures without fingers on one hand. The drawing's so bad it makes me laugh.

Rosie takes her phone back and goes to her Twitter account. "It's not funny. Look at this."

There's an actual picture of me. From where? Yearbook? Somebody's Facebook account? There's my face with a big X mark across it, #keepamericawhite. Funnier still. Like America's ever been white? Haven't they ever heard of the first Americans? The ones who'd been here for thousands of years before any of the "white" people showed up? How about how California was stolen from Mexico?

"Somebody's more than a little mad at you," Rosie says.

I shrug, hand her phone back to her.

We go for a bite to eat at a new Vietnamese place where Rosie has a two-for-one coupon. It's good, but I probably won't go back, at least not until they're giving out more two-for-ones. After Pho Quyen, we go back to Rosie's place. To Tilly. She wants me to watch this show with her, "Atypical," so I'll know music therapy's a real thing. We climb onto the big cushion, lean back against the wall, and Rosie finds the show on her laptop. I crack the window open just enough to let in a hint of clean night air.

"I'm going to skip ahead to the episode with the important part."

The series is about this high school kid who's autistic. He mainly wants to talk about penguins and the Antarctica. He doesn't have a clue about how to get along with people, and he wants a girlfriend. It's more of a girl show, probably nothing I'd ever watch on my own, but it's warm and cozy here in the trailer, and Rosie's leaning in close to me. We could be watching the Teletubbies or a blank screen for all I care.

"Look, here's the part, right here..."

It's people sitting around in a circle, in some kind of support group, and this one woman tells another how much music therapy has helped her autistic son.

"See," Rosie says. "It shows how important music therapy can be, how much it can help people."

"I don't know why you keep trying to convince me. I believe you."

"Yeah, but not everyone thinks it's a real thing, and it's great to see it in a TV series."

There's this scene where a bunch of kids are standing around some fat girl's locker, laughing at the girl. Her locker has "orca" written across it, and they're laughing and pointing at her and she's trying not to cry. Then the autistic guy's sister comes up to the group, sees what's going on, and punches the loudest one hard. In the face. And bloodies her nose. It's one of those super satisfying moments when an asshole gets what's coming to her.

"Serves her right," I say.

"I feel so sad when I see someone picking on someone else," Rosie says. "I hate how some people pick on Sofia and Fatima. They're both just the nicest people."

"Back when I was a little kid, this man totally took advantage of me, making me do stuff I didn't want to do, and always pushing me around. It hella pisses me off when I see that happening to anybody else. I want to smack 'em in the face like that guy's sister just did, only harder."

We watch a little more of the show, and then I pull Rosie closer, turn her face toward me, and kiss her on the lips, the way we like to kiss, a little bit of teasing tongue, and then a little more. The laptop slides to the side, and we scoot down until we're stretched out full length on the cushions, body to body, as close as we can get. We fumble around with sweatshirts and buttons and zippers, and our hands are everywhere, touching every inch of our bodies, and I'm asking, "Do you want to? Do you want to?" and Rosie is answering, "I want to," and we're both fumbling around for condoms that have to be within arms' reach but where? Where's the damn condom!!!! Finally, I grab my pants from where they've slipped to the floor, and find the condom in the back pocket. At practically the same time, Rosie pulls one out from somewhere in her backpack. And then it's more fumbling. And then I'm pushing hard into Rosie, fast and hard when she lets out a gasp that scares me, and I half pull out.

"Should I stop?" I say, breathing so fast I can barely get the words out. I feel her take a long breath in.

"Don't stop," she says, grabbing my butt and pulling me farther back into her.

So I go slower, easier, except it's impossible to do slow and easy. My body won't do slow and easy, and then it's over. "Rosie. Rosie. God how I love you," I say pushing her hair back and catching a dampness from her cheek. "Are you crying?"

"I'm okay," she says. "I don't think it's supposed to be good for girls the first time."

We're lying side by side now, and she takes my hand and slides it between her legs and moves it where she wants it to go until there's a different kind of gasp, a happy gasp, and we lie there, close, for a long time.

"This was the best feeling I've ever felt. Best in the whole world," I tell her. We kiss and scoot in closer. "I'm sorry I was such a fumbler, though."

She laughs. "We just need practice," she says.

"Lots of it. How about now?" I whisper.

"How about tomorrow night?" she says.

It's nearly one in the morning when I pull on my clothes and say goodnight. "I've never been happier," I tell Rosie.

"I'm happy, too," she says. "I'm glad we did it."

I'm smiling all the way home. Like lips stretched to the limit kind of smiling. Even when I walk into the house, I can't stop smiling.

William and Max are watching "The Fresh Prince of Bel Air," which is like their usual Saturday night watching after Imani's in bed.

"How was the new restaurant?" Max asks.

"Good," I say. Big smile.

"Must've been amazingly good," William says, appraising my smile.

" 'night," I say, eager not to answer any more questions.

In bed, I text Rosie: *Luv u luv luv luv u!*

A ding, and then, a string of hearts, followed by a stream of exclamation marks.

CHAPTER ELEVEN

I Can See Your House from Here

Sunday morning, the scent and sizzle of bacon gets me out of bed and to the table. William's making pancakes with his specialty Mickey Mouse pancake for Imani. She'd rather have Anna of Arendelle, but how could that happen with a pancake?

Max is sitting at the table, the newspaper opened to the movie section. "We're going to see the new 'Despicable Me' movie this afternoon. Wanna come?"

"Rosie and I are going for a hike," I say, reaching for the bacon.

With a stack of pancakes on the table, and Imani's Mickey Mouse pancake on her "Frozen" plate, William joins us at the table. "How about sharing some of the paper?" he says to Max.

"Help yourself," she says, lifting the "Entertainment" section out of the way. William slides the rest of the paper to his side of the table.

We're all munching away, enjoying the Sunday morning pancake/bacon treat, when William slaps his hand down hard on the paper.

"Of course, we are!" William says. "You can't have a president spouting hate and expect it not to mess things up!"

"Of course, we are what?" Max asks.

William pushes the newspaper out in front of him. There's a headline that reads "Blacks, Latinos are targets as hate crimes surge in the state."

Max reads out loud, "11.2 percent spike in total hate crimes. Second year of double digit increases in the state."

"What's a hate crime?" Imani asks.

William's voice softens. "Nothing you need to worry about, Baby," he says. "Hey! What happened to Mickey's big ears??"

Imani laughs. "I always eat the ears first!"

William folds his section of the paper and slides it over to Max. "And then there's this!"

"I know," she says. "That seems so wrong! More people voted for her than for him, but we got him instead!"

"What??? How can that happen??" I ask.

Max points to a section in the paper, and I read about the electoral college system, which maybe I'd heard of once in some government class. It must have been on one of those days when I wasn't paying attention 'cause I don't get it.

"I guess the good news is that the majority of the American people didn't vote for fear and hate," Max says.

* * * * *

Rosie's folks drop her off on their way home from church. We stuff sandwiches and water into our backpacks and take the bus all the way to the top of Lake Street. On the way up, we sit close, holding hands, and though we don't talk about what we did last night, it's there with us, keeping us tight together. Once off the bus, we follow the trail up to Echo Mountain. Near the top, we find a bench in the shade where we sit, looking out over the San Gabriel Valley and downtown Los Angeles.

"I can see your house from here," I tell Rosie.

"Liar," she says, punching me in the arm.

"Well, I can see where I could see your house from here if we had a telescope."

We watch a squirrel grab an acorn on the ground near us, then skitter up to the lowest branch where it sits on its haunches and munches away.

As I pull sandwiches from my backpack, a ten-pack of lubricated latex Trojans falls out onto the bench. "Max strikes again!" I say, but Rosie doesn't even hear me, she's laughing so hard. Which gets me laughing, too. You can't not laugh when Rosie laughs. It's like a virus. Rosie's laughter virus.

I stuff the package into the bottom of my backpack and unwrap the sandwiches on the bench between us. "Tuna or cream cheese and cucumber?" I ask.

Rosie scrunches her nose. "Tuna please."

I breathe deeply of the cool, piney air. A lizard suns itself on a rough log across the trail.

Rosie takes a bite of her sandwich and stares out over the valley. "I haven't thought about tests, or college applications, or that solo I've got coming up in choir. None of that since last night." She pauses for a moment, then says, "At least none of that until right now."

"I wish you didn't worry so much," I say.

"Me, too," she says.

"Look," I tell her, gesturing toward the view beyond us. "When you watch the city, and the cars on the freeway, and look at all the buildings from far away, especially on a clear day like today, everything looks clean and orderly and peaceful."

"I wish it was that way up close," she says.

She's starting to get that school-worried frown again when another squirrel races up the tree to the acorn-chewing squirrel and chases him out onto a branch. Just when it looks as if the chaser's about to catch up with the chewer, the first squirrel leaps to a far branch on another tree. It seems like he can't possibly make it. But he does. We both let out a long breath at the same time, then collapse in laughter. And Rosie's school-worried frown is gone again.

* * * * *

So, a near perfect weekend with Rosie, no worries, until Hockney calls about ten minutes after I get home.

"Come straight to my office at 8:00."

"Why?"

"We need to talk. You're not in trouble."

"I'm an aide zero period."

"I'll clear it with your teacher."

So, at 8:00 Monday morning, I wait in a chair outside Hockney's office long enough to read two more chapters of *The Grapes of Wrath*. I'm at the part where the guy who was in prison, Joad, goes to his family place and finds it all messed up and deserted, when Hockney finally calls me into his office. He tells me if I'd let the custodians take care of the sign, it would have saved everyone a lot of trouble. Says he understands my tires were slashed. He talks about the nasty online posts, says as soon as his tech aide takes one down, another one crops up. He tells me I don't understand how serious this situation is, blah, blah, blah. Here's what sucks though. Hockney tells me I can't be at school today. It's not safe.

"You're suspending me???"

"Not officially. It's just for your own safety, Mr. Barajas."

"That's so stupid! You think I can't take care of myself?"

"It's just a precautionary move."

Hockney glances at the clock, then calls Miss Suazo, the school secretary. "Would you please call Mrs. Benton, tell her I may be a few minutes late for the 10:00 meeting? Come along, Mr. Barajas. I'll take you home."

"I'll take the bus."

"No. You'll need a ride. If you don't want to ride with me, I can call someone to come get you. I think your mother's the emergency contact?"

Max is at work, probably scraping plaque from some careless flosser's teeth. I don't want her to have to leave work so I go with Hockney out to the faculty lot where he pushes a button on his key fob and a green RAV4 beeps.

He motions for me to get in. It's still got that new car smell. The dash display is about four times as big as the one in my old Honda. My dash tells me how fast I'm going. What the oil pressure is. What time it is and what radio station is on. His tells him all of that, plus tire pressure, and how close he is to objects when he backs up, MPG, and his location on a map. I don't even know what some of the dials show. Maybe it registers his blood pressure, too.

Hockney starts the car, backs up until there's a little beep-beep-beep, stops, shifts to drive, and we're on our way out of the parking lot and past the front of the school. I slump as low as my seatbelt will allow. Who wants to be seen riding along in the passenger seat beside the principal?

I start to give directions to my house, but before I can say to turn left at the next block, the voice of Barack Obama beats me to it. Does Hockney have every kid's address already programmed into his GPS, or is it only mine? It's kind of creepy. Not the Barack Obama voice, that's kind of cool. But that my address was already somewhere in Hockney's GPS is the creepy part. Well…it's creepy being alone in the car with a man who's not family. I can do it now, and I know Hockney's okay, but it still feels creepy.

Hockney asks me about WriteLight and Yoga, and I try to give more than one-word answers because I know that's what principals and parents and most adults want. But it's easiest if I can get them talking, so I ask about his son who I know plays football for S.C. That works. He tells me all about their latest game. Says he worries about head injuries, but his son lives for football. Besides, his son is officially an adult now so Hockney can't be telling him what to do. Talk of his son and football gets us all the way to my house.

Barack Obama tells him, "You have arrived at your destination. The route guidance is now finished." Hockney pulls over to the curb. "I'll wait to be sure you get inside."

"No need," I tell him. "I can get in."

"It's okay," he says, turning the engine off as if he's settling in for the morning. I get the spare key from under a potted geranium on the front porch. Hockney waits while I jiggle the lock a few times, then go inside. Buddy's waiting right inside the door.

"Hey, Buddy," I say, reaching down to scratch his butt. He leans hard into me, his comfort lean. It's been a while since he's done that, but it's like maybe he senses something I don't. "Release," I tell him.

I go to the front window and watch Hockney drive away. Buddy follows close behind, wagging his tail, like it's such a treat to have someone home at this time of day on a weekday. I know, it sounds crazy, like Buddy keeps a calendar and watches the clock, but he kind of does.

Cameron texts some Snapchat shit to me. Tells me there's more stuff on Reddit. I check it out. It's pretty much the same as before: purify the race, keep America white, stop white genocide. A bunch of stupid stuff.

I read for a while, eat a big bowl of leftover chili, get bored. Since I'm not officially suspended, I decide to go back to school for 7th period Yoga and then get a ride back home with Rosie.

I'm at the corner, waiting for the bus, when this blue pick-up comes driving slowly past me. Blue pick-up, white lettering on the side advertising landscaping, power mower and tools in the back—suddenly images of me in Denton's truck, him pushing my head down onto his open fly, me helplessly squirming, all flash before me. Can't catch a breath! Can't cry out! Choking! Chest heaving! Rapid panting! Pounding heart! Sweating!

I start the mantra. Slow down. Slow down. Slow down. I remind myself of the anti-panic attack drill. Hands on knees. Breathe. Slow, deep inhale. Slow, strong, exhale. Again. Remember I'm strong! Remember I'm powerful! I'm agile! Strength! Agility! Power! Mine! Breathe deep. Slow down.

The bus comes to a stop at the curb, and I manage to wave it on. Stay in the now. Slow breath in. Slow breath out. It's not then. It's now. Denton's in jail. I'm strong. Grown. No one could do that to me now. Stay in the now. Focus on now. Deep breath in. Notice the cool air as it fills my lungs. Deep breath out. Notice deflation, slow leak in a tough balloon. Empty the balloon.

I get up from the bench, take a slow step away, and turn in the direction of home. Slower breathing now. Still sweaty. I run my trembling hands over my dripping wet face, wipe them on my jeans. Stay in the now. Feel my strength.

When I get to within three houses of ours, I see Buddy, half standing, front paws on the sill of the big window in the living room. His head is turned in my direction. He sees me and disappears, rushing, I know, to meet me at the door. Inside, I sink to my knees and put my arms around his warm, sturdy body. He turns slightly, gets closer, leans his weight into my chest. Slowly, breathing returns to normal, sweat subsides, hands steady.

"It's okay, Buddy. It's okay." I ease up and go to my room, Buddy close behind. I stretch out on the bed, face down. Buddy jumps up and stretches out next to me, no space between us.

It's been a long time since I had a panic attack. I thought all of that was over—no more getting triggered by blue trucks, or a word or phrase. Once, just after I'd started school in Redville, a teacher asked me to "do something nice for him", a phrase Denton had used when he wanted a blow job. I totally freaked out, ran back to Josie and Hector's, locked myself in the bathroom and brushed my teeth like crazy, trying to get the taste of Denton out of my mouth. But that was eight years ago.

I change into sweats and running shoes, disappoint Buddy by squeezing past him through the door, and start off on a jog. Usually I'd take him, but he can't keep up when I run my fastest. I quicken my pace when I get to the track that borders the park, then full out run. I feel my speed, my strength, my stamina, and leave the panic attack behind.

Four laps. Then it's back to a jog, and a slower jog. I walk back home drenched in sweat, not panic sweat—strength sweat. The good kind.

CHAPTER TWELVE

True Patriot

Imani's in the living room, two inches from the TV, telling Ella she shouldn't keep Anna out of the room. Max and William are sitting at the kitchen table, talking softly, like they don't want anyone to hear. Max is in her after-work sweats. William's wearing a T-shirt and jeans, all scrubbed up. When I first started working with him, he was definite about how a painter shouldn't be wearing paint samples when he's not on the job.

I open the oven door. Meatloaf! I'm starving! I reach for the hot pads to take the pan out of the oven.

"Not yet," Max says.

"Looks done," I say.

"Turn the oven off. It'll keep. We need to talk," Max says.

"Okay," I say, leaning against the counter.

William nudges a chair out with his foot. "Have a seat."

Max looks at me, all serious, long enough to make me nervous.

"What?"

"Mr. Hockney called this afternoon."

"I didn't do anything!"

"He didn't say you did. Just said he brought you home to keep things safe."

"That's bullshit!"

"Eddie…there's a lot you didn't tell us, say, about all of that social media stuff, and who slashed your tires…"

"I don't know for sure who it was. I didn't see anyone do it."

"Yeah, okay," William says, his voice going way deep the way it does when he gets all serious. "You didn't see anyone do it, but you're probably pretty sure who it was. Right?"

Shrug.

"Mr. Hockney seemed pretty sure *he* knew who it was, not that he was sharing any names with us," Max says.

Silence.

"And who was it that posted a bunch of nasty stuff about you online?...Eddie?" Max says. "C'mon, Eddie. Make a guess."

"Well...I guess it was probably those Patriot guys. They're usually the ones that blast stuff like that on walls."

"Patriot guys?" Max says.

"Yeah. That's what they call themselves. Like at the Black Lives Matter thing? The P8RIOTs?"

William starts pacing around the kitchen. His face goes darker. How is that even possible? "Bad news. Those guys are bad, bad news."

"You know them?" Max says.

"Yeah—from the march back in September. Buncha stupid ass honky white supremacists, out there with their baseball bats and broken bottles, their storm trooper boots and pockets full of rocks."

"Those were high school kids???" Max asks.

"Some of them, yeah, school boys following their dumb-shit daddies...the Patriots," William sneers. "Here's a patriot!" he says, pulling up Max's right pant leg and showing the deep scar that runs all down the front of her shin from knee to ankle. "That's a patriot!"

He stomps into their bedroom, comes back out with two boxes, one a hand-carved wooden box and the other, one of those old cigar boxes. He dumps their army stuff out on the table—Max's Purple Heart, William's, too, and a bunch of other ribbons and medals. I don't know what they did to get the other ones.

"Patriots!" William yells. "Patriots fight *for* their country! Not against it!"

Imani comes to the kitchen, eyes wide.

Max is standing, her arm around William's shoulder. "William..."

"For equality! And justice!" he yells, even louder. "For democracy! Not for hate and racism!"

"William..."

He shakes his head and looks straight at Max, like he's just noticed she's there. "They're not patriots," he says, softly now. "We are."

She's got her arms around him, rubbing his back. They're locked together, and I see by the rise and fall of William's back that he uses that deep breathing trick to calm down, too. "God, I hate those bastards!" he says, in a near whisper.

"I know. I know," Max says.

Yeah, well, I know now, too. Probably the neighbors on both sides and across the street know, too. It's the first time I've ever heard William full blast. I've heard him mad before, but God! William's got some voice on him when he goes all out. The way Imani is looking at him, I'm guessing she's not heard him full volume before, either.

Max puts the medals and ribbons in their boxes and takes them back to their bedroom. William stares off into space for a moment, then reaches for the hot pads, takes the meatloaf from the oven, sets it on top of the stove and gets a knife from the drawer. I get the plates, three regular size, white with flowers, and one Imani-size, with Anna and Elsa. William cuts a small slice for Imani, puts it on her special plate, and hands it to her. She shakes her head.

"No, you have to have some, Baby. Just a little bit."

"That's too much!" she whines.

"Just try it."

She carries her plate to the table and sits staring at the meatloaf.

"Eddie?"

"Yeah. Please."

William puts a slice of meatloaf on each of the three regular plates and sets them at our places. I get utensils, Max puts a salad and bread on the table, and William pours water.

"Salad?" Max asks. I hold my plate within reach and she piles it on—lettuce, tomato, avocado, cucumber, croutons—then it's a spoonful for Imani, who gets right to work picking the cucumbers out. We eat in silence, like there's a moratorium on talking. Imani's not even doing her usual talk about Anna and Elsa, like: if they were at her school, she'd be best friends with Anna, but maybe Elsa and Ms. Lee would be best friends because Ms. Lee would know how to help Elsa manage her super powers, etc., etc. All silence. Awkward.

It's me and Max's turn for dishes tonight. I scrape, and she loads the dishwasher. Max is particular about how the dishes fit in the dishwasher. I wipe the table, and she puts leftovers away. We do that in silence too, until we hear William starting the bathwater for Imani, then Max takes up where we left off, before William got all heated about the Patriot stuff.

"I'm worried, Eddie."

"Max. Stop. They're nothing. They're cowards."

William comes into the kitchen to get a glass of water. "The guys in white who went around lynching black people were cowards, too. That didn't make the people they'd lynched any less dead," he says, taking the water back to Imani.

Max says, "People who are afraid are the most dangerous—especially those true-believer types…Mr. Hockney wants you to stay home from school tomorrow."

"That sucks! I'm not the one who should be suspended!"

"It's not a suspension. He says it's just…"

"It's a *suspension*. What else is it if he says I can't come to school?"

"Like all of a sudden you love school?"

"Some of it," I say. "Besides it's the principle. I don't mean like principal, like the principal is your pal, I mean it's just wrong."

My phone rings. Rosie. "I need to take this..."

Max nods, walks out to the living room. I take the phone outside.

"Hey, Rosie." I lean against the eucalyptus tree, pull off a leaf, crumble it between my fingers, breathe the strong, fresh scent.

"I heard you got suspended," Rosie says.

"Not officially."

I tell her the story, all but the panic attack. She tells me about new Patriot hate posts, and how everybody's talking about it, and how everyone is totally on my side. I change the subject with talk about the cornhole games we missed on Friday night. Rosie says Brent and Brianna seem to like each other. Meghan told Rosie that cornhole was actually fun.

"Brent says he's setting up a practice tournament this Sunday," I tell her. You want to come with me? Give it a try?"

"Maybe after church. But what do you mean, a practice 'tournament'?"

So, I explain to Rosie about Brent's bet with his dad. And starting this coming Friday, Brent's dad's off on business, somewhere in Canada. And Brent wants to practice, practice, practice while his dad's away—doesn't want his dad to see how much his game has improved. His dad's been practicing a little, but nothing like Brent.

"You talked to Brent? Does he like Brianna?" Rosie says.

"I don't know. We talked about cornhole."

"He must not like her, or else he'd have said something."

"He probably likes her. He's obsessed with cornhole, that's all," I tell her.

"Hey, I've got the car tomorrow," Rosie says. "Do you want a ride in the morning?"

"Sure. And do you think you could drop me at Big O's tomorrow afternoon? It's over there near First and Huntington."

"Okay. I'll have to get Zoe from school first, but then we can swing by the tire place."

Rosie says she's probably going to be up until after midnight what with an English paper due tomorrow. The paper will count for 15% of her grade so she's all stressed about it.

"I'm so tired of always feeling so much pressure about grades. I think I liked school back when we were at Palm Avenue, but now, I can't even remember how it felt to like school— not to always be worried about grades, and college, and the future."

"Yeah. I'm glad not to be worrying about that stuff. It must totally suck."

"It does! Maybe I should forget being a music therapist— just be a painter like you."

We both laugh at that, but I don't exactly like how she says, "...*just* be a painter..." like it's some loser job. I don't say anything about that, though. I mean, why sweat the small stuff?

"I better get back to my homework," she says, tapping her phone three times. I tap back: one (I), two (love), three (you).

Imani's in bed when I come back inside. William and Max are in the living room watching some TV news program. William mutes the TV and motions for me to sit down. Max has those deep worry lines, like the kind she wore constantly for months after she got home from Iraq.

"You're right about going to school tomorrow," William tells me. "You can't let fear of those guys keep you away."

"I'm not afraid of them," I say.

"Well, you can't let Hockney's fear of them keep you away, either."

"I don't know..." Max says.

But it's settled. It was already settled anyways—Rosie's picking me up in the morning.

CHAPTER THIRTEEN

Close Calls

I help Miss May get set up for writing before zero period and pass out notebooks while everyone goes quiet and watches me. We start the read-around: "Six Inches" by Jeff Coomer. Phong keeps his left index finger on the line he'll read when it's his turn. With his right hand, he pulls his phone out and nudges my thigh with it. I look down, see another anti-me post. May glances our way. Phong shoves the phone back in his pocket.

When it's Maryam's turn to read, she shakes her head. Miss May nods at Mark to take the next lines. Maryam's got some kind of agreement with Miss May about not reading things that could be offensive to her religion. Or something like that. It's no big deal anymore. Just like it's no big deal anymore that she wears a scarf thing. *Hijab*. That's what Rosie says it's called. I guess she knows because she's friends with Sofia and also with Fatima, another Muslim girl who's in choir.

But back to Write. We don't talk about the poems we read at the beginning of the period—like picking out symbols, or metaphors, or any of that regular English class stuff. Miss May tells us to let the words wash over us. Poems should be experienced, not laid out on the examining table and picked to death.

That's a relief. In Freshman English we spent day after day on some poem about this guy coming to a fork in the road and taking the one that wasn't so busy. Like what did the roads stand for, and decisions, and regret, and by the time we were finished examining every little piece of it, I'd filled a whole sketchbook with cats swimming and standing on their heads and chasing dogs, brushing their teeth, and one napping with his head resting on a big thick book of poetry. I got a C in that class.

"Six Inches" is about this guy, all relaxed, driving down a country road when all of a sudden, his car's off the road and totally wrecked. If he'd skidded six inches to the left, he'd be dead. Just six inches between life and death.

After the read-around, Miss May projects the writing prompt up on the screen. It's the usual routine:

The narrator of the poem writes about a close call. Think of any close calls you may have had, and choose one to write about. Your own story, or something fictional. OR...pull six or more verbs from the poem and weave them into a poem of your own. OR...write about anything else of your own choosing.

Close calls. I remember once when me and Angel, this kid who lived across the street, were playing on Tio Hector's tractor. It was parked out in the field, not far from the barn. Whenever Tio Hector was worried or upset, he'd go out and work on his tractor, oil the parts, clean it up. Sometimes he even waxed it. He didn't use it for farming any more, but he kept it, kind of like it was a special old friend. Me and Angel were just messing around. We were probably around eleven or twelve. Seventh grade.

So, we were sharing the driver's seat, pretend steering, pulling all the levers, and we knocked it into neutral. It started rolling, slow at first, but we were on a slight slope and it was picking up speed, going faster than you'd expect a tractor to go. At least that's how it felt. And we were headed straight for the barn.

Tio Hector came running out, yelling and waving his arms. "Turn the wheel! Turn the wheel!"

I yanked the wheel so hard to the left that we nearly tipped over, but we didn't, and the turn had us facing uphill and the tractor gradually rolled to a stop. Tio Hector ran up to us, breathless.

He reached in and pulled the brake back hard, wiped the sweat from his face and then, catching his breath, he said, "This is the brake." He released it, then said to me, "Pull the brake on," and I did. He released it again and said to Angel, "Pull the brake on," and he did. "First thing to know with any vehicle is where the brake is and how to use it." That's all he said. Then he took the driver's seat with us standing behind him and drove the tractor back to its usual parking spot—except this time, he parked it sideways, headed for the open field instead of the barn.

Tio Hector went back to the house, and Angel and I jumped from the tractor onto the soft weeds below and lay there, each of us seeing that other possibility. Crashing through the side of the barn, boards and debris slamming onto us, crushing us, or being hurled from the tractor onto the hard cement floor, or...and then we started laughing. Laughing, laughing, laughing until I peed my pants. I'm pretty sure Angel did too, but we didn't talk about it.

So, okay, I wrote about that, except the peeing our pants part. And writing about it got me thinking about Angel, wondering what he's doing now. Maybe I'll see him next time we go to Redville.

What will stay with me from today's writing is what Phong wrote about his great-great-grandfather's *kiem*—a double-edged sword that hangs over their fireplace at his house. It's been passed down for generations, and it's the one thing his grandfather took with him when he escaped from Vietnam at the end of the war. The *kiem* had rescued family men from close calls from many, many generations back. "I probably'd never even have been born if my grandfather hadn't had that sword for protection," Phong said.

Miss May is standing right in front of our desks when the bell rings. She tells me and Phong to hang on for a minute. After everyone else is gone, she holds her hand out to Phong.

"What??" he says, all innocent.

"Phong. What were you and Eddie looking at when you should have been following the read-around?"

He shows her. She looks at it, shaking her head, then finds the same posts on her own phone and gives Phong's phone back to him. "Next time you have something to show Eddie, do it somewhere beside in my class. Because if there *is* a next time in here, you won't get your phone back until one of your parents picks it up from the office."

Miss May writes a tardy excuse for Phong for his first period class and tells him he can leave. I start to leave but May calls me back. "Eddie, this has got to stop!"

"Why're you talking to me? I'm not the one posting this stuff. I don't even…"

The school phone rings. "Hold on a second," she says, reaching for the phone. "May here."

She's quiet, listening intently, then it's "Okay," and she hangs up. "You're not even supposed to be here!" she says.

So, it's another trip to the principal's office, except this time I don't have to wait on the plastic chair. And then it's another ride with the principal back to my house and a lecture along the way.

"Just give it today, Eddie," Hockney says. "We're getting this thing cleared up."

And now it's like Groundhog Day. Buddy's waiting at the door. I give him a pat and a few of his favorite scratches. He leans hard into me with his comfort lean. I watch through the front window as Hockney drives away. Buddy's all top-speed tail-wagging happy to have someone home again on a weekday.

Cameron texts with links to stuff on Reddit. I check it out. Same old thing—anti-Mexican, anti-genetically inferior (with images of a "defective" hand), purify the race, etc. Some of it's definitely directed at me.

I read. Eat. Get bored. Decide to meet Rosie in the parking lot after her soccer practice. I don't want to miss a ride home from Rosie.

3:15 and I'm at the corner, waiting for the bus. But this is where Groundhog Day ends. No blue pick-up. No panic attack. The bus comes to a stop at the curb. I get in, ride to within two blocks of the school parking lot, and find Rosie's car. I barely get there when I spot Rosie walking toward me. Cool.

It's the first time I've been in a car with Rosie driving. She backs out of the parking space at about .005 MPH and is almost as slow driving out of the lot.

"I need to get to Big O by closing time." I tell her.

"What time do they close?"

"10:00 tonight."

She takes her hand off the wheel long enough to smack me on the thigh, then gets super focused on driving again. We swing by Palm to get Zoe.

"Be right back," Rosie says, hurrying toward the courtyard where kids play tetherball.

I sit in the car, browse Snapchat and Reddit. The posts from this morning are gone, but there's a new one on Instagram. It's strange, getting so much attention all of a sudden. There's so much super mean stuff, but then there's all of this pro-Eddie backlash. People who barely even know me are posting stuff like what a great guy I am, and their posts are getting hundreds of likes. And there's a lot about how whoever sees hate graffiti anywhere should paint over it.

Rosie and Zoe come skipping across the lawn. I don't know. It's a thing they do. Zoe opens the passenger side door. "I get shotgun!" she says.

"Don't think so," I say.

She pulls at my arm, as if she can pull me out. She cracks me up. "C'mon!" she gives a yank. I laugh.

Rosie gets in the car and calls across to Zoe, "Get in the back."

"No! I hate riding on all these books!" She stomps her foot and pulls harder, which makes me laugh harder.

"Zoe! You can get in front when we drop Eddie off at the tire place."

Zoe gives one more pull, yanks the back seat door open, gets in and slams it with all of her might. "I feel sorry for Imani with a brother like you!" she says.

"I'm not Imani's brother," I tell her.

"Are too. Imani says."

"Doesn't make it true," I say. "We live in the same house, but we don't have the same parents."

"Well, I feel sorry for her anyway, having to live in the same house with you!"

Zoe's funny. Sometimes she loves, loves, loves me. Sometimes she hates, hates, hates me. Really though, as much as I complain about the pesty Imani, I sure wouldn't want to trade living arrangements with Rosie. For one thing, Imani always loves, loves, loves me.

At the tire place, I give Rosie a quick, Zoe-acceptable kiss, and go into the office to pay for my tires. Really, I've got Max's credit card, but I'll be paying her back a little bit at a time. I've already paid her $55.00 from my painting money. I'm soooo happy to have my car back. Now the trick is to park it where those fools won't notice it.

CHAPTER FOURTEEN

Challenges

Between the Hamilton High tech administrator tracking down and blocking posts, and social media companies generally being more careful about hate talk, the anti-me posts disappear by the end of the week. Like I said. No big deal.

Max and I spend Thanksgiving at my aunt and uncle's place up in Redville, like we always do. The whole family is there: Mario and his girlfriend, Francie, our cousin Vincent, Jordan, his wife, and their daughter Hannah, and, of course, Tia Josie and Tio Hector. We don't do the turkey thing. It's enchiladas for Thanksgiving and tamales for Christmas. William will be cooking a turkey back home, then taking it to his mom's house where he and Imani, and two of his sisters, will be for Thanksgiving.

Wednesday evening, we all have take-out Thai at Vincent and Jordan's. It's the first time the whole family's been together since before the election so there's a lot of talk about what the new guy's been saying about immigrants, and trade, and pulling out of the Paris climate agreement, and how every other country in the world takes advantage of us. And then there's how he treats women, and how he makes stuff up, and on and on. Everyone agrees that talk of politics will be off limits on Thanksgiving Day, though. Not that they'd be arguing and getting mad, but that the subject is so depressing.

Thanksgiving Day, we do what we always do, watch a little football, play horseshoes, Mario and I arm wrestle, two out of three, to see who gets the comfortable bed and who has to sleep on the floor in a sleeping bag. I win! Last year I finally beat Mario one round, the first ever. But this year, two out of three!

"Okay," Mario says. "It's double workouts for me starting Monday."

I flex my biceps.

After dinner and clean-up, we always watch a movie. It's a Thanksgiving tradition.

As usual, it takes longer to decide on a movie than it does to actually watch it. Tia Josie doesn't want violence. Jordan wants a classic. Tio Hector and Vincent want something funny. Mario and I waver between classic and funny. Hannah wants a musical. Max wants animation. You get the idea. After a lot of discussion and voting and drawing straws as a tie breaker, we end up with "Shaun the Sheep." Funny, animated, strange. I can't possibly describe it, but everybody ends up liking it. As great as it is to be with the Redville family, though, I can hardly wait to get back to Rosie.

As soon as we get home Friday afternoon, I drive to over to Rosie's, pretty sure I'll find her in Tilly, and I do. She's just sealed the envelope that holds her early application to University of the Foothills.

"I've been working on this since September," she says. "I'm worried it's not good enough."

"Here," I say, taking the envelope from her. I put it on the table, on top of the pile of books, and wave my hands slowly back and forth over it, casting a spell.

Abra, cadabra, this takes top spot,
Acceptance is certain, because she's so hot!

* * * * *

I tap the seal three times and hand the envelope back to Rosie. "There. You're in!"

She laughs and pokes. I laugh and kiss her. "Missed you," I say.

"Missed you, too," she says.

We're about to get seriously reacquainted when there's a pounding on the door. Rosie pushes it open. It's Zoe.

"Tell me a joke!" she says, looking at me.

"Zoe…" Rosie starts.

"Please!" she says, then turns to Rosie. "He promised me a Thanksgiving joke. Remember?"

"Ummm, yeah, I guess you did," Rosie says. "Before you left on Wednesday."

Oops. I *did* promise her a Thanksgiving joke if she'd leave us alone. Time to deliver if I want my joke promises to keep their power. "Okay, Zoe, but first I've got to go check my tires," I tell her.

She looks at me like she doesn't know whether to believe me or not.

"Really, I'll be right back," I say, and walk out to my car. I stand at the side of the car where she can't see me and quick search for Thanksgiving jokes on my phone, then sprint back to Tilly. "Okay," I say to her. "Did you have cranberries for Thanksgiving?"

"I don't like cranberries."

"But were they on the table for people who do like them?"

Zoe shakes her head, but Rosie says, "Yes they were. In that pretty glass dish. Remember?"

"Those were cranberries?"

"Anyways," I say, "Why did the cranberries turn red?"

"Why?"

I wait.

"Because they didn't want to be blue?" Zoe guesses. Sometimes her guesses are funnier than the punchlines.

I tell her, "No. The cranberries turned red because they were embarrassed that they saw the turkey dressing."

"Ha. Ha. Ha," Zoe says, and goes back to the house.

"I hope your application spell is better than your Thanksgiving joke," Rosie says, laughing.

We decide to hand deliver her application into the post office mail slot, so I take her to the big post office up on Main

Street. I do the abra cadabra spell again. Rosie kisses the seal and drops the envelope into the slot.

Then she wants to pick up a sweater that Brianna borrowed weeks ago so we go to Brianna's. Her mom says Brianna's with Brent, playing some beanbag game or something. She doesn't know where the sweater is.

We go to Brent's and sure enough, he and Brianna are playing cornhole. "We'll start over," Brent says. "Let's play partners. Brianna and I will beat the crap out of you and Rosie."

They don't exactly beat the crap out of us, but they win two out of three in close games. Brent for sure is getting better. I guess that old thing about practice makes perfect has some truth to it. He may still not be good enough to beat his dad, though.

The official cornhole tournament is set for December 10 so Brent's still got a couple of weeks of practice to go. And he's obsessed. Every day after school, all day on weekends, that's all he wants to do. Cornhole.

* * * * *

When we go back to school on Monday, there's more of those "14 Words" signs on the side of the gym, in black marker, about the size of a sheet of notebook paper. The same thing on the door to the boys' restroom and on a table in the quad. And "14 Words" is scrawled across the bank of lockers in the C Building. And then, when I'm putting away the mats after Yoga, I see "14 Words" printed in black on the floor, under the mat that Jason was using.

I get ammonia and a scrubber sponge from the supply closet and start scrubbing away, but you know permanent marker. Joe comes back to see what I'm doing. I point to the spot I'm trying to clean and tell him about the "14 Words" on the lockers. "I don't get it," I say.

"Count 'em," Joe says. "'We must secure the existence of our people and a future for white children.' That doesn't include you and me." He gets a wad of steel wool from the cabinet and brings it back to me. Then he runs his hand across the markings. "I thought maybe that kid was coming around," he says, turning back to his office.

I scour the marker off. I scour the floor's finish off, too—can't help it. A future for white children? Give me a break! How about a future for all children? Just shows Jason's an even bigger butthole than I thought he was.

* * * * *

Tournament day arrives. Brent's dad got new beanbags for the game, weighed them to the exact ounce.

"I want to be sure you guys haven't tampered with any of the equipment," he says with a laugh. I think he's only half kidding, though.

Mr. Bruno repeats the deal before they start the game. He says to Brent, "You lose, which you will, you lose and get a calculus tutor an hour a day, three days a week, for the rest of the school year. And, if you end up with less than a B in calculus, you go to math camp. Right?"

"Right," Brent says. "And?"

"And, if I lose, which I won't, no tutor, no math camp."

They shake hands. Mr. Bruno double checks the measurements to be sure everything is set up according to regulation.

We do a practice game, me and Zitter on one team and Brent and his dad on the other. Then things get serious. It will be two out of three, deciding Brent's fate.

Cameron and I stand on the sidelines. Brent and his dad are at opposite ends of the court. Two of his sisters, Brook and Bridget, bring out those grandma soccer game chairs.

"Hey, you guys want chairs?" Bridget says, looking at me.

"No thanks," I tell her. Bridget's the one who liked me better than she liked Brent, but that was a long time ago. I don't know if that's still true or not.

"I'd like a chair," Cameron says.

Bridget goes back to the garage, brings out two more chairs and unfolds them next to us. "You might change your mind if the game gets boring," she says to me.

Mr. Bruno calls me over and takes a quarter from his pocket. "You do the toss for us, Eddie."

Brent wins the toss so he gets to choose who goes first. "You first, Pops," he says. Mr. Bruno grabs a beanbag, stands beside the nearest board, places his feet just so, lobs the bean-bag high in the air, and we all watch as it drops cleanly into the hole.

"Lucky throw," Brent calls out, but I can see he's worried.

"Not too shabby," Mr. B. says, rolling his shoulders and stretching his calves and quads as if he's about to get into some tough, super-competitive soccer tournament, not a beanbag game.

Mr. B. starts out strong, 15 points to Brent's five on the first round. Besides practicing cornhole, Cameron and I have both been practicing calm, easy breathing with Brent, and pos-itive imagery, something Cameron's baseball coach pushes them to do. We've practiced everything we know to practice that might keep him from caving under pressure. Brent always caves under pressure. Like way back in the third grade, he'd get so worried about the Friday spelling test that even though he for sure knew every single word, he never got more than a C on the test.

Bridget and Brook jump up and down and cheer when their dad's beanbag goes through the hole. They do the same thing for Brent. I don't know who they want to win. Maybe they don't care. Or maybe they're not showing favorites for the sake of domestic tranquility.

Mr. B. wins the first game, but Brent got better after the first throws, so it was close. Just a two-point difference. I think Mr. B was surprised by that. It's not exactly a secret that Brent's been practicing, but most of the time he practiced when Mr. B. wasn't around.

Second game. Brent wins. He comes running over, high fiving us—well, high-fiving Cameron. High-two-ing me.

"God, I've got to get this next one. A no-calculus-tutor year! A no-math zone summer! The rest of the year will be dope!" Brent grabs a water and sits in one of the soccer chairs, staring at the court like he's willing it to be on his side.

Mr. B.'s standing at the back door trying to get Mrs. B. to come watch the game. She sounds mad. "This is the most stupid bet you two have ever made! You're going to be so upset if you lose, Brad. It's stupid to make a bet that will have you upset for months if you lose."

"I'm not going to lose! Come cheer me on!" When Mrs. B. doesn't come out, he saunters back to the court.

Bridget says to him, "I thought you weren't even going to have to play the third game, right, Dad? Huh, Dad? What happened?"

So, I guess I know whose side Bridget is on.

"Thought I'd give the little guy a chance," Mr. B. says, smiling. It's one of those barely skin-deep smiles, though.

In this last game, they're back and forth, within two points of each other all the way up to what's bound to be the last round. Both of them three points from game. Who knew cornhole could be so exciting? I guess anything's exciting if the stakes are high enough.

Cameron nudges me. "Does cornhole go into extra...you know...innings? Like in baseball?"

"I don't know. Check the rulebook—it's over there on the porch steps."

"I'll wait and see," Cameron says.

It's Brent's turn to go first, which means Mr. B. will get the last throw. With his fourth turn, Mr. B. is over game point. Brent is two points behind. He stands for a long time, deep breaths, doing that positive imagery, I hope. It looks like he's concentrating so hard his brain will break.

"You can do it!" Cameron yells.

I punch him. "Shut up! Don't distract him!"

Mr. B. stands a few feet away, watching, smiling, knowing he's going to get his way again with the tutor and math camp.

Brent pitches what looks to be a 3-pointer, which would put him ahead of Mr. B., but instead of being a 3-pointer, the beanbag clings to the edge of the hole.

"Already got a tutor lined up for ya," Mr. B. tells Brent. It's the last throw of the game. Mr. B. does that fancy lob thing again. A high clean throw. Almost clean. The red beanbag clips the side of Brent's blue bag, tips it into the hole without following it. There's a moment of silence, like no one can believe what happened, and then Brent jumps high in the air and yells, "Yes! Yes! Yes!" and then we're all jumping around him, high-fiving, high-two-ing, laughing. Bridget runs over to Brent and throws her arms around him.

"I can't believe you won!" she says.

Mr. B. comes over and shakes Brent's hand.

"Good game, son," he says. But he looks as puzzled as he did the day he walked into the classroom and saw Mrs. Calahan's black hair.

CHAPTER FIFTEEN

Watch Out

It's eleven a.m. on Friday, just before winter break. I'm outside the doors of the auditorium with my fourth period class and about a thousand other kids, waiting our turn to be let inside and herded to our seats for the annual winter concert. The full choir concert will be tomorrow night at a big Hamilton Heights church, but it's a long tradition to do a short band and choir program for the school on the last day before vacation.

The singers stand grouped together by a side door. The guys are wearing black pants with white shirts and red ties. The girls wear red dresses that, according to Rosie, nobody likes. "Everybody looks fat in those dresses. Nobody likes to look fat." Well, some of the girls look fat in those dresses, but only the fat ones. Most of them look good. Not as good as Rosie. But good. At least that's what I think.

Sofia and Fatima are wearing the same kind of dresses. They all come from the same catalog, or pattern, or something, because they've all got to be alike. But Sofia and Fatima also have shawls, made from the same material as the dresses, covering their shoulders. Their head scarves match, too.

Finally, with lots of shuffling around and chatter, we're all packed into our seats in the auditorium. Mr. Hockney walks on stage and stands in front of the microphone. He waits for things to get quiet. It's the usual, how lucky we are to have such fine music groups, and everyone should be sitting with their 4th period classes, and here are the exits, etc., etc. And now let's enjoy the concert.

The band director, Mr. Davenport, stands in front of the band with his arms raised. He waits, then brings his arms down, and the band starts with a jazz rendition of "Chestnuts Roasting on an Open Fire." I know that's what they're playing because it's listed in the program.

Cameron has a short drum solo in the middle of the song. It only lasts about twenty seconds, but I can tell he's pretty happy about it.

While the band's still playing, Mr. Taggerty, dressed in his tuxedo, comes over to where I'm sitting. I think wearing a tuxedo for a high school assembly is extreme, but that's Taggerty, all formal for choir concerts. He motions for me to follow him to a front seat on the right aisle, removes a "Reserved" sign, reaches under the seat, and pulls out a cardboard file box.

"Do me a favor. When the band finishes their last number, the lights will dim and singers will process in from the back of the auditorium, with candles, singing 'Silver Bells.' It's a beautiful opening," he says.

I'm waiting to hear what the favor is.

"So have a seat here until the first singer gets to about two rows from you. Then stand up and hold the box out so singers can drop their candles into it as they walk by. Not too complicated, huh?"

"They'll drop lit candles into this cardboard box??"

"Fake candles. You know. With *batteries*."

He's all sarcastic, like I should have known that. Why didn't he say fake candles in the first place?

"Got it, Eddie? Just sit right here, then stand with the box when the first singer gets close."

"Got it."

As applause for the band's last number dies down, Taggerty walks up to the center of the stage. He welcomes everyone, makes his usual remarks about being a respectful audience, then cues someone backstage to dim the lights. There's a faint flicker at the back of the auditorium as the first singers enter.

"City sidewalks, busy sidewalks, dressed in holiday style..." The sound is faint as the first few singers enter from the back, then gains in volume as others follow. It *is* pretty in the almost dark auditorium with the tiny lights and the full voices.

The first singer to walk past and drop a candle into the box is Brianna. Rosie's about five girls back, right in front of Sofia. I'm watching her, listening for her voice, when from somewhere off to the side, a guy jumps out, yanks Sofia's scarf from her head, stomps on it, yells "Go back where you belong, Raghead!" and runs in front of me toward the side door. Asshole!

I push into him, hard. He stumbles, nearly rights himself. I shove him down. Then Taggerty's there, pulling the guy up by the arm. Matt grabs his other arm. Then Hockney's there and Marcus.

There's lots of jostling around in the auditorium, some gasping, some calls of "Oh, no," and louder yells of "America for Americans!" and something about "illegals" and "faggots" and stuff I can't make out. I see Rosie stop to pick Sofia's scarf up from the floor. She brushes it off and hands it to Sofia. Security handcuffs the scarf-puller and walks him out of the auditorium. I don't recognize the guy, but it's a big school, and I don't know everyone.

Davenport's in front of the band giving a signal and they start blasting away at the "Star-Spangled Banner." By the time they get to "the dawn's early light," most of the kids are standing quietly for the national anthem, like we've all been taught to do since kindergarten.

Singers rush past me, not singing, dropping candles in the box as they hurry on stage. Some start to take their places on the risers, but Taggerty shakes his head and points them toward the backstage door. By "the twilight's last gleaming," the singers are no longer in sight. Taggerty stands at the microphone, silent, looking out over the student body. It is pin-drop quiet now. It looks like he's getting ready to say something, but then he just shakes his head sadly and follows the choir offstage.

Hockney takes the microphone. "Teachers, please take students back to your classrooms and proceed with your usual activities."

Then, his voice rising, he says, "Students! Anyone who does not return to his or her classroom for the remainder of fourth period will have an automatic three-day suspension starting January 2nd!"

I'm still standing with the box at my feet in the front row. I'm shaking. Not panic-attack shaking. Anger shaking. What a wimp-ass thing to do, rush a girl from behind and grab her scarf! I wish I'd given him a swift kick to the nuts. Or spit in his face when he was down or...Okay, deep breaths. Stop with the coulda, shoulda. Another calming breath and I go backstage to find Rosie. The girls are huddled together in a bunch, and it takes a minute to see her in the midst of the look-alike dresses. They're all in a close circle around Sofia and Fatima. The boys are mostly standing to one side, ties loosened, looking at their feet. Rosie's got her arm across Sofia's shoulder. Sofia's got her scarf back on.

I'm making my way over to Rosie when Taggerty stops in front of me. "Mr. Hockney wants you to come to his office," he says.

"Why?"

"Probably wants to talk to everyone involved in the incident. That was a brave thing you did, Eddie."

"Really? It's not like I thought about it."

"Well, then you've got good impulses."

Hockney's secretary shows me into his office. Marcus is there, too. And a policeman. With a notebook.

"This is Officer Christy," Mr. Hockney says. "He'd like to ask you a few questions.

"Officer Christy, this is Eddie Barajas, the young man who stopped the aggressor."

We shake hands. Christy takes a pencil from his shirt pocket and turns to a blank notebook page. "I understand you knocked the anti-Muslim boy down as he was running to the exit. Do you know who he was?"

"No. I didn't recognize him."

"Did he say anything?"

"Not to me. I heard him yell 'Go home, Raghead' at Sofia."

"And you just happened to be standing there in front when he ran past you?"

"I was collecting candles," I say.

"Candles?"

I explain about the candle collection job.

"Where did the guy who pulled Miss..." he checks his notes "...Khan's scarf off come from? Did you see?"

"He came from just a few rows back, on the other side of the aisle. At least, I think that's where he came from. All of a sudden, he was there, yanking at Sofia's headscarf."

"You were in the far right section, facing the stage?"

I nod.

"And the aggressor was coming from the middle section to your left?"

"Yes."

"You know, he would probably have gotten away if not for your quick action."

I nod.

"That's the pattern with this bunch. Strike fast. Run fast."

"What do you mean, 'bunch'?" Hockney asks.

"Well, you know. It's more than one person, the hate signs, the nooses, swastikas, the 'white lives matter' flyers. It's a whole group."

"Patriots?" I ask.

Christy glances over at me. "Can't say for sure," he says. "Wish we could." After a few more questions, Christy hands his cards around to us all, takes our cell phone numbers, and leaves.

At lunch, it's like everybody wants to talk to me about what happened. Some of it's "good for you," and high five/two-ing, and a couple are like, "Are you a Muslim now?" That's too stupid to even tell them how stupid it is.

Partly because Rosie keeps asking, and mostly because I want to change the subject, I try to talk to Brent about Brianna. I can't, though, because people keep coming to our table wanting to relive the assembly moment. Cameron's drumming the table like he's in another world and all I want to do is eat my lunch. I tell Brent and Cameron I'll see them later and take what's left of my lunch down to the yoga room.

Joe's in his office, shuffling papers. He glances at the clock. "Hey, Eddie. You're early."

"I need a quiet place to eat my lunch," I say, taking a seat on a bench against a side wall.

"No problem," he says.

Only five kids show up for Yoga today. The last day of school before vacation, and we're on a shortened schedule. Joe leads us through some stretches and then a series of poses. It helps, getting lost in yoga, focusing only on the yoga moment. The shakiness goes away, and my mind quiets. But here's something else. In warrior pose, when I turn my head slowly and gaze back over my extended right arm, I see that Jason, still farther back than anyone else, is doing the pose too.

We spend several minutes in child's pose, and I feel my neck, shoulders, and back release tension, totally relax.

As we sit in Sukhasana, Joe says, "Have happy holidays, Maricella, Alice, Miranda, Eddie, Jason." He pauses to hold eye contact with each of us as he says our names. "Be kind," he says. He bows his head and holds his hands in a prayer position. We do the same. "Namaste," he says. "Namaste," we respond. Except probably not Jason. I didn't hear his squeaky voice.

I'm rolling up the mats when Joe walks over. "I heard what happened at assembly," he says.

"You and all the 3,000-plus others here today."

"How are you feeling?"

"Fine."

"You did the right thing, but you probably made more enemies today, or at least made your old enemies angrier."

"I don't care," I say. "They're a bunch of chicken-shit cowards, that guy picking on a girl who's about half his size."

"You *should* care. He got arrested, probably will be charged with an assault designated as a hate crime. He's going to be really pissed. His friends are going to be really pissed."

"Yeah, well if they're that Patriot bunch, they're always pissed anyways."

"Okay, but watch out for them."

CHAPTER SIXTEEN

Solidarity

Max and William decided to go out somewhere, last minute, and I've got Pest Duty. We're on the floor with her Legos, building an ice castle, and I'm talking to Brent on my cell.

"C'mon, Blockhead. Brianna and Adele are both gonna be there. Take your pick."

"Right," Brent says, all sarcastic.

The pest wants everything in blue so it'll look icy. Except we're running out of blue pieces.

"I'll pick you up around 6:30," I say, as I watch my phone battery sink deeper into the red zone.

"Eddie!" Imani's grabbing my cell, trying to pull it away from me. I take it to the kitchen counter and attach it to the charger. "You're supposed to be playing with me!" Imani whines.

I go back to the Lego pile. "Look, I found two more blue pieces!"

She grabs the smallest one, twists it around, and manages to use it as a kind of steeple for the ice palace. As much as I complain about Imani, she's pretty inventive.

We're both admiring her work when Buddy rouses from his nap and lumbers over for a pat and a nuzzle, which makes him happy, which gets his tail wagging, which knocks the castle to pieces.

"Buddy!" Imani yells. "You ruined Elsa's castle! I hate you!" Buddy turns to her and licks her face. She's half crying, half laughing.

"Don't be talkin' smack about Buddy. He's the best dog ever."

"He destroyed Elsa's castle!"

"We can fix it," I tell her. "That was for practice. We can make a better one."

"There'll never be a better one!" she cries, but at the same time, she's gathering up pieces and locking them together for the foundation. I pull Buddy between my propped-up knees, a place he's happy to be and where he's semi-contained. I add a few pieces to Imani's foundation, then tell her, "Hey, Imani. I've got to go take a shower. You want to watch something?"

"You have to help me rebuild the ice castle!"

"No. I've got to get ready to go. You want me to set up the big TV for you or not?"

She pouts. I go into the bathroom. She bangs on the door. "Frozen!" she yells.

"What do you say?"

"Please!"

I open the door. "Just please?"

She sighs. "Pretty please. With sugar on it."

I set her up and go back to the shower.

I'm dressed, toweling my hair dry, when I hear some commotion in the living room. I stick my head out to see Imani and Olivia hugging each other and jumping around, and Max, William, and Carla standing by the door, watching. Carla's carrying a bundle of papers, and she looks like, what? I don't even know how to explain it. Like maybe she just lost her best friend? Or maybe she hasn't slept for weeks? However she looks, it isn't happy. Usually she's all bubbly, like Olivia and Imani are right now.

"Sorry we're a little late," Max says. "What time do you think you'll be home?"

I shrug.

"Text if it's after midnight," she says.

"Sure."

I grab my keys, wallet, and breath mints and head toward the door. "Bye, Ice Queens," I say to the girls.

Imani runs over to me, starts jumping up and down. "Olivia's sleeping over! Olivia's sleeping over!"

"Cool."

* * * * *

I pull into Brent's driveway and honk. That was another of Max's "Let's get this straight" dating demands for me. Walk up to the front door. Ring the bell. Talk to whoever opens the door. Wait patiently for the girl.

So, I do that with Rosie. But for a guy? For Brent? I honk. But I'm hella glad I talked him into going with me. I seriously want to be at the concert and hear Rosie's solo 'cause it sure didn't happen at school. But it's at a church, and I'd hate walking in there alone. I'm not sure I'll know how to behave. It'll be easier to walk in with Brent.

At St. Mark's, I hand the tickets Rosie gave me to the woman at the door. She gives us programs. We follow a group of grandmas inside. They're chattering away, taking turns bragging about what good singers their grandkids are. I never knew any of my grandparents. Maybe I've missed something.

"Hey, Blockhead." Brent slows and turns to me. "Do you have a grandma?"

"Are you nuts??? You know my grandma! Bleached hair? Purple shoes? Green fingernails?"

We sit in a middle row in front of the grandmas.

"Green fingernails? *She's* your grandma??"

"Dude! You know that's my grandma. She got me that Play Station when I was about eleven. Remember how pissed off my dad was?"

"Noooooo...I don't remember that."

"Oh, yeah...You weren't around then. But you've met my grandma."

"That joke about the dogs getting stuck or something?"

Brent laughs. "That's her."

"Do you like her?"

"Man, she's a crazy old grandma, but yeah, I love her! I mean, she thinks I'm perfect. Nobody else in my family thinks I'm perfect."

"Right. Nobody else in the whole world thinks you're perfect."

The lights dim, and it gets quiet. It's a strange place, this church. I mean, maybe not strange to a lot of people, like people who go here, but it's strange to me. The air feels funny, cool and fresh, but also like maybe it's been hovering around near the high ceiling for a long time. I'm glad Brent's here. It would have been way too awkward to be in here by myself. I mean, not by myself. There are a lot of people in here. But I would still have felt alone if Brent hadn't come.

Some old guy comes up front, a priest, I guess 'cause he's wearing the kind of round collar like you see on priests in the movies. He says what a happy occasion it is to have such a fine choir in this sanctuary. He says it's a place where everyone is welcome, no matter color, creed, gender identity, rich, poor, etc., etc. That's nice. I hope it's true, not just sort of true like at Hamilton High.

Mr. Taggerty takes the mike after the round-collared guy. He says pretty much the same stuff. I check out the people in front of me—mostly old people, but I see a few Hamilton High kids. Rosie's parents and Zoe are sitting up near the front. Over to the right is Sofia's family. At least, I think it's Sofia's family. There are three headscarves in a row, then a man on the other side. And maybe that's Fatima's parents? Another man and another head scarf.

Mr. Taggerty turns to face the side of the stage, motions, and the boys walk out, single file, to the center of the stage. There are six in the back row, then another five boys come out and stand in front of the line of six—black pants, white shirts, red bow ties. There's a brief pause, then the girls come out. They're all wearing their concert dresses, but with light shawls around their shoulders—and matching head scarves, just like Sofia and Fatima have.

The place goes super quiet, like maybe people have stopped breathing. Then someone up front starts to clap, and it spreads, and then people are on their feet and the applause fills the building.

"Why are they dressed like that?" a grandma behind me says.

"Why not?" a quieter voice asks.

"That's just weird!" Brent says.

"I bet it's not weird to Sofia or Fatima," I say.

Taggerty's standing before the choir, arms raised, waiting for the applause to die down before he gives the downbeat. Downbeat. Another choir word I learned from Rosie. She's learning paint colors from me.

First, it's some corny old song about how all this kid wants for Christmas is his two front teeth so he can say "Merry Chrithmas." Whenever they sing "my two front teeth," the boys give wide open smiles and point to their two front teeth which have been blacked out to make it look as if their teeth are missing. They're total hams on that one.

Next is a Hanukkah song which the program says is from the Jewish tradition. Then a Nasheed from the Islamic tradition. At the end of the last long note, the grandma behind me says, "That music sets my teeth on edge! It's not even music!"

"Hush, Harriet," the quieter grandma says.

There's a brief lull while the singers reposition themselves. Brent elbows me in the arm. Hard. "You dragged me to this, and Adele's not even here!"

"Yeah she is! On the end of the second row, and Brianna's right in front of her."

Brent looks up at the group, then back at me, puzzled.

"On your right, Blockhead!"

He looks again, like he's concentrating as hard as he used to do during those third-grade math tests. "She looks so different," he says, staring harder. "They both do."

Finally, it's time for Rosie's solo, "O, Holy Night," from the Christian tradition. She steps forward, pauses, then gives a nod toward the piano, and Sofia plays an introduction.

"At last! Some real Christmas music!" the loud grandma behind me says. Then the whisperer: "Shush!"

Rosie's voice is strong and pure. "O holy night, the stars are brightly shining..." Her mom and dads—"real" and step— sang in choir in high school. I guess Rosie comes by singing naturally.

It's strange not to see Rosie's shiny, chestnut hair framing her face. I like her face. But I miss her hair. I hope this is only a one-time thing.

During intermission, Brent tells me, "I'm over Adele."

"Really?"

"For sure. She doesn't look so good without her hair. Brianna looks prettier. Plus, Brianna's nicer."

"Just like that, after all these years, you're over Adele because you saw her with her hair covered?"

"Yep. And because Brianna's the one who likes me. And because no math tutor! No math camp!" He raises his hand for a high five/two.

* * * * *

After the concert, the chatty grams walk out behind us. The chattiest one, who I now know is Harriet, is talking about how her granddaughter, Cherise, should have had the solo Rosie sang.

The quiet grandma says, "I thought the girl who sang did a beautiful job."

"Hmph. Cherise said everyone thought *she* sang better at the audition, but the other girl is the teacher's pet..."

Brent taps me on the shoulder. "Earth to Eddie. Earth to Eddie...As I was saying...What is it I was saying again??"

"Ummm..." I stop eavesdropping and turn my attention to Brent.

"What was that about? Did all of the girls convert to Muslims or what?" Brent says.

"Islam," I say.

"Islam, Muslim, same thing."

"Islam's the religion. Muslims are people who belong to that religion," something else I learned from Rosie, who. learned it from Sofia.

"Whatever..."

Ding. A text from Rosie: *Meet at Matt's. Party. 9*

Me: *big house on Primrose?*

Rosie: *thumbs up*

Me: *with Brent?*

Rosie: *K*

Me: *K*

Rosie: *heart*

"9:00 at Matt's," I tell Brent. "Brianna will be there. And your ex."

"Choir party?" Brent says. "Like I'd fit in at a choir party?"

"That last party at Matt's? There were a bunch of people there who weren't in choir... I'm just going to hang out with Rosie. You can hang out with Brianna. There'll be plenty of food."

"Yeah? Okay, then," he says, lifting first one arm, then the other, sniffing his pits. "I better get a shower before I get close to Brianna."

The grammas stop at a car in a handicap parking space, and Brent and I walk on to the back of the lot. The last I hear of them is Harriet spouting off about how if she'd known there was going to be so much foreign music, she'd have stayed home and watched reruns of Andy Williams' Christmas show.

Maybe it's fine not to have a gramma. I guess the quieter one might be okay, but what if she was a Harriet? Besides, I've got Tia Josie. And her chocolate chip cookies, and her soft-body hugs. She's sort of like a gramma.

I take Brent to his house and wait in the car for him to come back out, clean and deodorized.

* * * * *

Matt's got a floor-to-ceiling Christmas tree, all decorated and lit up. I walk close and take a deep breath. Yep. It's real. We've got a real tree, too, but it's a baby tree compared to this one. And this tree's got fancy ornaments. Ours has some fancy decorations too, but it also has a paper ornament that Imani made in school and some other old, faded paper ornaments that Mario and I made a long time ago.

Most of the choir kids are here, but not Sofia or Fatima. They weren't at the last party, either. Matt's dad comes in, congratulates the choir on a great concert, tells everyone to have fun, and leaves.

I make my way over to where Rosie's standing in the middle of things. The girls are talking about how it wasn't until the last minute that Sofia's parents decided to let her be in the concert tonight, and how it felt to wear the scarves, and why would anyone do that to Sofia? And then, it's "Oh, my God! Eddie!" and how brave I was, and how if it wasn't for me, that guy would have got away with what he did, and nobody should get away with that bullying stuff and…and…

I stutter and stammer around, and then Brent looks over at Brianna like it's a big surprise to see her here, and says, way loud, "Brianna! Hi!" It's so loud that everyone pauses to look at him. Some of the girls giggle 'cause I guess there's been some talk about Brent and Brianna, like isn't it cute, and isn't it great that Brianna's got someone special, so, much to my relief, the attention shifts. I pull Rosie away from the group and over to the food table. We load our plates and find a quiet corner near the tree.

Rosie talks about how glad she is that the concert is over, how nervous she was about her solo, and then how nervous everyone was after all that happened with the choir on the last day of school, and how relieved she is that we've got a two-week break, and…and…and…

It's funny about Rosie. When she's nervous or stressed she talks nonstop about whatever it is. The opposite of me. When I'm stressed, I get quiet. I mean like silent. So, I guess we're a good balance. And I like that Rosie talks a lot because then I don't have to. I'm sitting close to her, enjoying her monologue, when she spoils it by telling me that I'm her hero.

"Don't say that," I tell her.

"Why not. It's true. You were so brave…"

"I wasn't brave. It was a reaction. I was pissed at the guy, and then he was running right past me. Probably anyone would have brought him down if they'd been standing where I was."

"I don't care what you say. You're a hero."

"And I don't care what *you* say. I'm not."

We both laugh, but it's not exactly funny. I hate that hero shit.

I glance over to where Brent and Brianna are standing. He's gesturing all over the place, and he's got that big, silly grin. He's telling her all about the cornhole tournament. I'm sure of it because he's actually demonstrating an underhand pitch, except not with a beanbag.

* * * * *

After everyone's played some silly games and danced and mostly coupled up, and it feels like it's about time to leave, all of the choir kids get in front of the Christmas tree. Matt plays a note on the piano, kids hum the note, he takes his place with the boys, counts one-two-three, and they sing the alma mater. I don't know why, but it gets to me, maybe because I'm a senior and almost finished with Hamilton High, or maybe it's the harmony, or all of the emotion of the past few days. Whatever.

When they're done, the singers do a big group hug, and then there are shouts of Merry Christmas, and Happy Holidays and see you in two weeks, and it's like everybody leaves at the same time.

Brent asks if we can take Brianna home, so we do. Maybe he's finally getting a girlfriend for real. When we pull up in front of her house, Brianna says "bye" and gets out of the car.

"Walk her to her door, you blockhead!" I tell him.

"Why?" he says, all confused.

"Just do it!"

So, he gets out, slow and puzzled like, and walks with her up to her front porch. She fumbles around for a key, or something. I take the opportunity for a long, true kiss with Rosie and don't notice Brent until he gets back in the car.

"That was awkward," he says.

I can see that I'm going to have to give him Max's "Let's get this straight how-to-treat-a-girl" talk. But not right now.

CHAPTER SEVENTEEN

Not Just Criminals

When I get home from the Christmas party, I'm surprised to see that Max and William are still up, sitting at the kitchen table with Carla. There are a bunch of papers jumbled around on the table and everyone looks worn out. Not just Carla.

"You have a good time?" Max says, kind of absentmindedly.

"Yeah. Good concert. Good party," I say as I walk past them to my bedroom. I'm already in bed, half asleep when there's a soft knock on my door.

"Yeah?"

"Okay to come in?" Max asks.

"Sure."

She sits on the side of my bed. I lean up on my elbow. "This is only between us. You can't tell anyone. Not even Rosie," she says. I wait for her to go on but she says, "Promise?"

"Yeah. Okay."

"I want you to know what's going on, but this is important, Eddie. You can tell absolutely no one."

"Okay. I got it."

"We've just finished a lot of paperwork with Carla and Arsenio. Guardianship for Olivia and Ivann. Adoption papers."

"What??? Olivia and Ivann are moving in with us?? I don't wanna share my room with Ivann, if that's what you're thinking!"

"Calm down, Eddie. We've got the papers in case we need to use them, but nobody wants that to happen."

"Why even have the papers then, if nobody wants it to happen? That doesn't even make sense."

So Max tells me Carla and Arsenio are undocumented. Olivia and Ivann were born here so they're citizens, but Carla and Arsenio aren't. They've been trying to get green cards, going through all of the paperwork. They're on a waiting list, but now, with all the talk about sending immigrants back where they came from, and stereotyping Mexicans as drug dealers and rapists, and increased ICE enforcement, they're scared of being arrested and deported and separated from their kids.

"But I thought they were only arresting criminals."

"Really, Eddie? I know you're busy and in love, but I don't know how you've missed this!"

"That's what it said on TV. Only people with criminal records."

Max pokes around on her phone, then turns it so I can see the screen. "Okay, so this is only one story out of hundreds, but you'll get the idea." It's this story about a family living in L.A. Kids ten and fourteen, both born in the U.S. Pictures of the kids at different ages, family gatherings, birthdays at the park, "Teacher Aide of the Year" plaque framed on a wall.

The parents came illegally sixteen years ago. They hoped for a better life, and that's what they found. The dad ran a landscaping business, the mom was a teacher's aide, they helped out at school fundraisers. One of their kids, the girl, the fourteen-year-old, was in a special science program, and her team won a district award for the robot they built. The boy was a Little League star. The parents helped their neighbors. They paid their taxes. Neither of them had ever even had a traffic ticket. They'd been trying to move toward citizenship for the past eleven years, but there were all kinds of delays. It took money for lawyers' fees to move things faster, but they couldn't always afford legal help.

And then at six one morning, ICE came to their house. Arrested both parents. Took them away from their terrified kids. Called children's protective services to take the kids to foster care. The parents are trying to get the kids back to them in

Mexico, but whatever money they have is frozen in bank accounts in Los Angeles.

There are pictures of the kids, looking so lost and sad, each in a different foster care home, no longer living in their old neighborhood, going to different schools where they don't know anyone...

"Stories like this are coming out every day," Max says.

"That sucks!"

"Yeah. It does. Carla and Arsenio are scared to death that they'll be separated from their kids. That they'll lose everything they've worked so hard for. And Carla's afraid they're passing their fear on to Olivia and Ivann—keeping the doors locked at all times, telling them never to answer the door no matter how many times someone rings the bell or knocks or calls to them. Always keeping the windows locked and the shades drawn. Carla's afraid to go outside to water her garden!"

"Really?"

The arm I'm resting my head on is tired. And my neck is getting stiff. I plump my pillows against the headboard and scoot up to a sitting position.

"ICE has their address from all of their applications for citizenship. They could show up at any time to arrest them."

"But the garden?"

"ICE can't come into the house without a search warrant, which they almost never have. But if Carla or Arsenio are out and about, ICE could arrest them and send them back to Mexico within days."

Max says Carla and Arsenio want to be sure their kids don't end up like the kids in the story we just read. Separated and sent to schools where they don't know anyone. That's why they've filled out the paperwork that gives Max official guardianship of Olivia and Ivann. It can't be Max *and* William because they're not officially married, but they'd be in it together.

Max says, "We've got birth certificates, doctors' records, certificates of immunization, insurance policies. The same stuff I had to get together for you and Mario when you went to Carmen's. For sure, we'd take better care of Olivia and Ivann than Carmen did of you, but it'd still be terrible for them. I wanted you to know, though, not just have this mysterious secretive stuff going on. Carla's spending the night here, too, and then we'll take her and Olivia home in the morning."

Max says the papers will be in a metal file box, in the left-hand corner of her closet. She can't imagine a time I'd need to get them but, if there is, I'll know where they are.

As tired as I am, I have a hard time getting to sleep after all Max told me. It seems like a lot has changed over the past year or so. Like people are meaner. And more racist. And more scared. Or maybe it's always been this way, and I'm just now noticing. I turn on my bedside lamp and take *The Grapes of Wrath* from the table. I'm at the place where the Joads are being called "Okies" and totally hate-talked, and I think maybe people aren't meaner now. Maybe they've always been that mean about immigrants. Not that the Joads are exactly immigrants. They're all Americans, but I guess you could say they emigrated from Oklahoma to California, and they sure weren't welcome in California, and even though the Joad story took place a long time ago, the hate part reminds me of right now.

* * * * *

On Sunday, Brent, Cameron and I decide to go to the beach. It's not exactly beach weather, but at least it won't be crowded. Cameron wants to go to Laguna because of the cliffs. Brent wants Balboa because he's got a thing for the Ferris Wheel at the Fun Zone. I decide on Santa Monica. That's kind of a compromise because there's a Ferris Wheel on the pier and you can see cliffs from the beach, but the main thing is, it's the shortest drive.

The first thing we do, like at the lake, is strip down and run for the water. It's take-your-breath-away cold, but the surf is good, not killer but not wimpy, either. I swim out to what I think is the right spot to catch a wave, dive under three waves before I catch one. I swim with it, and then, as I feel the push of its power, I hold my body stiff, angled upward, and am propelled nearly to shore.

I watch for a minute as Cameron tries and misses, then see Brent get a ride halfway in. I swim out again, tread water watching for another perfect ride. Finally, after a bunch of misses, I catch an okay ride. Not like the first one, but it brings me in. I run to my towel and wrap up. I'm freezing! Cameron's already wrapped.

"You're blue," I say through my chattering teeth. Brent's out now, too. The three of us stand shivering, our towels wrapped tight around us. Down the beach where the real surfers are, the board surfers, those guys are all wearing wet suits. There's a reason. We go to the restroom on the pier and change into dry clothes.

Brent tries to talk us into riding the Ferris Wheel with him. I think maybe I will until we get there and I see that it costs $8.00.

"It's worth it!" Brent says. "It's a great view!"

"Yeah, well. It's either the view from the Ferris Wheel or lunch. I'll stick with the view from the pier."

"Meet us at the food court!" Cameron calls to Brent as he's getting on the $8.00 ride.

I guess the ride doesn't last long, 'cause Brent's already found us by the time we're placing our food order. We all have bowls of hot chili. That helps.

We watch old guys fish from the pier for a while, then wander along the sidewalk where there are a bunch of little stands with people selling stuff they've made. I see a necklace, silver, with a heart. It would be a perfect Christmas present for

Rosie. $45.00, but a necklace like that would probably be twice that much at a regular jewelry store.

Cameron's a few stalls down, looking at potholders for his mom. That seems like something a little kid would give his mom but, hey, at least it's a gift.

I wander down where Brent's looking at ceramic cups. I could get a cup for Max that says #1 Mom, except she's already got about five of those. Brent's grinning his cornhole grin and holding a black cup with a big #2 on it.

"Maybe I'll get this for my dad," he says.

"Ummm. He might not see the humor."

"I know," he says, still grinning.

I go back to the necklace place. The woman at the stall says, "I could let you have it for $40.00." Awesome.

"Could you hang on to it for about ten minutes?"

She nods and puts the necklace under the counter. I sprint to the car for my emergency money. This *is* an emergency. I open the trunk, pry the rim off my donut tire, take the two twenties from the hidden envelope, and put the empty envelope back in its place.

Back at the stall, I hand the lady my cash. She writes a receipt. $40.00 plus $3.00 sales tax. Shit! I forgot about sales tax. I reach into my pocket, pull out a dollar bill and a handful of change. $1.72 to be exact.

"Hang on," I say, and run over to where Brent's trying on a camouflage jacket.

"How's it look?"

"Like an idiot Patriot. Can I borrow $1.30?"

He takes two ones from his pocket and hands them to me. "Thanks!" I say, sprinting back to the booth.

"You owe me! Don't forget!"

I hand over the tax money. The lady gets the necklace from under the counter. "Would you like this in a gift box?"

"Sure!"

She puts the necklace on some kind of padding that fits the box perfectly. She arranges it so the heart is in the center of the box, puts another piece of padding on top. She adds the lid and ties it closed with a satiny Grasslands Green fancy bow. Cool. I go back to Brent, who's put the camo jacket back and is trying a leather jacket.

"What do you think?"

"Better."

"Maybe I'll get it." Brent always carries one of his dad's credit cards with him, for emergencies only, supposedly.

I look at the price tag. $175. The sales guy tells Brent he won't find a jacket of that quality for less than $250 in any of the stores.

"Emergency?" I ask.

I look down the sidewalk to where Cameron's standing outside some place that sells wind chimes and incense. He's talking to two girls, laughing with them.

"Look at that," Brent says. "Maybe it's the Tough Skins jeans?"

He takes off the jacket and hands it back to the salesman. "$165?" the guy asks.

"I better not," Brent says, walking away. "I'm warmer now," he tells me.

On the way home, Brent and Cameron talk about their college application essays. Brent says his dad's making him apply to top engineering schools, even though there's no way he'll get into any of them. Cameron's parents say it's up to him where he goes to college, as long as it's ranked in the top fifty. He wants to major in music with an emphasis on performance jazz. His parents are cool with that as long as he minors in education. So he'll have something to fall back on, they say.

Pretty soon the college talk turns to background noise, and I'm thinking about what Max told me about Olivia and her family. That would so suck. Like it sucked when Max was shipped off to Iraq, and we had to go to our Aunt Carmen's. At least

Max and William would take good care of Olivia and her brother, not like Carmen did with us. But it would still suck.

Cameron wants to be dropped off first because maybe Meghan's going to pretend to go out with some girls but come climb through his bedroom window instead.

"I thought your dad nailed your window shut when he caught you with that sophomore girl after the Harvest Festival," I say.

"He did, but it's easy to take nails out with the other end of a hammer."

"Doesn't he ever check?"

"Not yet," Cameron says.

So I drop him off first, then Brent. At home, I take the box with the necklace out of my pocket and tuck it into the top drawer of my dresser. I can't wait to give it to Rosie. Maybe I won't wait for Christmas. Maybe I'll give it to her when I see her tomorrow night.

CHAPTER EIGHTEEN

A Reverse Mohawk

It's near the end of our walk, and Buddy's sniffing at every fence and lamppost, checking his pee-mail. I swear he pauses longer to sniff next to the tree where Peppy habitually does her business. That's what Yoga Joe calls it, "doing her business."

The moon is nearly full, and the air is clean and fresh, and I'm thinking about Rosie, like I always do, and thinking we can get in a little Tilly time tonight when...pounding feet behind me and before I can turn to look, I'm down, smashed in the back by something hard and heavy. Buddy growls, yelps. I roll, spring up, connect a kick to a guy's groin, pivot, karate chop to a guy's face, and I'm down again. A kick to my head. Another. I roll into a tight ball, hands and arms over my head. More blows to my back, my head, try to roll away, hits keep coming. Buddy barking, growling...

"Enough," someone yells. "Let's get outta here!"

Another kick. Screeching tires. Fast, heavy footsteps. Someone yanked off me.

Running feet, fading.

"Eddie. Eddie. Are you okay?"

It's William, his ear to my chest, fingers feeling pulse, checking my head, arms, legs. "Talk to me, Eddie."

I try to say something, but nothing comes out. I hear the click of his phone. "Send an ambulance! Hanover, between Cloverly and Alessandro. My son's badly beaten. Unconscious." Then, more screeching brakes. Footsteps.

"Get your hands in the air!"

"He's hurt!" William yells.

"Put your hands up, and get away from him!"

I feel William move away...

"Drop it! Drop it!!" More voices.

I hear something drop. His cell???

"Up against the car! Spread eagle!!"

"Robbery in process, black male..."

"Get help!!" It's William.

I try to call out. They've got to know William saved me...William! but nothing comes out.

I hear rustling around, then..."I'll run a check on his license...put the knife in an evidence bag."

Somebody else is next to me, running his hands over me. I'm trying, trying, trying to call out.

More rustling. "Let me go to him!"

A smack. "Don't move!"

"William!" finally, a voice. I've got a voice. "William! Dad!"

"The kid knows him," the guy near me calls out.

"Don't mean shit," another guy says.

"Let him go."

"Dad!!"

William's there, beside me. "Help's coming, Eddie. Help's coming."

"Buddy," I whisper.

"He's okay. He's tough, like you."

Sirens, then nothing.

* * * * *

Murmuring. Soft voices. Max. William. I'm cold. Something's stuck in my arm. I blink, blink, try to keep my eyes open. Grey light.

"Eddie!"

I blink.

"He's awake! Eddie, it's me. Max!"

I try to turn my head to the sound of her voice, but it hurts.

"Look. He moved! Eddie?"

My lips are stuck together. Dry. I'm so dry. "Water," I manage to croak out.

Max dabs my lips with water. I run my tongue over my lips, trying to get things working. More water dabbing at my mouth, maybe a cloth? A sponge?

Slowly, the room comes into focus. Max in a chair beside me. William sitting next to her. "Where...?" My voice is all raspy.

"You're in the hospital," Max says.

My head feels strange. I reach to rub my forehead, but Max takes my hand and gently puts it back on the bed.

"You've got stitches," she says. "A big bandage around your head holding a gauze cap...You got beat up. Remember?"

I start to shake my head no, but damn! It hurts!

"Do you know who it was?" William asks.

I close my eyes, let the voices fade. "Let's not push that now," Max says.

I drift further away. Then there's a light shining through my eyelids. I blink. The light moves away. I blink again, then focus. A man, gray hair, tiny pointy beard at his chin, bending over me, smiling, holding a small flashlight. Max, still in her chair beside my bed.

"Hi, Eddie. It's Eddie, right?"

I give a nod, a tiny one, so it doesn't hurt.

"What's your last name?"

"Barajas," I creak out.

Max dampens what I now see is a sponge and gently wipes my lips. She puts a straw in a glass of water and holds it to my mouth, but I can't manage to get any water through it, so it's back to the sponge.

"Eddie, I'm Dr. Googooian, your neurologist. I'm here to help figure out how you're doing. Okay?"

A tiny nod.

"I'd like you to follow this light with your eyes. Understand?"

Nod.

He shines the light to my right, clear at my edge of vision. I look as far to the right as I can manage without turning my head. He slowly moves the light from the right to my far left, then up and down, then in slow circles. I follow. He turns the light off, then sits in the rolling chair where William was sitting before, and rolls to the foot of the bed where I can see him without turning my head.

"What's your address?" he asks.

"406 North Cloverly Avenue, Hamilton Heights, California."

He looks at Max. Eyebrows raised.

"Right," Max says.

He asks a whole bunch more questions, grade in school, names of friends, how many donuts in a dozen, etc., etc., etc. "You're doing great, Eddie!" he says, smiling.

Then it's stuff like wiggle your toes, hold up your left index finger. Right index finger. Just a slight pause when he sees I don't have a right index finger. Then he makes a quick adjustment to right thumb. When he's finally finished with his version of Simon Says, he asks, "Now, do you know why you're here?"

"Hurt," I say. Like every single inch of my body hurts, but I don't want to say that many words.

"Do you know how you got hurt?"

"No."

"Okay. That's to be expected after any traumatic experience. Your memory of that time will probably come back in the next few days, or weeks. What's the last thing you can remember before you woke up here in the hospital?"

I think back through blank time.

"Friends? School?" he asks.

Was it Miss May's class? Yoga? "Yoga?" I say.

"What day was it?"

"Wait. The beach."

"What day was it?" he asks again.

Can't think.

"Sunday," Max says.

"Sunday?" Dr. G. asks.

Tiny nod.

"Tell me more about the beach," he says.

Everything's murky, like trying to drag memory from the bottom of a muddy lake. I close my eyes, try to see Santa Monica... "Cold," I say.

"It was cold out?"

"Cold water."

"Were you alone?"

I'm being sucked back into the murk.

"Eddie? Can you tell me if you were alone?"

I manage to mumble, "Friends."

"I'll be back a little later," the doctor says, touching me lightly on my shoulder. "You're doing fine." He takes what looks like a TV remote from the table beside me. "We'll raise your head a little," and then, as if by magic, the top part of my bed rises a few inches. He puts the glass with the bent straw in front of me, and I manage a swallow.

"I'll check in with you tomorrow," he says, and is gone.

* * * * *

It turns out, I have a broken metacarpal bone on my left hand—that's a small bone that goes from my wrist to the first knuckle of my middle finger. For that, I've got a half-cast thing that goes from below my elbow to where my fingers start.

A cracked rib—painful but will supposedly heal on its own. I've got a black eye that goes from my forehead, past my cheek, to the edge of my jaw. A black eye that's more a cross between a Deep Aubergine purple and a Constellation Blue. They might be pretty accent colors on a side wall in one of those big San Marino houses, but on a face? Not so pretty.

The worst injury is to my head—a concussion—plus I've got about a four-inch wide shaved-bare strip of baldness with 27 stitches running down the top of my skull. Sort of a reverse mohawk.

Three nights in the hospital—Sunday, Monday and Tuesday—and Wednesday morning I go home. Max is on one side and William on the other, steadying me, as I hobble from the car, through the back door and into the kitchen. I get a whiff of chicken soup and realize how hungry I am.

They lead me to the living room and help me get settled in William's recliner. Pretty special because nobody but William ever sits in his recliner, unless it's the pest on his lap while he's reading to her.

Buddy comes limping in on three legs, his right hind leg in a splint, wrapped tightly in bandages. He tries to stand on his good leg, trying, I think, to get close enough to lay his muzzle on my thigh like he likes. He can't manage that with only one working hind leg, though. He gives a big Buddy sigh and lies down at my feet.

Max ties a dishtowel around my neck and brings in a bowl of soup on a lap tray. It's the best thing I've ever tasted in my whole life. Two bowls, a pain pill, and I drift off to sleep.

Rosie comes over later in the afternoon. She rushes to me, arms out for a hug, then freezes in shock, dropping her arms to her side. "Oh, Eddie! Oh my God!"

She reaches toward me again. "Where can I touch you that won't hurt?"

I manage to lift my least hurt hand and point downward to you-know-where.

"Eddie!" she says, then busts out laughing. I laugh, too, though it hurts like hell on the side with the cracked rib.

She takes my pointing hand and guides it gently to her face, where she kisses it and holds it against her cheek. "I'm so sorry!" she says, tears welling to the brink of overflow. "Who did this?"

"Didn't see."

"But why???"

"Don't know...Missed you," I say.

"I wanted to visit you in the hospital, but your mom said it would be better to see you at home...I left a card for you at the nurse's station, though. Did you get it?"

"Yeah. Thanks," I say, managing a smile. Rosie sits beside me then, telling me of the hassle of more college applications, and how the guy who teaches the Music Therapy class is giving her and Brianna good recommendations and she's sure that will make a difference for that program and...I'm not sure what else because I guess I drifted off. When I wake up, there's a folded piece of notebook paper leaning against my water glass. "I'll see you tomorrow. Love you. Rosie. Xxoo." The border is decorated with hearts.

* * * * *

As Doctor Googooian predicted, my memory slowly returns. At first, it's like the sound track of a damaged film, parts clear, parts scratchy, frames of silence. Buddy's yelp. William calling my name. Someone yelling, "Enough!" Sirens. Screeching brakes. Hands up! Then, slowly, things begin to fall into order. And I get a new memory of William's voice yelling, "Get off him!" and pounding footsteps running away.

When William gets home from work that evening, I tell him, "You saved my life. I'm remembering you saved my life."

"You saved *my* life," he says, which makes no sense at all, like maybe he's joking, but I see he's not. He says, "Yeah. Remember Devon Parker? Last year?"

I nod. Everyone remembers Devon Parker. He was the reason for the Black Lives Matter demonstration back in September. He'd been pulled over for a broken taillight. Just a few miles away—south Hamilton Park. Two cops. Cop asked for his license. Devon pulled it out of his pocket—one of those no-hack metal wallet things. Metal caught the light. Cop yelled

"Gun!" and shot him dead. Thirty-two years old. Everybody remembers Devon Parker. Even the pest remembers Devon Parker. They kept the news from her, but kids learn a lot in school that parents don't want them to learn.

"What about him?" I ask.

"The cops thought I'd jumped you, robbed you, said I was going through your pockets, not that I was trying to check for bleeding and breathing, to see if anything was broken, frantic to get help. I'd beaten and robbed you: that was their take on it, and I was on my way to meet Devon Parker."

William looks past me, toward the window, but his eyes are somewhere else, back at the side of the street, I guess.

"I was handcuffed against the car and the roughest cop had his hand on his gun, and I was bargaining with God, please let me live to raise Imani. I'll go to church. I'll paint the whole place for free. Just long enough to see her in college.

"I felt the cop pull his gun from his holster, and then I heard you shout, loud: 'William! Dad!' and the other cop got it, called his partner off, uncuffed me, let me go to you…"

I don't want to look straight at William, and I don't want him to look straight at me either because I know we're both crying. And then he pulls me close to him, and even if it hurts my beat-up arm, it feels warm and safe and we're both crying without caring, and I'm smelling the lingering paint and cleaner, the sweat and soap, the goodness of William, and maybe he really is my dad.

And then the pest comes running in and stops cold. "Who stopped 'Frozen'?'" And we pull apart and start laughing, wiping our eyes.

"I was watching it! I just went to the bathroom and you turned it off! No fair!"

"We're tired of 'Frozen,' Imani," William tells her.

"Can I watch it in my room, then? On my tablet?" she whines.

William sighs. "Okay, Baby, for twenty minutes."

"What if it's not over then?"

"Then it's not over. It's not like you don't already know the ending."

"But I want to *see* it!" She stomps back to her room. "Twenty minutes doesn't start yet!" she says.

William laughs. Sets the timer on his phone for 22 minutes, and I think, "What if? What if he wasn't here to raise her?" How sad that would be! It's more like William saved my life than I saved his, but either way, I'm glad he's alive.

* * * * *

It's strange, this in and out stuff. Like I drift off, and when I wake up, I've got another piece of memory back. And this time I remember. It was Jason. Jason's squeaky voice yelling "Enough! Let's get outta here." I'm sure it was Jason.

Late in the afternoon, Brent stops by, looks me over, then says, "I've never even seen a face that color."

"What color?" I ask.

"What? You don't know what color your face is? You haven't looked in the mirror?"

"Yeah, I have. But what color would you say it is?"

"I'd say it's the color my arm was after that guy hit me with a baseball bat."

"That was an accident."

"Still turned the same color…What'd you tell the cops?"

"Everything I know, which is nothing."

"Bro! You know who did it!"

"I don't know. They came from behind. I didn't see them!"

"It had to be those Patriot guys! They're so pissed at you…"

"They're pissed at everybody. Well…maybe not you, white boy, but everybody like me—or more like everybody who doesn't look like them."

"Yeah, but they're *hella* pissed at you."

Max comes in from the kitchen, hands me a glass of water and two pills. "Hey, Brent," she says.

"Hey, Mrs. Max."

"You want anything to drink? Lemonade? Sparkling water?"

"No, thanks."

Max leaves, and Brent starts in again about how it had to be those guys.

"Can we please change the subject?"

"Okay, but..."

He's quiet for a nanosecond, then, "My dad says he'll buy me a car if I'll get a calculus tutor, go to math camp, you know, let him off the hook for his lost bet."

"Some bribe," I say.

"I'm not going to do it."

My head is pounding so hard I can hardly follow what Brent's saying.

"I mean, I really, really want a car, but I really, really don't want a math tutor, or to go to math camp, so forget the car..."

I wake to a kind of gray outside the window and wonder if it's morning gray or evening gray. God, my head hurts, and my whole right side, like the crack in my rib has spread to all of my other ribs. Can that even happen? The light's on in the kitchen. I hear Max and William shuffling around out there, catch the scent of the special sauce William always makes for pork and beans, so it must be evening, not morning. And it must be Wednesday 'cause, you know, pork 'n beans.

Brent. I guess I drifted off while he was here, like with Rosie, except there's no heart-lined note from Brent resting against my water glass.

CHAPTER NINETEEN

The Lie

It's no longer like climbing Mt. Everest to walk to the bathroom and back to the recliner. My mind's cleared enough that I can read a few pages of *The Grapes of Wrath* before I get drifty.

After dinner (chicken and greens, so it's Thursday) I'm back in the recliner and Max is on the couch near me, remote in hand, looking for a movie that might get us laughing. She says we can all use a few laughs.

We've just started "Young Frankenstein" when Joe stops by with more healing tea and a special cup that has a strainer and lid that go with it. Max pauses the movie.

"You've got to let it steep for at least five minutes," he tells Max.

"Thanks," Max says. "We'll give it a try."

Joe moves closer, looking down at my head. "That's one ugly gash you've got."

"Thanks," I tell him.

He laughs. "Peppy misses you," he says. "She was okay with Jason today, though."

Wait. What did he say? Jason? "Peppy was with Jason today?"

"Yeah, well, you were in no shape to walk her, and Tuesday, you know, long day for me."

"But Jason?"

"Hey, I know you don't like Jason, but that didn't bother Peppy. She liked him okay."

Again, I hear Jason's high-pitched Miss Piggy voice in my head, "Enough! Let's get outta here!"

"He..." I want to tell Joe not to trust Jason with Peppy—not to trust Jason at all, but I can't find the words.

"What?" Joe says.

"Jason's..."

"What???"

"You shouldn't trust him," I manage to say.

"I know he's caught up with the wrong crowd, but I'm not sure that's who he is in his heart."

"It *is* who he is," I say. "Mr. 14 Words."

"Well, you'll be back on the job soon. Now drink one full cup of that tea before breakfast and another before bedtime. That'll speed things along."

As if on cue, Max brings in the tea cup and sets it on the tray beside my/William's chair. "Tea for you, Joe?" Max asks.

"No, thanks. I need to get back home." Joe makes the Namaste gesture to me and leaves.

Max starts the movie again, but as funny as "Young Frankenstein" is, I drift off, not waking until the monster's doing some song and dance thing.

"Bedtime?" Max asks. I nod. She raises the recliner to a sitting position. With her helping on the left side, and me using the right chair arm for support, I manage to stand, inch back to my bedroom, and ease myself onto the bed. Max brings in tea, a glass of water, and my bedtime pill.

"You should drink the tea, too," she says, after I down the pill.

I take a sip and hand it back to her. She sets it on the table beside the glass of water, my phone, and a box of tissue. She fluffs my pillow, straightens the covers, pulls them up to my shoulders, kisses me on the forehead, and tells me "Sweet dreams," like she used to do back when I was a little kid.

So tired. Fuzzy. I'll be glad when I can get out more than a short sentence. When I can talk sense. When I can convince Joe that it's crazy to trust Jason with his dog and in his studio.

Third day home. We sit around the table in the dining room. Six of us. Me, Max, William, Officer Harvey, Officer Romero, and Mario. I'm glad Mario was able to switch shifts with someone so he could be here for this interview. I mean, I know I didn't do anything wrong or anything, but it's still kind of scary to be grilled by the police. Mario knows cop-talk.

Introductions around the table, then chatter, who wants coffee, nice weather for December, how am I feeling...

Officer Romero is short and fat, with streaks of grey in her hair. She's one of those special cops who's always present when a minor is involved. Like Officer Goodridge back when I was only nine and had to make a statement about the pervert.

Officer Harvey is the guy who figured out William was a good guy, not one of the attackers. He starts off. "Tell us what happened on December 23, the night you were attacked."

Mario takes a small tablet and pencil from his shirt pocket, like the tablet and pencil that Harvey has sitting in front of him.

"What were you doing right before you were attacked?"

"Buddy and I were almost home from our walk."

"Then what?"

"I heard someone running behind me, and then I was slammed to the ground."

Harvey checks his notes. "One person, or more?"

"More."

"Did they tell you to empty your pockets? Give them your wallet?"

"They didn't say anything, just pushed me down and kept beating me."

"Then what?"

"I don't know. I woke up in the hospital."

"Think back. Did you see anything? Anything at all?"

"Everything was black."

"You couldn't see anything, but what were you hearing?"

Ever since yesterday when a time was set for the interview, I've been thinking about what they might ask. What I might answer. Trying to find more memory, but there's not much there.

"Try to relax, Eddie," Mario says. "Any little detail might help."

Long pause, then Harvey says, "Do you think your injuries came from fists? Clubs? Any ideas?"

I try to remember what I felt, run my fingers lightly along the long gash in my head. "Kicks. Boots, maybe," I say. "I remember rolling into a ball, covering my head. I guess that's how my hands and arms got so messed up."

I glance over at Max, who looks like she could cry. She says she'll bring coffee refills and goes into the kitchen.

"You think maybe someone was kicking you?" Harvey says.

I nod. "And Buddy..." At the sound of his name, Buddy slowly gets up off his bed next to William's chair, limps over to me and leans against my leg. I give him a scratch and a pat. Harvey sits watching, pencil ready to go. "I heard Buddy growl, and then yelp."

"What else did you hear?"

I think, try to remember, then... "William. I heard William close to me, asking where I was hurt, but I couldn't talk."

"And then?"

"Screeching tires, shouts at William to get away, lots of shuffling around..."

"And then?" Harvey asks.

I shrug.

"What's the next thing you remember?"

"Max's voice. In the hospital."

"How about the ambulance? Did you hear the siren?"

I try to dredge up any other details. Did I hear the siren? "Okay. Yeah. I heard a siren, and a lot more shuffling around, and William telling me over and over that I was going to be okay. Oh, and before that, I forgot to say that I heard William yelling that I was his son."

Max and Mario both turn to look at William, who's looking at me. We haven't talked about the son thing since we used it to get the cops off him.

Harvey flips back through his notebook and glances at a few pages. "Okay. Good, Eddie. Now tell me…"

Officer Romero glances at her big-faced watch. "Let's take a short break."

"Just a few more…" Harvey starts.

"A short break," she says, giving him one of those "Don't mess with me" looks like the kind Max has perfected.

I stand. Slowly. Everything hurts. I get my phone from the tray next to William's chair. A text from Rosie: *after sch?*

I text back a thumbs up. Better. I feel better knowing I'll see Rosie in…I check the clock…in about three hours.

Max has again topped off coffee for William and Harvey. Romero skipped the top-off. Max brings out a plate of cookies that look homemade but aren't.

"Just a few more questions," Harvey says, motioning me back to the table. I hobble over and lower myself into the chair. Damn, I hurt!

Harvey reads his notes, reminding me of what I've said so far—I heard running, was thrown to the ground, beaten, kicked, maybe with boots, heard Buddy yelp, heard William ask where I was hurt, couldn't answer, heard screeching brakes, shouting at William to get away, William yelling that he's your dad, a siren, William whispering you'd be okay, then waking to your mother's voice in the hospital.

"Have I got that right?" Harvey says.

I nod.

"Yes or no?"

"Yes."

"Anything else? Anything at all?"

I shake my head.

"What about from whoever jumped you. Any sounds from them?"

"Just running coming up behind me."

"Nothing else?

"No," I say, even as I'm hearing Jason's Miss Piggy voice in my head.

"Okay," Max says to Romero. "It's time for Eddie's pain meds, and he needs a rest."

Officer Romero nods. Max tells me to get comfortable. That would be William's chair. She brings me one of those little plastic containers of applesauce, fresh water, and a pill. I take them all in that order, recline back, close my eyes, and doze off to the murmur of voices, Harvey asking William a bunch of questions, Max fussing around in the kitchen, Mario's occasional comments.

Again, I remember the kicks, hear Jason's squeaky voice, "Enough. Let's get outta here," and I'm filled with a white-hot anger at Jason.

I should have told Harvey about that too, I guess. But maybe it seemed like it would take too much energy. The telling. The questions and more questions. Maybe another time, I tell myself.

Next thing I know Max is standing over me, nudging, whispering, "Rosie's here. She can come back later if you're too…"

"I'm not tired," I say, raising the recliner, trying to look wide-eyed and awake.

"Come on in," Max calls to Rosie. She, Max, fluffs my pillows, takes dirty dishes from my tray and goes back to the kitchen as Rosie comes in.

"Hey, Rosie," I say, my voice hoarse and weak sounding.

"Hey, Eddie," she says, giving me a tight smile. She stands a few feet away, watching me, like maybe I scare her or something.

I pat the arm of the recliner. "Sit. What's up?"

She half stands, half sits, all stiff like, on the arm of the chair, facing me. "How do you feel?" she asks.

"Better." I'm not sure that's true, but I want Rosie to think I'm better, to stop being afraid to touch me, or look at me. "What've you been doing?" I ask.

"Well...I took Zoe shopping so she could get something for Mom and Dad for Christmas. That was a pain."

"Why?"

"She wanted to get them a 'Frozen' jigsaw puzzle and her favorite Bundt cake, never mind that it'd be stale by Christmas. I tried to get her to think about what *they* might like, the joy of giving a gift that someone might actually like rather than something that she'd end up getting the benefit from."

"She's so like the pest," I say, managing a small enough smile that it doesn't hurt.

"And then we go to the bookstore to find something for mom, and she decides on a book about dolphins 'cause, you know, dolphins are Zoe's next big obsession after Elsa and Anna." Rosie laughs and relaxes onto the chair arm, letting her legs dangle above the floor.

I didn't even notice I was holding my breath, but I guess I was because as soon as I feel Rosie relax, I exhale a double lungful of stale air.

I have less to talk about than ever. I slept. I sipped soup. I took my meds. I answered some police questions. I slept. I sipped soup. I took my meds. I mean, how boring is that?

"What else?" I ask Rosie. "What else have you been doing?"

"Sofia's parents are talking about transferring her to St. Francis. Fatima's, too."

"Because of that scarf-pulling asshole?"

Rosie nods. "But Sofia wants to stay at Hamilton. Especially for choir and soccer."

Text ding. Rosie glances at her phone. "Gotta go," she says. "Give me a joke for Zoe?"

It's funny how I can barely remember stuff from when I got beat up, but all of those corny jokes are still stuck in my brain. "Did I already give you some bird jokes?"

"Just the one about elephants being smarter than chickens."

"No, I mean jokes with real birds, like the kind that fly around."

"Chickens are real birds!" Rosie says.

"Okay, so why do birds fly south for the winter?"

"Why?"

I wait. Rosie always tries to get out of guessing, but no guess, no joke. She looks up at the ceiling. I look at her.

"Ummm…because winters are warmer in the south?"

"Nooooo. Because it's too far to walk."

* * * * *

I wake to the scent of soup. Still chicken, I think. And not that I don't like chicken soup, but I wish I could chew again. Mario comes in with a bowl of soup and a slice of bread, and clears a space on the tray. I raise the recliner.

"Wanna milkshake?" he asks. "Help replenish a little fat?"

I nod.

By the time I've soaked up all of the bread until it's soft enough to eat, then tipped the bowl up to drink the rest of the soup, Mario's back with two tall vanilla milkshakes. He pulls a chair up beside me. After a big gulp of the shake, he lets out a long, satisfied, "Aaahhh."

"I'm practicing my culinary skills," he says. "Francie says that when we move in together, we'll be sharing kitchen duties. So far I've mastered milkshakes and cereal."

I laugh. It hurts.

"Listen, Bro. I know you're tired of talking about this, but you must have at least heard *something* from those guys the other night."

I take another sip of milkshake. Something about the look on his face, intense concern? Curiosity? He looks like the seventeen-year-old brother who so wanted the truth from me back when I was nine. I trust him. I should tell him. But then what? The police take control? Suddenly, I realize the reason I've kept the Jason part of things to myself. I don't want the police to deal with Jason. *I* want to deal with Jason *myself.* I finish the milkshake, feeling better than I have since before I got beat up. I smile at the thought of giving Jason what he has coming.

"Eddie?" Mario says. Eyebrows raised in a question. "You're sure? Nothing?"

"Nothing," I say. God, I hate lying to Mario, but not as much as I'd hate not getting my chance at Jason.

CHAPTER TWENTY

A Late Christmas

Ten days after Christmas, we gather around the tree as if it's Christmas Eve. They've waited until I'm strong enough to laugh and to play a lame—literally lame—round of fetch with Buddy out in the yard. He's got a lighter splint now so he hobbles a little more easily. And I've still got a cast on my left arm, and my right hand still hurts so I don't throw the ball very far.

Max and William and the pest waited until I was strong enough to join in before they opened any gifts. Well, that's not quite true. Imani got to choose one gift to open on the real Christmas Eve. Some kind of "Frozen" backpack, I think. But all the rest of the presents are wrapped and waiting, like on a real Christmas Eve.

It's dark out and only the lights from the Christmas tree and the little blinking lights across the mantle are on. White lights on the mantle and the tree. William has a thing for only white lights on the tree, maybe because she's constantly dealing with color, mixing colors, painting a color a customer wants, then painting over it because it's not what she (usually she) wanted after all. So, the tree is all lit up with white lights, and Christmas music from Max's phone is playing through the Bluetooth speakers. We're sipping hot spiced apple cider from Christmas cups, like we always do on Christmas Eve. In the glow that is Christmas Eve, even if it's a delayed Christmas Eve, I think how lucky I am to have this family, this warm, safe place. How lucky I am to be alive. It could have been different.

The tradition for opening presents is that the youngest goes first. Imani rips open her first package, lets out a squeal, then pulls this big, velvet cape thing out of the box. It's reddish-purple, Cherry Cola, I'd say, with Cornstalk Gold trim. She drapes it over her shoulders and runs her hand across the velvet.

"You like it, Baby?"

"Thank you!" she says, then runs to William and throws her arms around him.

"It's from Maria, too," he says.

She runs to Max and gives her an equally enthusiastic hug. "Thanks, Mommy!" Imani twirls in a circle and the cape billows out, then wraps around her. "I'm Anna of Arendelle!" She twirls in the opposite direction. "I'm never taking it off!"

"Well...you might change your mind come summer," William says.

"It's beautiful, isn't it?" Max says. "Look at the lining, and the gold beading. Carla's such a meticulous seamstress."

"Aunt Carla made this?"

"We couldn't find anything like it in the stores," Max says.

Imani wraps the cape closer around herself.

"Your turn, Eddie," Max says, bringing a big, fancy-wrapped box over and setting it on the couch beside me.

I feel bad. In all the pile of presents under the tree, there's not much from me. The only present I bought is the necklace for Rosie and I haven't even given it to her yet. I want to save it for a private time, and there haven't been any private times in weeks. Feels like years. Soon though.

"Open it, Eddie! I hope it's Kristoff's furry coat!"

I shake the package. "Maybe it's Simba's mane."

"No! Open it!"

I look over at Max. "I'm sorry..."

"Just open it, Eddie," she says with a laugh. "We know you've not exactly been up for shopping."

I tear off the paper, open the box, and find it crammed full of art supplies: different sizes of sketch pads, ArtGraf stuff from Portugal! Graphite sticks and a whole bunch of special pencils.

"They didn't have Simba's mane at the store," Max says, "and Carla was too busy with capes to make a mane."

"This is awesome," I tell her. "Thank you!"

"It's from William, too."

"Thanks, William."

I open the sketch pad and lightly outline Simba in a crouched, hunting position, then start on the background.

Imani finds a package for Max under the tree and takes it to her.

"Aren't we going in order of age?" William asks, pretending to be offended. Imani gives him a puzzled look. "I'm younger than old-lady Maria," he laughs.

"Doesn't look like it," Imani says.

"Thanks, Imani," Max says.

Imani finds a package for William and takes it to him.

"No, you first, Maria. I've been waiting weeks for you to open this," he says, flashing her a big smile.

She looks at the box. "Nordstrom?" she says.

"Open it."

She carefully removes the fancy ribbon and lifts out a sweater. "Baby blue! My favorite color!"

"Ocean Front Blue," I say.

"Umm. Maybe closer to Chill Blue," William says.

Max feels the sweater, rubs her face against it. "Cashmere? William…?"

"Don't worry about it," he says. "Customers were generous this season."

She gets kinda teary. Max is like that sometimes when someone does something extra nice for her. Like maybe she doesn't deserve extra nice. But she does. Everybody who knows Max knows she deserves extra nice.

"Not that you don't look great in that Target sweater, but what do you think? Like it?"

"Oh, I love it!"

She leans into William and gives him a long kiss. I look away. I mean, I'm glad they love each other, but that part of it's kinda weird.

"Yuck!" Imani yells. They pull away, laughing. "Your turn, Daddy! Open mine first!" Imani reaches past two larger packages from Max to get a small red and green gift bag.

William opens it slowly, making a big deal of "What could this be?" and "If it's a jacket, I hope it fits..." No way could a jacket fit in that bag, and Imani laughs and laughs at William's remark. He takes his time, poking around in the bag. "I wonder..."

"Daddy!! Open it!!"

William reaches in and pulls out a small metal thing, about four inches long. Imani grabs it away from him.

"It does twelve things, Daddy! See. It's a screwdriver, and a bottle opener, and a knife, and a keychain..."

William eases the gadget back. "Cool!" he says. "This will be so useful! Go get my keys, Sugar."

She runs into the kitchen and grabs William's keys from the hook by the door. He switches key chains. I remember what he said about how he could have ended up like Devon Parker and how awful it would have been if he couldn't raise Imani. It totally sucks that Devon Parker doesn't get to raise his little boy.

Imani hands the last two fancy-wrapped packages to William. They're from Max. The first is a set of wireless headphones, so he can listen to music when he's working and not have any wires get in the way. The second is a book by Barack Obama, *Of Thee I Sing: A Letter to My Daughters*. He thumbs through it, remarking on the beauty of the illustrations, then hands it to Imani to look at. He leans in for another of those kisses with Max and I look over Imani's shoulder at the book. It's about thirteen different American heroes—Abraham Lincoln, Sitting Bull, Helen Keller, Martin Luther King, even Cesar Chavez.

"Hey, Imani," I say. "Hand out the last gifts, will you?" She looks puzzled. "Those big envelopes under the tree."

Since I couldn't get out shopping, and I had plenty of time on my hands, I did cartoons for everyone. Imani opens the one with her name on it and starts laughing. It's Simba the cat, eyes gleaming, ears back, pulling the pants off the pompous Duke of Weselton. William's is a bossy-looking Simba in a paint spattered cap, sitting on William's shoulder. William is in his usual painter's clothes, roller in hand, and Simba's pointing out a place William missed.

For Max, Simba is dressed in one of those white coats that dentists and hygienists wear. He's standing on the dental tray, next to Max, a long strand of floss pulled between his front paws, ready to floss the patient's teeth. The patient, who's reclined back with an overhead light shining into his mouth, is a scared-looking William. Well...I don't do people well, so Max and William aren't exactly recognizable. Everybody's laughing and making a big deal about the cartoons. I feel a little better about not having any real gifts for anyone.

Max starts gathering up trash and empty cider cups when William says, "One more thing." He goes into their room, then comes out holding a brown paper bag. He sits on the arm of the couch, next to Max.

"Your book is perfect," he tells her. "I've been thinking about heroes ever since you told me about Eddie's WWCCD bracelet. Our country's in such a bad place right now—so many leaders spewing out hate and fear that the people who admire them decide it's okay to shoot up synagogues, and churches, and mosques..." He shakes his head slowly. "So, I've been thinking a lot about people like the ones in this book. Leaders who help us do the hard work to make our country better...so..."

He takes something from the bag, looks at it carefully. "Here," he says, taking Max's hand and slipping a colorful woven bracelet onto her wrist.

"It's beautiful," Max says. "All shades of blue from the lightest to the darkest, all woven together! I love it."

"Look closely."

She studies the bracelet for a moment, then smiles. "WWDHD."

"Good choice?" William asks.

"Perfect. Dolores Huerta's one of my all-time major heroes, always standing up for women and for poor people."

"Tara, the high school girl at the job over in Alhambra, makes these bracelets that she sells at craft fairs and on Etsy. Usually they're just colorful designs, but I commissioned her to do some special bracelets for us."

He hands a bracelet to Imani. It's thicker than Max's, full of pinks and reds and purples. He leans down to help her fasten it. "See, you've got a hero from make-believe," he says, reading the letters WWAOAD to her. "What Would Anna of Arendelle Do?"

Then he twists the bracelet so the other side is on top. "WWMOD. What would Michelle Obama do?" Imani twists it back so the WWAOAD side shows.

"Okay, so say something happens at school," he says. "Like maybe you see a kid take another kid's lunch money from their desk. And you know it's not right, but you don't want to be a snitch. Now your bracelet will remind you to think about what Anna of Arendelle would do. Or what would Michele Obama do? And it might help you figure out what *you* should do."

"What *would* they do?"

"I don't know for sure," William says. "That's for *you* to think about."

William turns to me. "I know you already have a bracelet, but I thought you might like a less clunky update."

He hands me a bracelet in light tans and greys, WWCCD spelled out in deep brown, or...in Baronial Brown, with a

background of Buckwheat Flour and Sail Cloth. I slip the bracelet on my wrist. "Cool."

William looks at me like he's trying to figure out if I mean
it.

"Really. It's cool. Thanks."

"What about you?" Max says.

William slips a dark colored bracelet, Midnight Black, In-
digo Blue, and Virtuoso Purple, over his left wrist.

"And?" Max asks.

"Well...you know, WWMLKD."

* * * * *

The day after our late Christmas Eve, after Max and William and Imani leave for lunch and a movie, I text Rosie to
come over. She says she's got too much to do to finish some
college application. I call her. "I thought you applied already,"
I say.

"I put in an early decision application to UOF, but I need
to have back-up applications for second tier choices."

"Second tier?"

"Yeah, for if I don't get my first choice. Really though,
there's UOF as my first choice and all the rest would be like
my thousandth choices. No place else has the kind of music
therapy program I want."

"You'll get in," I tell her. "With your grades and test
scores, and all of the extra-curricular stuff you do? Plus, you're
beautiful. Did you send a picture?"

Rosie laughs. "The thing is, I don't have an instrument. I
only sing. It would be better if I played the piano, or guitar, or
something. But I know I can help a lot of kids with music therapy. I for sure want to help kids."

"I've got a present for you," I say, using the singsong-y
voice I use when I'm trying to get Imani all interested in some
surprise.

"What is it?"

"You have to come see," I singsong-y say.

"I've got to get the rest of these applications out of the way."

More sing-song. "You're gonna like it."

"Well…" She laughs, says she has something for me, too. She can't stay long but, yeah, a break from the applications would probably be good.

It's around two when Rosie comes in, carrying a package wrapped in shiny red paper, tied with a fancy silver bow. I hold out my little package to her.

"You first," she tells me, then takes my hand and draws it closer to get a better look. "Cool bracelet."

"William gave it to me. He gave one to Imani and Max, too…" I tell her what the letters stand for.

"Hmmm, if I had a bracelet, I wonder whose initials I'd want on it?"

"Come on. Open your present," I say.

She sits, staring at my bracelet.

"Rosie…"

"I know!" she says, all smiles. "Beyoncé! WWBD!"

"Beyoncé?"

"Yeah! She helps a lot of people, especially girls and women, and she does it through music!"

"Really?"

"You know. Her songs make you think about stuff, and they stay with you. And she makes about a zillion dollars off of every album, and she gives a lot of it to places that help girls become leaders, and she speaks out for gender equality and against police brutality and…"

"Would you PLEASE open your gift??"

She laughs. "After you," she says, handing me her package. Now it's her turn to use the singsong-y voice. "Please? Pretty please??"

So, I open her package. Inside is a small box of those kiddie candies that are shaped like hearts, and a CD of the last choir concert. I check the list of songs and performers, happy to see that Rosie's solo is on the CD.

"I didn't have much money, and I didn't..."

"This is perfect!" I tell her. "Whenever I'm missing you, I can hear your voice."

And then, finally, she opens my gift to her. She loves the locket. I mean she seriously loves the locket. Teary-eyed loves it the way Max loved her cashmere sweater.

It's the first time we've been alone since before I got beat up. The first time we've had a real kiss, not one of those quick, made for public viewing, pecks. I pull Rosie closer, move over to make room beside me. She starts to scoot in, then pulls back. "I'm afraid I'll break you," she says.

"No. You'll put me back together," I tell her, again pulling her toward me.

This time she wedges in beside me, her body close against mine. She's warm and soft next to me, her hand stroking my face.

"I've missed being close to you so much," I tell her. I slip my hand under her blouse. She moves in closer, her thigh pushing against what wants to be pushed against.

I'm not like one of those locker room guys who talks about how they've done all of this sexy stuff with some girl. I'll just say we didn't do the full Tilly, but close enough to feel hella good. Rosie, too. I like that Rosie feels hella good, too.

Later in the evening, while Imani is giving me a scene-by-scene description of "Despicable Me #3," Max comes to sit beside me on the couch. Imani is talking on and on about Gru and Dru, and some diamond-powered robot, and a kidnapping, and and and... It's a welcome shift from "Frozen," but I'm mostly spacing out when I feel the warmth of Max's hand on mine. I look over at her and see tears welling in her eyes.

"Max..."

She shakes her head and turns her face into my shoulder.

"Max?? What's wrong?"

"I can't help thinking about how you could be dead now!"

"I think about that, too, sometimes—how much I'd miss if I didn't get to live my life."

"You're not even listening!" Imani yells at me. "I'm not going to tell you how it ends!" she says, stomping off to her room.

Max and I both laugh. She wipes her face on my shirt. "I'm so glad you're here," she tells me. "I don't know what I'd do without you."

"You'd choose the sweetness of life," I tell her.

She shakes her head. "I hope I'm never put to that test," she says.

We sit for a while, quiet, then Max says, "I don't understand why anyone in this world would want to hurt you, Eddie. How can that be?"

"I guess not everyone likes me as much as you do."

I hear a text ding and reach for my phone. It's Rosie. Max gives me a motherly pat on the leg, then goes back to Imani's room.

Rosie: *who made your bracelet*

Me: *someone william knows*

Rosie: *phone?*

Me: *don't know*

Rosie: *find out?*

Me: *k*

I go out to the garage where William's shifting paint supplies, getting ready for tomorrow's job. He won't give out customer's phone numbers, says it's important to respect their privacy. But he looks through his account book and gives me the bracelet maker's email.

Two days later, Rosie has a WWBD bracelet, and Brianna has WWJD, like the kind I wanted when I was a little kid. By the end of the week, Cameron has WWLRD. That's for some drummer that he says is the best. Brent has WWCMD, for Christopher McCandless, that *Into the Wild* guy he's been talking about so much lately. That's how tense things are at Brent's house now that he's refusing to be bribed into getting a calculus tutor or to sign up for math camp. He keeps telling his dad, "A deal is a deal." I guess that's not going over so well.

The Tuesday before school starts up again, everyone's parents or guardians, or whoever, get one of those mass emails from the school—from Hockney, to be exact. It's a reminder that Hamilton High is a hate-free zone, that all students are welcome, whatever their race, religion, gender, ability, or country of origin. He asks that families remind their children that every single person is worthy of respect whether or not we agree with them. Students who deface school property with hate signs or symbols, who participate in hate speech, or promote hatred in any other way, will be immediately suspended, followed by expulsion.

CHAPTER TWENTY-ONE

Too Soon

"Are you sure you don't want to stay home a few more days?" Max says, as she pulls up in front of the school. "Get a bit stronger?"

"I'm good," I say. "Thanks for the ride."

"You're *sure* Rosie can bring you home after school?"

"Max..."

"Okay. I know. I just..."

"I know. You worry. Stop it. Go down to Nunamakers and get an ice cream cone." We both laugh, knowing I'm talking about a lot more than ice cream.

My face is still bruised, but Max says no one will notice. I guess my skin's dark enough that the bruises have reached the color of blend. I still walk with a limp, but I'm down to only one pain pill at bedtime, so at least I can stay awake in class during the day. If I want to.

Miss May does one of those cartoon doubletakes when I show up before zero period. It's a quick double-take, though, and then she's all, "Great to see you—so glad you're back—the tables are a mess, the cupboards are a mess—hard to get along without you!"

"Thanks," I say, starting on the daily routine, tables first, then putting whatever May has for us today at each place.

"What's with the cap, Eddie? No caps."

"Hockney said it'd be okay, as long as it's an HH baseball cap," I tell her.

She looks doubtful. I take my cap off and bend my head to show her the hairless strip in the middle of my head and the still stapled-up gash.

She turns away. "Okay, okay! Put the cap back on." Once I've covered my stitched-up bald head, she asks, "Are you all right? I heard you were hurt pretty bad."

"Yeah. I'm all right."

"I missed you."

I focus on straightening the tables in the front of the room.

The class is all quiet as I pass out notebooks and today's reading. Like people can't talk and get a good look at me at the same time? A couple of the girls look at me like "poor Eddie." I hate that!

I scoot into my desk next to Phong and half-listen as May talks about choosing our favorite writing for the next WriteLight collection.

Phong leans close and whispers, "You look like shit."

I laugh, thinking "You look like shit" is a lot better than "poor Eddie."

"Who's that?" I say, pointing to the WWKTTD on Phong's wrist. I guess that girl who makes the bracelets must be getting rich by now because a lot of people are wearing them.

"You know. KT Tatara, that Asian comedian guy?"

"Wait. Asians can be comedians?"

Phong pulls back his hand as if to smack me, then drops it. "There's no safe place to hit you, is there?" He looks me over again. "It was probably those Patriot guys."

"Don't know."

"Probably though."

I shrug, finding the lines of the poem that Naomi just read, counting down to the place I'll read when it's my turn. "I would show you/the invisible tokens/of sorrow and joy." It's good that Miss May always reads the whole poem when we finish reading around because everybody mostly only concentrates on their own lines when we do the read out loud thing.

I wonder if it's a coincidence, or if May chose the poem with me in mind. "Scars" for today's writing prompt. Ours or someone else's? Internal or external? I've got a lot to choose from. There's the scar down the middle of my right hand from the surgery back when I was four years old. The surgery that was supposed to give my hand greater flexibility and range of motion. But didn't. Max says there was only one, highly questionable, advantage that came from that surgery, and it wasn't a better working hand.

The pain pills made me sick, and sometimes after the surgery, I'd wake in the middle of the night, screaming in pain. And the only thing that could distract me were Mario's farts. So, Mario became an expert fart master. He was in 7th grade back when he was on regular fart-duty. With so much practice, he soon became the fart hero of Palm Avenue School. He's twenty-five now, and he says the fart-hero designation doesn't carry as much weight as it once did. He says Francie shows no respect for this highly developed skill. Sometimes, though, when it's just the two of us, and we're outside somewhere, Mario lets loose with his favorite long, rhythmic, melodic release of gas. And, like always, or almost always, I bust out laughing. He likes to wait until I've taken a gulp of soda, so he can get that soda-snort from me, too, but it's harder for him to find perfect fart conditions now that he's grown up and I'm almost grown up.

I said I *almost* always bust out laughing, because there was a time, back when I was nine, when I stopped laughing at Mario's farts. That's what tipped him that there was something seriously wrong in my life. And when I started laughing at farts again, he knew I was going to be okay. Max says that if the surgeon had told her, no, the surgery wouldn't make my hand better, but it would turn Mario into a fart king, well, she could have saved me a lot of pain and saved herself a lot of much needed money.

That old hand scar's not the scar I'll write about today, though. Maybe I'll write about the scar that runs from the top of my forehead past the crown of my skull. That's a "doozie."

That's Dr. G.'s word, not mine. He says it remains to be seen whether or not hair will grow back in the strip. Rosie says she'll love me with or without a full head of hair, but I for sure don't want to have this reverse mohawk thing for the rest of my life. Max says it will be distinctive, but what with my stub of a hand, I don't need any more weird distinctions.

So, what scar to write about? Maybe the scar of betrayal by a once-trusted adult? Nah. The hand scar, the hairless head scar, the heart scar...Does Simba have a scar? I'm not sure. It doesn't have to be real...

Imani, also known as the pest,
Has a scar left by Simba, in jest.
A scratch thin as his whisker,
No blood, not even a blister,
But the pest cried bloody murder.
Even the neighbors heard her,
Neosporin and band-aids
Lessened her tirades,
Consoled with ice cream and kisses...

...to be continued. Bad last line, and I want to get something in there about rewarding Simba with tuna, or fish? Fish would be easier to rhyme.

Phong and I make our way through the jammed-up halls toward Earth Science.

"I heard you didn't tell the cops who beat you up."

"I don't know who beat me up."

"Would you tell if you knew?"

"I don't know."

"But what I'm asking is *would* you tell if you did?"

"I don't know. I mean, I don't know if I'd tell or not."

"But..."

"Could we talk about something else? Like the weather, or something?

"Hmmm. Was it raining that night you got beat up?"

By the end of third period, I'm totally done in. I guess that shouldn't be too surprising 'cause all I've been doing for the past two weeks is walking from William's recliner to the kitchen and back, watching "Parks and Recreation," thinking I could be dead, dozing, walking from the recliner to the bathroom and back...You get the idea.

I drag myself to the lunch court and flop down at the table across from Brent, who is in agreement with Phong's earlier assessment. "You look like shit."

"I feel like shit," I tell him.

Cameron puts his tray on the table and sits next to Brent. I look into my lunch carrier, take out the bottle of water, then zip it up again. Nothing looks good.

"I heard the cops were here again this morning, grueling those Patriot guys about beating you up," he says.

"Where'd you hear that?" Brent asks.

"You know. Monica. She's an aide in the office. She knows stuff. She says they brought five of those guys in and had them wait outside Hockney's office. Then they called them in, one at a time. Everyone knows they did it."

"I don't know they did it. I don't know *who* did it," I say.

"Yeah, well, you for sure know you pissed them off," Cameron says.

"What else did Monica say? Who all was in there?" Brent asks.

"She didn't know their names, just that they were the guys who were wearing 'Make America Great' hats back when school started," Cameron says.

Meghan comes over and sits down next to Cameron. "Can I talk to you?" she says.

"Sure," Cameron says.

"I mean, like private?"

"Oh. Okay," He takes the last bite of his white bread sandwich, empties the remaining Cheeto crumbs into his mouth, slides his tray to the end of the table and follows Meghan to a spot over by the tree, away from everyone else.

"More drama for Cameron," Brent says. "I don't know why he gets so much girl-drama."

"Maybe it's the tie," I say.

"Maybe I'll start wearing a tie," Brent says.

I unzip my lunch carrier and look inside again. Just like before, nothing looks good. Brent watches me for what seems like too long. "Really, you look worse than shit."

"I'm hella tired. I wish I was home."

"Well...go home then."

"I'm riding with Rosie, and she's not out 'til after 6th period."

"Well, at least you can sleep through dumbbell math."

But instead of going to math, I go down to the yoga room and meet Joe coming out.

"You don't look so good," Joe says.

"That makes it unanimous."

He gives me his raised eyebrow look.

"Phong. Cameron. Brent. That's been their greeting today. Before hi, or how's it goin', it's 'you look like shit.'"

"Aren't you supposed to be in class this period? What brings you here?"

"I just...I'm tired..."

"Well..." He holds the door open for me. "I'll be back in a few minutes."

I sit at his desk, lean back in his chair, and try to get comfortable. I shove a huge stack of stuff to the back of the desk, make a space where I can lay my head. For a Buddhist, Joe's got a lot of shit piled around. God, I'm tired. When am I ever not going to be so tired?

The buzz of the bell cuts through my sleep. I don't open my eyes.

"Eddie. Eddie. Wake up," Joe says, nudging my shoulder.

I open my eyes.

"Come on. Sit up. If Mr. Hockney sees I'm letting kids sleep in my office, that'll be the end of me."

I lift my head, push myself back into the chair.

"What're you doing here, anyway? You shouldn't be back at school yet."

"I was bored at home."

"So? Is this better?"

I shake my head. Just a little, not past the hurt line.

"You should go home."

"Have to wait for Rosie," I tell him.

"Call your mom?"

"She's at work."

Joe glances at the clock, then back at me, then at the clock again. "Come on. I'll walk you to the nurse's office. You can stretch out in there until Rosie can take you home."

"It's not her day."

Joe gives me the question look again.

"Tuesday/Thursday. She's not here on Mondays."

Joe sighs, "Okay. You may as well hang out in here as go sit on one of those hard chairs in the office." He stacks three mats against the wall, rolls another one up for a pillow. I hear him on the phone to the office, telling someone that I'm with him. I drift off.

At dinner that night, Max—who's not usually an "I told you so" mom—says, "I told you it was too soon for you to go back to school."

"Yeah, well, I'd finished all 10,123 episodes of "Parks and Recreation."

"What'd you hear about the guys who beat you up?" William asks.

I shake my head, take a bite of salad and concentrate on chewing. At least I can chew again, sort of.

"C'mon, Eddie. There's got to be plenty of rumors flying around. It's high school. Right?"

I take another bite of salad.

"Eddie…" Max starts.

I turn to Imani. "Hey! I wrote a poem about you today. Wanna hear it?"

"About me? Tell me it!"

"It's in my notebook."

"I wanna see it!"

"I'll get it, but I'll have to read it to you 'cause it's all messed up, stuff crossed out, writing in the…"

Imani runs to the living room, grabs my backpack from beside William's recliner, rushes back and shoves it at me. "Tell me it!" she says. Then, as an afterthought, "Please??"

"Imani. Sit down and finish your dinner," William says.

"But I want to hear my poem!"

"After dinner, Sugar," William tells her.

I finish my dinner in peace, now that the subject of who beat me up got shifted to the poem. I hadn't meant to read it to the pest, but it was a great distraction.

"I'm done!" Imani says. "Tell me the poem!"

I get my notebook out. Uh-oh. This needs some quick editing. I can't call Imani "the pest" in front of William. I turn the paper around, then back, like I can't read my writing. All the time I'm stalling, thinking pest, best, jest, rest… I scratch out the first line and make a quick substitute.

> Imani, who won't say dis or dat,
> Has a scar left by Simba the cat.
> A scratch thin as his whisker,
> No blood, and no blister,
> But she cried bloody murder.
> All of the neighbors heard her.
> Neosporin and band-aids
> Lessened her tirades,
> Consoled with ice cream and kisses…

"It still needs a last line," I tell her. "What rhymes with kisses?"

"Umm, Disses? Hisses? Misses? Pisses…"

"Imaaani," William says. It's his warning voice.

"I'm just going through the alphabet, Daddy! Now you made me lose my place!"

"You were at P," Max says.

"Sisses," Imani continues. "Wishes. Is that a rhyme? Wishes?"

"Close enough," I say.

"Then dishes, fishes…" and it's through the alphabet all over again.

Max has scraped garbage onto one plate and stacked the others, so dinner's officially over. "May I be excused?" I ask, pushing my chair back.

"Sure," Max says.

I put my notebook back in my backpack, get *The Grapes of Wrath* out, and take the ten steps to the living room where I flop down into William's recliner. Really, this is where I've wanted to be all day. I've barely read the first sentence of Chapter 23 when William comes in, gives me a thumb over the shoulder gesture and says, "Out!"

I look up at him, thinking he's kidding.

"Out! If you're well enough to go back to school you're well enough to sit somewhere else"

"I don't think I'll go to school tomorrow," I tell him.

"Out! Your lease is up!"

I drag myself into my room and stretch out on my bed. I don't know why my head still hurts so much. Maybe they left a piece of gravel in there or something. I rub my stub-hand along the fuzz strip in the middle of my head. Dr. Googoooian says I'll be more comfortable when all of the stitches are dissolved but I don't know when that will be.

I go back to the living room, sit on the couch next to Max. "I'll take my pill now," I tell her.

She glances at the clock. "It's not even eight o'clock. You get the pill at nine."

"C'mon, Max. I'm ready to go to bed."

"I'll bring it in to you at nine," she tells me. "If you're still awake, you can have it then."

"But..."

"No buts, Eddie."

"I'm not Gordon, or whatever his name was. You know?" I say, angry. "I'm not turning into some addict because I want a pill an hour early."

The pest looks up from her tablet. "Who's Gordon?" she asks.

"I'll see you at nine," Max says, all mad.

William watches as I walk across the room to my bedroom.

"Who's Gordon??" the pest asks again.

I close the door behind me and sit on my bed. I probably shouldn't have said what I did about Gordon. He was a guy they both met at some veteran's thing. He'd been in Iraq when they were, and they got to be friends. Gordon and William used to play basketball sometimes. And then they heard he'd OD'ed. I guess it was cold of me to say what I did, but it pisses me off how Max is all dedicated to being the pill cop.

I find my phone to call Rosie. Battery's dead. That kind of day.

It's as if the fluorescents inside my skull flicker on and off. On and off. I wonder if that's how it's going to be from here on out. I wonder if something moved around when I was unconscious, and it's never going to find its place back to the right spot. All I know is, something doesn't seem right in my head.

I plump the pillows behind me and start on Chapter 23 again. It's one of the chapters that's about migrants in general, comparisons to where they've come from, their awful conditions. Sometimes I skip those chapters because I want to keep reading about the Joad family. Tonight, I do a quick skim of

Chapter 23, then get back to the Joads in 24. I remember where I left off. They'd found a place in a camp that was clean and where people treated each other right. The kids saw flush toilets for the first time. I can remember what I read, but I'm worried about math. I hold my place in the book with my stump thumb, gaze at the ceiling, and, starting with the sixes, go through the multiplication tables. That works, all the way through the twelves. Those were always the hardest for me, but 12 x 6 is 72, and 12 x 12 is 144, and 12 x 9 is 108, and all the rest are still the same. But why do I feel so fuzzy? Floaty?

My phone rings. I get it from the charger. Finally, after one phone call and three texts, it's Rosie. "Hey, Rosie."

"Hey, Eddie."

"What're you doing?'"

"The times tables."

"What????"

"You know, 12 x 12 is..."

"I know what the times tables are. Since the 4th grade I've known that. Didn't you?"

"I was testing myself. That's all."

"God. I wish that was the test I was studying for. Calculus is killing me, and I've got to keep my A or..."

"I thought colleges didn't even look at your senior year, especially not second semester."

"So, I should just blow it off?" She sounds irritated.

"That's not what I said."

"I've got to go, Eddie. I've got studying to do."

"But..."

"I'll call you tomorrow."

I lie back down. 8 x 9 is 72, 11 x 12 is 122. Shit. It seems like Rosie's just waiting to get mad, like something's changed, and I don't even know what it is.

CHAPTER TWENTY-TWO

Strength

When Max talked with Dr. G., he said I shouldn't go back to school for another three weeks. And they set it up so I can't get back in without a release from the doctor. So, okay. Three weeks. I'll work on building my strength and stamina, a little bit at a time. Weights, and some yoga moves that are strengthening, and taking Buddy on walks, a little longer each day for stamina. Yeah, and practicing a few karate moves, too. It's been a while since I practiced karate, but you never forget that stuff. Even if your brain doesn't remember, your body does. Next week I'll start working with William again. Just a few hours at a time to begin with. Rosie picked up homework for me from my teachers. It's sitting in a big pile on top of my dresser.

Mainly, I work on all the body stuff, but what about...I don't even know what to call it. My mind? My spirit? My heart? Whatever it is, I've got a lot of time to think, and I keep thinking what if? What if I'd been killed? Would my life have counted for anything? And what if William had been killed? And why did anyone want to hurt me so bad? Or, why can't we all be like the good camp in *The Grapes of Wrath*, where everyone helps each other out and works together instead of being in one of the bad camps where groups of people are fighting against each other?

By the time Dr. G. releases me to go back to school, I'm strong again. Fit. My reverse mohawk has grown out some, but it's all uneven. I've always done the basic barber thing, but then Max heard about this cool barber that one of the dental patients goes to. So, the Saturday before I go back to school, she takes me to the Cut Above barber shop, and now I've got a low fade on the sides and a low brush cut on top. It looks strange, like

I'm trying to be all stylish or something. Rosie likes how it looks, though, so that's good. Also, she says she likes how it feels when she rubs the buzzed top of my head. Calls it a "fringe benefit." Get it? "*Fringe* benefit"?

I'm good. No more pain. No more pain pills. Buddy and I are back to walking our longer route. I still have to wear a belt to keep my pants up, but I don't have to pull it as tight as I did a couple of weeks ago.

Besides taking me to Cut Above, the day before I go back to school, Max takes me to Nunamakers. January is a little cold for ice cream, but tradition is tradition. I get the big sundae because even though I'm strong and fit, I could still stand to gain some weight, and besides, I like it. Just remembering it has my mouth watering right now. So, me and Max talked about hard times, how my getting beat up scared the shit out of her. And how it made me want to hurt somebody back, the way I'd been hurt. We talk about how hard things are for Carla and Arsenio, and how sad it is that people like the Patriots are so scared of change that their fear turns to hate. We talk about families being separated at the border. Wars. Famine. Climate change.

After all of that, we go on to the sweetness of life and the goodness of people. All of the bracelet people, and the people in William's *A Letter to My Daughters* book, but more than that, just everyday people. Whenever there's an accident, people always rush to help. It's natural. And help poured in for people who lost their homes in last summer's fires.

"And, a little thing," Max says, "but think about how all of the choir girls wore hijabs and stoles at the winter concert so the Muslim girls wouldn't feel alone."

I'm glad for the ice cream talks. They remind me that the bad stuff that's come my way is only a tiny piece of my life. So, yeah, glad for the ice cream talks, and glad for the ice cream.

* * * * *

I'm out of WriteLight before the passing bell stops ringing, managing to catch Rosie as she leaves the choir room. She smiles, reaches up and passes her hand lightly over the top of my head.

"Fringe benefit," she laughs.

Brianna comes rushing over to Rosie, jumping up and down and screaming.

"Why weren't you in choir this morning?" Rosie asks.

Brianna keeps jumping up and down. "I got it! I got the letter Saturday! I'm in at UOF!"

Rosie hugs Brianna and smiles weakly. Brianna steps back. "Did you get a letter?"

Rosie shakes her head.

"It'll probably come today!" Brianna says.

Rosie nods. "I hope," she says.

"It will! Your grades are better than mine! SAT's better than mine! Oh, I'm soooo excited!!" she says, then rushes away to spread the news.

The hall is crowded with kids rushing to first period in a maze of different directions, the sound level beyond what's acceptable for hearing health. I lean in to give Rosie a quick kiss before I turn toward Earth Science. Her eyes are watery.

"Hey," I say. "What's wrong?"

She shakes her head and walks toward her English class. I catch up to her.

"Rosie! What's wrong?"

I put my arms around her, hold her in a tight hug, feel her strong short breaths against my chest, and I know she's crying. We stand clenched together in the middle of the hall, kids walking around us, paying no attention. There's always drama in the halls of HH, and ours this morning is just one more drama. Pushing back a bit, I move us closer to the wall, out of the busy middle. "What is it?"

"What if I don't get in?" she gasps. "It's the best music therapy program in the country, and Brianna and I've planned this together since we were freshmen and…" Sobs. "It's all I've ever wanted!"

"You'll probably get your letter today, like Brianna said." Rosie wipes her face and walks off toward class.

At lunch Brent's as happy about his college letters as Brianna was about hers. "M.I.T. No! Cal Tech. No! Georgia Tech. No!" he laughs.

"I bet your dad's pissed," Cameron says.

"My dad's been pissed since the cornhole tournament," Brent says, "or maybe since I got a C in Algebra when I was thirteen."

"What're you going to do, then? Hamilton Heights Community College?" Cameron asks.

"I'm pretty sure I'll get into Chapman or Occidental, which are *my* first-tier choices. Maybe major in history. The ones that don't want me were all my dad's first choices, not mine. Trouble is, I've spent so much of my school life fighting against engineering, I've hardly ever even thought about what I *do* want to study."

There's more talk about colleges while my mind wanders around the quad, back to this morning's classes. Except for that one day a few weeks ago, it's been almost a month since I've been here. The quad, the halls, the classes, the people, it seems strange being here, like I've stepped back into some past life where I maybe don't belong any more.

I go through the motions in afternoon classes. Before I help set up the yoga room 6th period, I step on the scale and am happy to see that I'm up to 147 pounds. Five more pounds and I'll be back to my pre-attack weight.

After dinner, I go over to Joe's studio. The lights are on. I peer in the side window to be sure he's not teaching a class, then tap lightly on the door. He's barely got the door open a crack when Peppy squeezes through, barking excitedly, jumping on me, running circles around me. I pick her up, laughing, and nuzzle my face in her soft fur. She wiggles around and licks my face. Joe's laughing now, too.

"I guess she missed you," he says. "Come in."

He leads the way into the studio and sits cross legged in Sukhasana. I grab a bolster pillow so I can do a modified Sukhasana 'cause my left leg's still a little stiff. Peppy settles onto my lap. "The doc's cleared me for all regular activities," I tell him.

"That's good," Joe says. "You look lots better than you did a few weeks ago."

"Feel better, too," I say, rubbing Peppy's ears the way I know she likes. It's funny. Dogs. Buddy loves a belly rub. With Peppy, it's ears. She never rolls over on her back the way Buddy does, begging for a belly rub. But then, Buddy's not big on ear rubs.

"I can help out at the studio again on Tuesdays and Thursdays and watch out for Peppy on your long day away."

"I'll only be needing you on Thursdays now."

"What about Tuesdays, when you're gone until late at night?"

"Well, you know, since you were laid up so long…"

I keep rubbing Peppy's ears, watch while her eyes slowly close halfway, then pop back open. Her head rests lightly on my knee, and I know that with two more ear rubs she'll be totally asleep.

"Jason'll keep covering Tuesdays."

"Jason!" Peppy jumps awake. "I told you! You can't trust him!" Peppy jumps off my lap and goes to her bed.

Joe pulls his knees into his chest and leans forward. He gives me a long, searching look, then says, "Calm down. Deep breaths."

"Fuck deep breaths! Cameron would have walked Peppy, or Brent, or anyone else!"

I push up from the bolster. Joe stands to his full height, feet planted firmly on the floor. Arms slightly bent. Fists tight. Fight stance.

"You. Need. To. Calm. Down," he says, in a tone I've not heard before. Maybe it's his prison tone.

"You trust Jason? You don't know shit about Jason!" I say, and I'm outta there.

I start toward my house, then take a turn. Two blocks up Elm Street, toward Palm Avenue. I wonder, why are some streets called streets, and others avenues. And then there are boulevards. Oh, yeah, and drives. There's Peach Drive over by where Rosie lives. Who decides what's a street, or an avenue, or a boulevard, or a drive?

A nearly full moon shines through the leaves of one of the giant elm trees that line the sidewalk edge. I guess that explains the Elm in Elm Street. The February air is crisp and chilly, and I pause under the partially moonlit elm and take ten deep cleansing breaths. Not because Joe told me to. Because I want to. Because it's like I need cleansing. Body and soul.

A text ding. I hope it's Rosie. It's Joe.

Come back. Talk.

I stand under the elm for a long time, breathing in fresh air, not wanting to talk to Joe. Like how could he trust Jason to watch out for Peppy? Why would he even let him inside the studio? Another text.

Please.

So, okay. I go back to his place. Joe leads me into the kitchen. Peppy glances up from her bed, then goes back to sleep.

"Tea?" he asks, pouring a cup for himself and waiting for my answer.

"Okay."

We sit across from each other at the kitchen table, sipping peppermint tea. After a long silence, Joe says, "I don't understand what got you so upset."

"And I don't understand how you could substitute Jason for me."

"Look. I know you two got off to a bad start..."

"He's a dick."

"Eddie. Hear me out...Jason could use a little work, and I needed some help with you out of commission. I know I could have used Brent, or Cameron, or any other number of kids. They would have been fine. But I have a sense that Jason's a guy who needs something good in his life, and I'm pretty sure Jason needed work in a way the others didn't."

Every time Joe says Jason's name, I hear that squeaky voice in my head saying, "Enough! Let's get outta here." It plays in my head at the weirdest times.

Joe goes on, "I know you can pretty much get as much work as you want with William, and cutting you back a day shouldn't be a big deal. I still won't charge you for yoga..."

"Wake up! Jason's a scumbag!"

"I know you don't like him..."

"I fuckin' hate him!"

"That's a little extreme, isn't it?"

"No!"

I get a heart pounding surge of adrenaline and want to shout out the truth about Jason, that he's one of the guys who jumped me. But first...I wanna give Jason a taste of what he gave me.

"Forget it," I say.

"He's been doing a nice job on Tuesdays. Peppy..."

"Just forget it."

* * * * *

Only three days back at school, and then it's a long weekend for Martin Luther King, Jr. Day. There's always a big MLK march down Main Street past City Hall to Dodsworth Park where there's music and dancing and a big BBQ dinner, unless it rains. Then everything shifts to a church that's close to the park and has a big covered outdoor space. Max and I've been walking with William and Imani every year since they moved in with us. It's a reminder of what MLK stood for, and it's also a big party.

People may not be in as much of a party mood this year, what with the decision not to press charges against the cops who shot Devon Parker. And then last week, police in L.A. shot and killed another black guy who came at them with a pocketknife. The guy's wife had called 911 asking for help—said her husband hadn't been taking his meds lately and he was acting all crazy. When the police got there, the guy was outside his wife's house stabbing at the door with his pocketknife. When the police called to him to drop the knife and put up his hands, he lunged at them, and they shot him. So, the guy was a nutcase, but did they have to kill him? Between that, and all of the white supremacist talk going around lately, the MLK march will be serious.

Rosie's going to the march, too, with her church group. She invited me to walk with them, but, as much as I like to be with Rosie, I'm not into the church group thing. We'll meet up at the park after the march. But today, Saturday, she's in the garage with me and Max and Imani and William, making signs. We always make a bunch of extra signs for the march for people who don't bring their own. Besides, William's got all of the paint and clean-up supplies, and masking tape and heavy-duty knives, and with the overhead garage door open, we get plenty of light and air.

Text from Cameron:

Helping Dad paint the kitchen. Borrow a ladder?

I show the text to William. "Sure, as long as it's back by Tuesday morning."

K, I text back.

Imani has painted two signs. One says "We're who MLK" and the other says "dreamed about." She and Olivia plan to walk side by side. Rosie's sign is "Standing on the Side of

Love." She says that's what her church is emphasizing this year. Max's sign is "Together We Can!" which was one of the mottoes of Cesar Chavez and the farmworkers. William's is "Live together as brothers, or die together as fools." Imani doesn't like it.

"It should be brothers and sisters!" William looks at her blankly. "Live together as brothers and *sisters*, Daddy!"

Rosie high-fives Imani, who adds a fist bump.

William nods, gets the white paint, covers the quotation marks, and changes it so it reads: "Live together as brothers and sisters, or die together as fools."

My sign says. "3 Words" at the top and "Equality for All" beneath it. "3 Words." It's a good contrast to the "14 Words" I'm still seeing all over the place. William and Max have painted a few more signs to hand out at the march: "No Justice. No Peace." "Know Justice. Know Peace." "Black Lives Matter."

The signs are laid out to dry on the garage floor when Cameron stops by for the ladder. "Whoa! What's all this?"

"What holiday are we out of school for?" I ask him.

"Oh, yeah," he says, walking around the garage to read the signs. "For the march? But isn't that mostly…?"

William's stopped painting and is watching Cameron, whose face turns pink.

"I mean…" Pink turns to red.

"The march is for everyone who wants Dr. King's vision to be real…The ladders are over there," William says, nodding toward the wall where six ladders hang from giant hooks. "Take your pick."

Cameron chooses the six-foot ladder. "Thanks," he says to William.

William picks up the "We must live together as brothers and sisters, or die together as fools" sign and hands it to Cameron. "Take this, too."

"Daddy…!"

"I know, Shug. I'll make us another one."

Cameron holds the sign, looking puzzled.

"Go on," William says. "Take it with you. Sleep on it."

"Well, okay," he says to William, "Thanks. See ya," he says to me and Rosie, as he walks past us, taking the ladder and sign out to his dad's car.

CHAPTER TWENTY-THREE

Revelation

I wait for Tuesday, knowing Jason will show up at Joe's around 4:15 to walk Peppy. Knowing what CC would *not* do, I leave my WWCCD bracelet in my top dresser drawer.

By 4:00, I'm standing close to the wall by Joe's back steps, a place where I can't be seen by anyone coming from the direction Jason will be coming from.

Tense. Adrenaline pumping. I feel the regained strength in my body, feel the rage that's been building over hate signs, and bullying Muslim girls, and most of all over hearing that squeaky, "Let's get outta here," as I lay crumpled on the ground. I replay that night, the sudden attack from behind, the fists, the kicks, the weeks of pain and fogginess that followed...

Jason glides around the corner of Joe's house on his bike, rests it against the side of the wall, and walks toward the door. I step from the shadows and walk toward him, blocking his way. He steps back, tries to walk around me. I step in front of him.

"Tuesday. It's my day to walk Peppy!" he squeaks. His face is red. Fists clenched.

I'm lightning fast with the karate fist to chest. He takes a swing. I block it. Chop to the throat. Kick his legs out from under him. He's on his knees. I kick him in the face. He's down, curled in a ball.

"Get up you cowardly piece of shit!" I kick him again. And again. "How does it feel??"

"I didn't want..."

I draw back for another kick and, wham! I'm pinned flat against the wall, staring at Joe's face.

"What the fuck are you doing???"

Peppy is barking, barking, barking behind the door. Joe's face is so close I can smell his gum. Minty. Over his shoulder, I see Jason on his hands and knees, trying to get up.

"He started it," I say, like I'm back to pre-school days.

Joe looks back at Jason, half up now, but not quite. "You stay right here, Eddie. Don't move!"

He turns to give Jason a hand up, guides him a few feet to one of the patio chairs. He checks Jason's head and a bloody spot on his cheek. "Where do you hurt?" Joe asks him.

Jason whispers something back, but I don't get what he says. My breathing's slowed. Adrenaline's subsided. I get Joe's key from the fake rock. Peppy's all over me as I open the door. I attach her leash and walk back outside.

Joe notices. "Hey! I told you to stay there!!"

"Peppy needs a walk," I say.

Joe looks from me to Jason and back to me. He takes a step toward me. "I want to know what this is about!"

I walk Peppy down the driveway and onto the sidewalk. Joe doesn't stop us. I feel good. Like for the first time since I got jumped, I feel good. Payback feels great.

Well…when my shoe connected with Jason's face, it felt weird. I've never hurt anyone in a fight before. Karate, that's only for self-defense. But this *was* self-defense. Delayed self-defense. And at least I didn't have a bunch of other guys with me. I didn't do that chicken shit jump from behind thing. One on one, face to face, like it's supposed to be.

Peppy finds her pee place and squats. I take her another two blocks, then turn back. Aware of the strength and power within me, I'm calm. Relaxed. It's starting to drizzle, and the light rain feels good. Cleansing. When we get back to Joe's, I scuff the soles of my shoes back and forth on his doormat, then hold Peppy in place and wipe each of her feet on the mat. I tap lightly on the door. Joe doesn't call to me to come in, like he usually does. Instead, he opens the door and stands looking at me like maybe he doesn't know me. Maybe he doesn't.

"Are you over whatever kind of fit you just had?"

"I'm through with Jason, if that's what you mean."

He pushes open the screen door and stands aside. I unhook Peppy's leash, and she rushes into the kitchen. I turn to go but Joe takes my arm. "Come in," he says. "Have a cup of tea. It'll calm you."

"I'm calm," I tell him.

"Well, come in anyway."

I let him guide me into the kitchen. Jason's sitting at the table, staring into a teacup. Joe pours tea for me and sets it on the table. He pulls out a chair. "Have a seat."

I stand, leaning against the counter. After a pause, Joe puts my teacup on the counter beside me and sits at the table across from Jason, who's still staring at his cup. He's got a scraped place on his left cheek. Other than that, he looks okay. As okay as he ever looks, anyway.

"I want to know what this is about. Who wants to go first?" Joe says.

Silence.

"Well, okay. How about you go first, Eddie? You obviously were the attacker. You shouldn't even have been here today."

Silence.

"Well? Eddie?"

"He started it," I say.

"Jason?"

Jason shifts his gaze from his teacup to the window over the sink, like there's something fascinating out there.

"Well...?" Joe says, leaning so far across the table he's probably also giving Jason a whiff of his minty gum.

Jason's eyes dart toward me, then quick back out the window.

"Okay, Jason. You started it? Like Eddie happened to be in my yard, on a Tuesday, when he doesn't belong here, and you started fighting with him? And then you let him beat you to the ground?"

Long silence.

"I don't buy that you started the fight, Jason. Did you?"

He nods his head, just barely, and continues staring out the window. "Maybe. Sort of." I can hardly hear him, he's speaking so softly.

"What? How???"

"Before. Not today."

"Way back when you decided you didn't like each other? Back when you gave him the finger?? That was a long time ago!"

"Not then..." Jason says, shaking his head.

"Well, then, when?"

Silence. More silence.

"C'mon guys," Joe says.

I take a deep breath. "Back when he and his buddies jumped me. Back when they kicked the shit out of me. That's when he started it."

I sip my tea. I think I'm getting used to Joe's tea. Joe looks at Jason, then me, then back to Jason.

"Wait. I don't get it. Jason, you were part of that bunch that jumped Eddie? I know you guys have had it in for each other since the beginning of school. But getting a gang of guys to jump Eddie? From behind? Because you don't like him?"

Jason looks at Joe. "It wasn't like that."

"It was like that!" I say. "I heard you! You and your fucked up squeaky voice!"

"No. I mean...it wasn't because I don't like you."

"What then?" Joe says.

"It was...Eddie gets in the way."

"What????"

"You know. We're Patriots. We fight for our country. For everyday working American men."

Joe sits rubbing his tattoo.

"I tried to get them to stop! One of the guys kept kicking him, and I told him it was enough—it was time to go. I knew they were hurting him bad."

Jason puts his head down on the table. At first, I don't know if he's laughing or crying, but he's crying. Sobbing. Really hard. Peppy leaves her spot by Joe and sits close to Jason, her paw on his thigh. I pick her up. Rub her ears. Watch Jason cry. What the fuck is *he* crying about?

Joe walks to the counter, refills the electric pot with water, dumps in a handful of tea leaves, and plugs the pot in. Deep breathing, organic tea, yoga. Joe's answer to all that's fucked up. Sometimes that's not enough. He gets a box of tissue and sets it in front of Jason, who takes one and wipes his nose and face. "I didn't want to," Jason says, looking at me. "I'm sorry. I'm sorry."

"What?? You didn't want to??? Someone was holding a gun to your head telling you to jump me and beat the shit out of me???"

"Not exactly...kind of..."

And then he tells this weird story about his dad and these Patriot guys who're on a mission to give pure white men their rightful power. To secure a future for white children. Between all of the Mexican immigrants sneaking in and taking jobs, and the Muslim terrorists, and the Jew conspirators, and the faggots and, worst of all, the nigger hoodlums who're trying to take over with their Black Lives Matter thugs, it's up to the Patriots to crush the scum who are ruining their country. They've got to squash anyone who gets in their way.

And I got in the way of their message, painting over their sign. And if it hadn't been for me, their fellow Patriot who taught that raghead girl a lesson would never have been arrested. So Jason, along with four other Youth Patriots, were sent on a mission to stop me. Not to kill me, but to hurt me so bad I'd never get in their way again.

"There were five of you?" Joe asks.

Jason nods.

"And you're all like…Patriots??"

Jason nods.

"Why do you hang out with those guys, anyway?"

And then the story gets even weirder. He says he was living with his mom in Texas. He hadn't seen his dad since he was six, when his parents split up. His mom was a druggie, sometimes selling to pay for her habit, sometimes being away for two or three days at a time. But that was okay. Really, he liked things better when she wasn't home.

A few years ago, some nosy neighbors filed a complaint with Child Protective Services, saying they thought Jason was being neglected, and when CPS came to investigate, they didn't like what they saw. But his mom managed to put on a good act, and nothing happened. But then, in high school, Jason started cutting class and getting in trouble. And when he and some friends were caught drinking beer in one of the guys' cars, in the student parking lot during school hours, that got the social worker back on their case. And that scared his mom all over again. With CPS sniffing around, the next step would be the cops. And she decided Jason was too much of a liability. That's what she'd told him. He was a liability.

So then, with the help of some friend from a long time ago, his mom found out where his dad lived. She told Jason to pack up. They drove twenty-three hours from Texas to Hamilton Heights, and when she stopped at the dad's address, she told Jason to get out of the car. She took him by the hand and pulled him up to the door, rang the doorbell and pounded on the door, and when his dad opened the door she yelled, "Your turn, Sam," shoved Jason inside, ran back to the car and peeled away.

It's like someone has turned the talk faucet on, and Jason keeps talking and talking. He says it was strange. Even though his mom had burned all of his dad's pictures, Jason recognized him right away. Eleven years without even a picture. And his mom would never talk to him about his dad, and she'd smack him in the face if he ever asked about him. Eleven years in a total dad blackout, and he still knew his dad right away. And his dad knew him! Threw his arms around him and hugged him tight. He was so happy to see Jason, he was crying, just holding him and crying. His dad told Jason he'd wanted to take him with him when he split from the mom, but Jason's mom took off with him. No forwarding address. His dad told Jason his mom hadn't wanted him. She'd only wanted to hurt the dad.

It wasn't news to Jason that his mom didn't want him, but it was total news to him that his dad did. No one in his whole life had ever wanted him before. And he got a family. Uncles and aunts and cousins, and his dad had a lot of friends, too, who were almost like uncles to Jason. For the first time ever, he had a family that did things together. A big Patriots family all working to make things better for the real Americans. On weekends they did all kinds of training. It was great.

And then he goes quiet until he says, "But I don't like hurting people. My dad says the ones we hurt aren't people anyway. Not like us. But I don't like that part of it."

Joe pours more tea. Peppy gets squirmy. I put her down and hear the click of her toenails, then the flap of the dog door as she takes herself outside. When she comes back, she goes to Jason. He picks her up. Rubs her ears.

Text ding from Max: *are you ok?*

Me: *thumbs up emoji*

Max: *where are you?*

Me: *Joe*

Max: *I'll come get you when you're ready to leave.*

Me: *No need.*

Max: *Yes. Need.*

Me: *No.* I send it seconds before the phone battery goes totally dead.

Joe's watching me do the text thing.

"Sorry. I had to answer that, or Max'd go all crazy. Calling everyone. Running around looking for me. She doesn't want me walking alone anywhere at night anymore. Not even home from your place."

Joe nods. "I guess that's understandable."

"It's a pain."

"You're lucky to have a mom who cares," Joe says.

"I know that. It's still a pain," I say.

Joe looks across at Jason. Shakes his head like he can't wrap his mind around all that Jason's said. I can't either, but who could make that shit up?

Joe turns to me. "What about all of those interviews with the cops? Why didn't you tell them?"

"Because I knew they wouldn't believe me. I didn't *see* him. And, you know, a Mexican guy's word against a white guy's?"

"C'mon Eddie. Your brother's a cop. You can't be that prejudiced against cops. You know better."

"I know they were about to do a Devon Parker on William that night. If I hadn't come around enough to yell 'Dad' at him, it would have been bad news."

"Dad? I thought he was only 'sort of a stepdad.'"

"Yeah, well I wasn't in any shape to give details. I mean, as fuzzy as I was, I knew yelling 'Dad' would let the cops know William belonged with me—let them know they could stop treating him like he was a dangerous criminal who'd just beaten me up and was robbing me."

"Well, you've got to tell the police," Joe says.

"No!" Jason says. "The Patriots! They'll know I was the one who told! They'll kill me! I know my dad loves me, but it's all about the cause!" He glances at the clock. 8:50. "Gotta go! My dad'll send somebody out to find me if I'm not home by 9:00." He rushes out, calls back, "Don't tell! Please!"

I rinse my cup, leave it in the sink. Joe watches me.

"You've got to tell the police."

"I don't know…"

"You've got to! That bunch needs to be stopped."

"What if they *would* kill Jason? I wanted revenge, but..."

"I'll give you twenty-four hours. If you haven't told by then, I will. But it should come from you."

I go blocks out of my way so I can cut through the park. Being in the middle of all of those oxygen-exhaling trees and bushes always helps clear my head, and I could use some help with that tonight. That first blow to Jason brought a flood of relief from my long-building anger and frustration. I wanted to hurt him like he'd hurt me, but I never wanted him dead. Would they kill him?

I wander over to the swings and take a seat, remembering how Mario always used to push me on my favorite middle swing while we waited for Max to get off work. I sit, scuffing my shoes in the sand, barely moving back and forth, wondering what it would be like if no one ever wanted me. I can't imagine how that would be. And what'll happen if I tell the cops? What'll happen if I don't? Joe always means exactly what he says, so I guess one way or the other, the cops'll know pretty soon.

I watch a blinking satellite cross the sky overhead, then start walking toward home. I'm a few blocks away when I see Max and William in the distance, walking toward me. William's swinging a flashlight. Max is carrying her old walking pole thing that she hasn't used for years. I wave both arms overhead.

"Eddie?" Max yells.

I pick up the pace to meet them. When I get close, Max rushes to me and grabs me in a tight hug. Is she crying? She's crying!

"What's wrong?" I say. Like maybe there's been some awful phone call from the Redville family, or maybe Olivia's parents have been arrested, or...?

Max loosens her hug. "It's just, we worry," she says.

I take another look. The flashlight in a neighborhood with streetlights. The long, pointy walking pole that Max no longer needs. Weapons. They're carrying weapons.

"I texted, and you didn't answer. I called Joe, and he said you'd left about fifteen minutes ago. We just..."

"Sorry," I say. "My battery went dead."

We turn and walk back to the house. As soon as we come through the door, Imani yells, "No fair! I wanted to call 911!" She slams William's cell phone down on the sofa and clomps back to her bedroom. "Be glad you didn't have to," William calls after her.

So, Max and William had gone looking for me, fearing the worst. If they weren't back within twenty minutes, Imani was to call 911. William had written careful instructions for what to say to get responders out looking for them. For us.

I get Buddy's leash, snap it on. Max follows me to the door. "I'll go with you," she says, grabbing her walking stick again.

"No. I'll be fine! No hovering!"

"Take this, then," she says, shoving her walking stick at me.

"I'll take the flashlight," I say, and leave as she calls after me to be careful.

So, my body's all healed, but there's still, what do they call it in the military? Collateral damage?

CHAPTER TWENTY-FOUR

A Lie Revealed

With my cell plugged in and charging, I sit on the floor, back against the wall and call Rosie's number. No answer. It's after ten. She's not supposed to use her phone after ten, but sometimes she does. I text: *Goodnight. Love you.*

Remembering the swings, remembering that Mario has always had my back, I call. He picks up right away. I hear the smile in his voice. "Hey, Babbler. What's up?"

"I want to talk with you about something, you being a cop and all."

"Yeah?"

"Well…I sorta knew who one of those guys who beat me up was."

"You sorta knew, or you knew?"

Even though we're not face-timing, I know exactly what Mario's expression is right now. It's the raised eyebrow, straight-lined mouth expression that says: stop with the modifiers, the "sortas," and "almosts," and "maybes."

"I knew."

"All along when you said you didn't see anyone, you were lying?"

"I didn't see anyone. I heard someone."

"Tell me about it."

So I do. I tell him what I heard, and how I worked to get strong again to get back at Jason, and the fight this afternoon, and then everything Jason said, and how Joe said if I didn't tell the police within 24 hours, he would.

"Joe's right. The police need this information."

There's a silence that's starting to feel awkward when Mario says, "I'll come down. Go with you to the police."

"You don't have to…"

"Yeah, I do. I've got background on these guys that may be helpful. And I want to be sure you get to the right people when you tell your story. Most of the Hamilton Heights guys are good, but there're a couple of doofuses on the force, and we don't want them screwing things up. We've got to be sure that Jason's protected, so we want to be careful about what we say, when, and who we say it to."

Mario says he's tired. He's not going to start the two-hour drive at midnight, plus he's got to take care of a few things at the station and arrange for someone to cover his shift for him.

"I'm an early riser," he says. "I'll get there by nine, ten at the latest."

He says to be fake sick and stay home 'til he gets here. He says not even to tell Max what's up. We can all go to Dimitri's when she gets off work and talk then.

William bangs on my door around 6:30. "You're late!"

"I don't feel too good!" Which is true. My stomach is all trembly about going to the police station. Not as trembly as it'd be if Mario wasn't going with me, though.

7:00. Text ding. Rosie: *Where r u?*

Me: *sick*

Rosie: *sad face emoji*

Minutes later, another text ding.

Joe: *Are you telling or am I?*

Me: *me*

Joe: *thumbs up emoji*

Mario pulls up in a squad car a little before ten. He's wearing his uniform and badge. He reaches over and opens the passenger door for me.

"What's with the squad car?" I ask.

"The chief told me to make it official."

"Why?"

"There's an active Patriots group up our way, too, but we can never get anything on them. A trans kid was killed a couple of months ago. Super bright, talented, killed on their way home from a night class." Mario pauses, shakes his head. "It had to be the Patriots but no witnesses. No evidence."

We do the drive-thru thing at Starbucks. Mario gets a large espresso, and I get a medium hot chocolate. Mario gets a protein box too, but I'm not hungry.

We park in a shady spot so Mario can eat his breakfast before we go to the station. He says he called ahead to be sure we'll be talking with the right people. "Officer Harvey, who you already know," he tells me. "And another guy, Mr. Chang, who specializes in hate crimes."

We talk about not much while Mario finishes his breakfast. Traffic. The weather. Tio Hector's smaller than usual garden. Mario notices my bracelet, and I tell him about William's gifts.

"Better than your old one," he says, looking closely at the letters.

I don't tell him I gave the bracelet a vacation yesterday. But me and Cesar? We're good again.

We dump our trash and drive to the police station, past the entrance where the red, white, and blue flag flies at the top of the tall pole, and the California bear flag flies below. We park in the back, one dusty little sheriff's car in the middle of a row of big, shiny police cars. Mario texts Harvey that we're here, and after a minute or two, he and Mr. Chang meet us at the back entrance. Chang's not wearing a uniform.

Basic greetings and then we follow them up a short staircase and back to a room about the size of our dining room, a yuck green color, probably Celery Verdure. In the middle is a round wooden table with six rolling chairs around it. Harvey pulls two chairs off to the side, spaces the others equally, and motions for us to sit down.

"Coffee?" Mr. Chang asks.

"No thanks," Mario says. "We made a Starbucks stop before we got here."

"Wise move," Harvey says. That gets a laugh from the three of them. Maybe cops don't make good coffee.

"I'd like to record this, if it's okay?" Harvey says, taking a small recording device from his shirt pocket and placing it in the middle of the table.

"Sure," Mario says. "Me, too." He takes a similar looking device from his own shirt pocket and sets it across from Harvey's.

"Fair enough," Harvey says.

"All right, Eddie," Officer Harvey starts, "You remember something more than you told us about earlier?"

I nod.

"Yes or no. For the recording."

"Yes."

And then we go through the whole thing again. Everything I told Mario last night, except I don't name Jason.

Then Chang takes over.

"You say this kid—X, we'll say—is part of a group that's called the Patriots?"

"Yes."

"What do you know about the Patriots?"

"Nothing, except they hang out together and wear flags on their camo jacket sleeves."

"What kind of flags?"

"American flags."

"What else do they wear?"

"Sometimes they wear boots with their pants tucked inside."

"Does X dress like that?"

"Sometimes one of those jackets."

And on and on, asking the tiniest details. Did I know they were the ones who slashed my tires? No. Did I think they were the ones who slashed my tires? Yes. When I was attacked, what time was it? What day was it? Where was I? Hypnotically dull, and then, in the same dull tone of voice, Chang says, "Name of the kid you heard?"

I almost blurted out Jason's name. Caught myself just in time.

Mario's out of his seat. "That's it!"

I roll back. Stand beside Mario.

Harvey shoots Chang a dirty look.

"A kid's life is at stake, and you're trying to trick my brother into saying the name? And then what, you'd rush out to arrest him, but he's not there, and the next day he turns up dead??"

Mario shoves his chair back, grabs my arm, and pulls me out the door with him. Down the stairs, through the parking lot, and into his squad car in a flash. Harvey's in the parking lot now, yelling for us to wait.

Mario backs up, and makes a quick turn, onto the street. My heart is racing, but Mario's all calm now.

"I'm proud of you," he says. "That trick is older than dirt, but it often works on inexperienced witnesses."

"It almost worked on me."

"But it didn't...What an unprofessional asshole." Mario glances in the rearview mirror. "Here comes Harvey."

Harvey is right behind us as we pull into the driveway at my house. Crap. Two cop cars in our driveway?? That'll get the neighbors talking.

Harvey follows us to the door. "Can we continue our conversation?"

"No Chang!" Mario says.

Harvey nods and follows us inside. Once again, we're at the dining room table, except this time it's only the three of us. Harvey takes out his recorder. Mario shakes his head. Harvey puts the recorder back in his pocket and takes out the little notebook I guess he always carries with him.

"Tell me about the kid who beat you up," Harvey says.

Should I? Is it true Jason's dad will kill him if he finds out about what Jason said? I ask what's most on my mind. "What'll happen to the guy?"

"Good question," Mario says.

Harvey glances at Mario, turns back to me.

"This is a group we've been watching for a long time. They're in other places, too, like up where your brother is, and down toward San Diego. They don't all call themselves the Patriots, but they're connected. White supremacists. Wherever they are, they're plastering walls with 'Stop White Genocide,' and all kinds of hate signs targeting Muslims, Jews, Blacks, anyone who's not of the 'pure white race.' They beat up on people. Sometimes kill, but so far, we've not been able to prove anything. "

Mario chimes in, "They're also after LGBT people, immigrants, people with disabilities, you name it."

"But what will happen to...X?

"I'm getting to that," Harvey says.

He goes on to say how the incidence of hate crimes rose during the campaign, when there was all of that anti-immigrant fever, and rose even more after the election. "Like that sign you painted over," he says. "Wasn't that shortly after the election?"

I nod.

"As soon as we get some solid evidence, or a solid witness, we can move in on these guys. Stop them. That's why Mr. X's story is crucial.

"But..."

"Yeah. I know. What will happen to him? We've been in touch with the FBI regarding Patriot activity around here."

"Yeah, we've also been in close communication with the FBI in Redville County," Mario says.

"They're monitoring hate crimes all over the country," Harvey says. "They're spread pretty thin right now, won't come unless there's a strong case for arrest and conviction..."

"But what...?"

"Okay. Once X tells us his story, we'll place him under protection, first with us, then with the FBI."

"What if he won't tell? He doesn't want to get his dad in trouble."

"If he won't tell, we'll pick him up, interrogate him in the presence of you and Joe. Ultimately, he'll tell us his story, but it would be a lot easier to protect him if he meets us somewhere willingly."

After listening to a lot of hows and what ifs regarding how Officer Harvey and Mario can meet with Jason without having to actually pick him up publicly and take him to the station, I come up with the idea that we could get him to come home with Joe, then meet him there.

"How's that gonna work?" Mario says. "I thought he was a Tuesday guy."

"Well, Joe could have some emergency and need someone to take care of Peppy for a while. Joe can bring X to his house and we can be there." I glance at the clock. "Yoga'll be over in forty minutes so we better call pretty soon."

"Do you have a better idea?" Mario asks Harvey.

He shakes his head. "You?"

"Nope."

So, I call Joe and tell him to pretend some emergency came up and he has to leave immediately for San Diego or wherever, and he needs Jason to watch out for Peppy. I'm away, so Jason is the only one who can help.

And Harvey calls the FBI.

CHAPTER TWENTY-FIVE

In Custody

Rosie texts and invites me to come over this evening. Her parents are taking Zoe to dinner and to some new animated movie.

I call her. Tell her I can't do that tonight.

She says we'd have the whole place to ourselves, and I won't need to get all weirded out about everybody knowing how we're using Tilly. She says that in her sexy voice and, man, I want to drop the phone and race over there. But...

"God, Rosie. Can't you talk them into going tomorrow night instead?"

"Why can't you come over tonight?"

"I just can't."

"Why?"

"I'll tell you tomorrow."

"Why do you always have to hide things from me?"

"I don't! When have I ever hidden anything from you?"

"Now."

I can't stand when Rosie's mad at me, and for a second, I think why not just tell her? And then I think again. "I swear, Rosie, this'll all make sense tomorrow, or maybe Friday. At least by Friday."

"I may be busy tomorrow, and Friday," she says, all angry.

"Rosie..."

"Bye," she says, and cuts off.

Crap! Why am I stuck with this anyway?? Why do I have to be here? But I know—first hand witness and all that. Plus...Jason. I never liked the guy. Hated him after they jumped me, but to never have anyone care about you, or want you around? I feel sorry for him.

I follow Mario and Harvey to the police station where they park their official cars. They'll ride with me back to my house. No need to have black-and-whites sitting in the neighborhood, broadcasting that something's up.

Harvey texts Officer Romero, who meets us in the parking lot. On the way to my place, he fills her in on the situation with Jason.

"We'll need to notify CPS," she says.

Harvey gets a text ding. "Okay. FBI'll be here in an hour or so," he says, then texts something back.

My phone dings, and I pass it to Mario to read. I'm sure not going to look at a text while driving with three cops in my car. "Joe says they're at his place," Mario says, so I take us there.

Before we get out, Harvey tells Officer Romero that the FBI says not to contact CPS. They're bringing an FBI-selected social worker for Jason.

Peppy's her usual happy self when Joe opens the door, but when Jason sees us all file through the door, he starts pacing. Harvey stops just inside the door, blocking it. Mario takes a few steps toward Jason and sticks his hand out.

"Mario Barajas," he says, "Redville Sheriff's Department."

Jason stares at him. His face is Chantilly Lace white.

Mario reaches for Jason's hand and gives it the standard shake. Jason just stands there, eyes darting from one person to another.

"You're...?" Mario says, still gripping Jason's hand. Finally, Jason gets it.

"Jason Paulson," he says, his voice squeakier than ever.

Harvey walks over and extends his hand. "Jack Harvey, Hamilton Heights Police."

Jason takes Harvey's hand. "Jason Paulson."

"Have a seat, Jason," Harvey says, motioning to the armchair.

Harvey turns to Joe, introduces himself, then sits on the couch across the room from Jason. Mario sits on the couch at the other end from Harvey. Romero scoots a chair over next to Jason. "I'm Officer Romero, Juvenile Division. I'm here to help," she says, smiling. Jason looks away.

"Eddie, bring in a couple of those director's chairs from the studio, would you please?" Joe says.

Everyone situated, Peppy circles the room running from person to person, sniffing, standing on her hind legs, pawing for attention. Joe takes her back to the kitchen and puts one of those dog gate things across the door. She barks and whines and makes a fuss.

"She'll calm down in a minute," Joe says. And she does.

Harvey moves a side table in front of Jason, a few feet away. On that table he puts his recorder and another device that's going directly to an FBI agent. Mario adds his recorder to the table. Harvey assures Jason that he will be protected from harm.

"Whaddya mean?"

"You'll be under FBI protection before we leave here."

"What about my dad? Can I call my dad?"

Harvey shakes his head. Jason looks away.

"I mean, I'd like to at least explain. At least tell him…" he pauses, takes a deep breath, chokes out, "…tell him I love him."

Harvey shakes his head. Jason looks at Romero, who also shakes her head. Joe sets a cup of tea on the side table beside Jason, but when Jason lifts the cup his hands are so shaky, he puts it back down.

They start with the details of the attack. Then details of the Patriots, everything Jason said last night and, with Harvey and Mario's questioning, more. Jason says they're preparing for a race war. Take back America. Every weekend they go to a place in the desert where they have maneuvers. Maybe thirty or so men and boys. The wives and moms don't ever come to the desert, but they always have a big dinner waiting for them.

Everybody eats together when they get back from maneuvers. They practice target shooting, handling weapons, hand to hand combat. It's fun with his cousins and the other juniors. They have bench press contests. The first time Jason went to the desert with them, he could barely press ninety pounds. Now he's up to 180.

During the week, sometimes they all meet at his dad's house or sometimes at his uncle's house. They talk about the work they've done the previous week, in addition to spray painting threats to let certain kinds of people know they're not welcome. They also put up flyers for White Lives Matter, and Stop White Genocide, and America for Americans, etc. Some of the flyers have contact information. They've got to educate white men who don't understand what's happening. In addition to the signs and flyers, they review other ways they've let inferiors and intruders know they're not welcome, sometimes beating people up, or painting messages on their houses or cars, or on mosques and synagogues.

They strategize about what's up for the next few weeks and how it fits in with their long-term calendar. Sometimes they work out with weights on those nights, too. They've got to be tough for what's to come.

I can't believe my ears, but no one else in the room seems surprised.

After about an hour, two FBI agents show up at the door and flash their badges at Joe. They don't look like the FBI guys you see on TV—all dark clothes, shades, and expressionless. There's a black guy—tall, in khakis and a Canary Yellow pullover. The woman's even taller, in a longish Dove Grey skirt with a plaid jacket. She's white. Maybe Moroccan Moonlight. They're both carrying heavy briefcases. He's Nathan Thompson and the woman is Madeline Franks.

They must have been listening in their car on the way over because they seem to know everything that's been said. Franks asks Jason if he can tell them the address of the house they sometimes meet at. Jason shakes his head. She reaches into her briefcase and pulls out a detailed map of the greater Los Angeles area, including Hamilton Heights. Together they figure out the general vicinity of the place, then Thompson takes a computer from his briefcase, does the Google Maps street view thing, and before long, Jason's found the place for them. They bring up a street view of Jason's address so they can be sure that's actually where he lives with his dad and some of the others. It is.

Harvey says they've been watching those places for months. Then it's the same thing with the desert where they go for "maneuvers." Jason shows the general vicinity, they narrow the street view, and Jason identifies a familiar shack.

"Anybody live there?" Thompson asks.

"Just some old guy."

"What's his name?"

"Everybody calls him D.R."

"D.R.? What do the initials stand for?"

"Desert Rat."

Franks and Mario pull their chairs together in the back corner where they talk for a bit, then identify some Redville places with Google Maps.

I think I've said everything I need to say. Maybe I can still get in a little Tilly time with Rosie? I stand. Stretch. It's a long time sitting in a crowded room. "I'd like to get to Rosie's before it's too late," I tell Mario.

"We're not finished yet," Thompson says. "We'll tell you when."

There's another knock at the door. This guy's Hank Vargas, a social worker.

Joe brings another chair in from the kitchen and sets it down. The new guy moves it over right next to Jason's chair and gives him a big, flashy, smile.

"You can call me Hank," he tells Jason. "You and me are gonna be best friends for a few days. I'll be with you 24-7, making sure you stay safe. Every single movie you've ever wanted to see on Netflix, we're gonna see."

"I've seen all the movies I wanna see," Jason says.

Officer Romero looks over at Harvey, who gives her a nod. She stands, smooths her skirt, says goodbye to Jason, who still doesn't look at her. "I'll call the station for a pick-up," she says. "I'll wait outside."

"Okay. Thanks," Harvey says.

*   *   *   *   *

Around 9:00, Jason's cell rings. He reaches into his pocket, but before he can answer, Hank takes the phone, shuts it off, and tosses it to Nathan.

"I want to talk to my dad," Jason says. Hank shakes his head. Jason looks slowly around the room—police, sheriff, FBI, no more cell phone, and it's like he gets that his whole life is changed now, and there's no going back. He does another scan of the room, then bolts to the bathroom.

Joe's place is small, and you can hear everything from every room even with doors closed, so we all hear Jason puking. And puking. And rinsing and rinsing. Hank goes into the hallway and taps lightly on the bathroom door. The rest of us pretend we're not hearing the noises.

Joe and I talk about what he wants me to do when I clean the studio tomorrow. Damp mop the hardwood floors, brush off the bolsters and rearrange them neatly in the bolster cabinet. Refold the blankets and stack them, same side out, on the shelves. It's what I always do, but it gives us something to talk about instead of listening to Jason dump his guts.

The rest of the group talks about the addresses they've got, what they might find there. When Jason and Hank come back into the room, Jason is paler and shakier than ever. Hank keeps telling Jason everything's gonna be okay, but I'm pretty sure Jason doesn't believe it. I wouldn't either.

"We about done here?" Hank asks.

"You two are," Nathan says.

"Okay Jason. Let's go watch movies."

"Where?" Jason asks.

"Someplace you'll like."

"I need to call my dad."

"We'll talk about that when we get where we're going. C'mon."

Jason nods, then goes into the kitchen where Peppy's half asleep in her bed. I'm sitting near the passage to the kitchen, so I see him pick her up. He buries his head in her fur, and I see his back heaving with sobs. Peppy squirms around so she can lick his face, and they stay there like that until Hank goes in and puts his hand on Jason's shoulder.

"We have to go now."

I step into the kitchen and ease Peppy from Jason's arms. Joe goes to Jason, hugs him, and tells him how much he's appreciated his help, what a great job he's done in the studio and with Peppy. Jason nods. Joe faces him, puts his hands in prayer position and says, "Namaste." For what I'm pretty sure is the first time ever, Jason returns Joe's Namaste.

Jason turns to me. "Sorry, man," he says.

"Me, too," I tell him, and I mean it.

I watch Hank guide Jason through the door, wondering what the hell's going to happen to him.

"Let's call it a night," Thompson says. "We'll check in with you guys in the morning."

Harvey shakes hands with everyone and leaves. Mario shakes hands with everyone. I follow him to the door. Thompson stops me.

It turns out only the law enforcement guys can go. Joe and I are under surveillance for at least another twelve hours. What that apparently means is that one or the other of the FBI agents has to be watching both of us at all times, and we have to be "incommunicado."

So, Mario and Peppy go back to my place, and probably sleep in my bed, while Joe and I are put in the back of an FBI van like a couple of criminals. They take us to a Holiday Inn where we can be under the constant watchful eyes of Thompson and Franks.

* * * * *

It seems like I've barely fallen asleep when I hear noises coming from the other room. It's light out, so morning. The seven o'clock news. I'm in one of the two beds in the room. Joe chose to pull the blankets from the second bed and sleep in a pallet on the floor. Someone, Franks or Thompson, or sometimes both, have kept watch from a little sitting area outside our room. The TV's so loud, no way can I go back to sleep. I wander into the other room to see what's up.

The morning news guy is talking about a raid. "Combined efforts between local law enforcement and the FBI led to simultaneous FBI raids on four separate properties, one in Central California and three in Southern California. Large stores of weapons, ammunition, and explosive devices were confiscated. Also on the properties were masses of white supremacist materials." Twenty-four men and five women arrested. Six juveniles taken into custody. Details to follow.

Then it's on to traffic reports and a four-car pile-up on the 210.

Franks and Thompson high-five. Thompson tosses us our phones. "Let's go. We'll take you home."

I text Rosie: *Watch the news!*

CHAPTER TWENTY-SIX

Celebration

It's Saturday and I'm working with William, painting the outside of his mom's house in a kind of rundown part of Pasadena. It's hard to believe William and his two sisters grew up in this house. It's small enough to totally fit into the great room of that last place we worked on in San Marino. There's a ton of prep work to do before we get to the fun part. William power-washed the place yesterday and now we're scraping and sanding away at chipped paint. His mom went to stay with his sister out in Riverside so she doesn't have to live with power-washing and paint fumes.

Even though there's a lot of prep, this isn't half as bad as the church down the street that we finished last week. That took three Saturdays. But William kept his promise to God about painting the church if he could live long enough to raise Imani. The promise about going to church every Sunday? He watches some Christian program on TV every Sunday morning now, before anyone else is up. I guess that counts.

My cell pulses against my butt.

"I got in! I got in! I got in!" Rosie yells.

"What?"

"The mail just came! I got accepted! I was so worried, but I'm in! UOF!

"Well...good news," I say.

"Aren't you happy for me?"

"Sure," I say.

"You don't sound happy about it."

"Well...you know...I'll miss you..."

Rosie sighs. "I'll miss you, too, but...I got IN!"

William comes around the corner with a fresh supply of sandpaper and makes a small circle motion with his free hand, meaning "wind it up". I nod and turn away from him.

"We're quitting around 6:00," I say. "See you at seven?"

"Can you get off any earlier? My parents are taking me to Bistro 17 to celebrate. They invited you, too."

"How early?" I ask.

William taps me on the shoulder as he walks past and does that circle thing again.

"My dad made reservations for 6:00. Please, Eddie? It won't be a celebration without you."

"I'll check with William. Call you back."

Instead of asking William right now, I go back to scraping and sanding. He should see me working again before I ask to get off early.

It's a little after noon when William puts the small ice chest on the patio table. We sit under the umbrella, eating sandwiches and fruit, and drinking the sparkling water that he packed before we left this morning.

"Bistro 17??? They're taking you to Bistro 17?" he says. "Man, I'd have to skip a month's car payment to afford anything on that menu!"

I ask to leave by 5:00. Twenty minutes to home, ten minutes to shower. Another fifteen minutes to the restaurant, five minutes for parking. Ten minutes cushion.

After telling me I'd better give myself time to go buy a suit, and to get a lesson from Max on which fork to use when, William says he doesn't want to stand in the way of my fine dining experience and, sure, I can leave at five.

Finished with my sandwich and fruit, I take the last swallow of sparkling water and start back to the spot I was sanding.

"Wait a sec," William says, motioning for me to sit back down. "I need to talk to you."

We sit in silence long enough to get me worried, like maybe he's going to fire me or something? Maybe those weeks I couldn't work he found someone better?

"So, I've been thinking...about when I said you were my son. And you called me Dad. Remember?"

"Sure."

"Well...I want you to know, you can call me Dad, if you want to. I'd be proud to be your dad."

"Thanks. I guess..." I stop, not knowing what to say.

"Or stay with William. Either way."

"It's what we're used to," I say, "but could I just think of you as my dad?"

"Like I said. I'd be proud."

We share an awkward hug, and I get up to go back to work.

"Hang on," William says. "I've been wanting to talk to you about something else, too... You know how everyone's always saying how you have so much potential, and you should be going to college?"

I nod.

"Well, you should feel free to change your mind if you want to. You're the best worker I've ever had, and you'll be good at the business end of things, but..."

"I don't want to change my mind. I like painting with you. I don't want to be stuck behind a desk. I like doing something physical."

"Yeah. It's physical all right," William says, rubbing his shoulder. "You should think about that. You're a whiz now, but the work gets harder as you get older. I'm only thirty-seven and sometimes I feel like an old man already."

"I'm not changing my mind. I like how we make things look so much better. I like color."

"Well, okay then." William smiles his widest smile, and we go back to work.

Once home, I shower, dress in a clean shirt and jeans, go out to the living room where Max sits reading and give her a kiss on the cheek. She raises her head, looks me up and down.

"You're going to Bistro 17 wearing that?"

"Yeah. Why?"

"No," she says, taking me by the arm and leading me back to my bedroom. She gets out the dress pants, shirt, and tie I wore to Mario's graduation from the academy last summer.

"You can't wear everyday clothes to Bistro 17. It's not that kind of a restaurant."

"I wish I wasn't even going," I say. "Let Rosie go with her parents."

Max unbuttons my shirt and hands me the dress shirt.

"Okay. Okay! But I'm not wearing that tie!"

"You want to borrow one of William's?"

"No! I'm not wearing any tie!"

Max laughs and goes back out to the living room. I do a quick change and interrupt her reading again to say goodbye.

"*Ai*, you look so handsome, *Mio*," she says, tearing up.

I make a run for the door, not wanting to see her tears and hear "You're so grown up and only yesterday..." I mean, I like that she loves me, but the teary stuff is kind of uncomfortable. I don't know why. It just is.

* * * * *

It's a little before six when I get to the restaurant and Rosie's waiting for me right inside the door. She gives me a big, glowing smile, and I realize it's been a while since I've seen that smile. Maybe it wasn't anything about us that was causing her to seem grumpy and distant. Maybe it was only that she was so stressed about getting into college. Whatever the reason, I'm glad to see her smile again.

I follow her through a dimly lit room, past tables with white tablecloths and candles and wineglasses, and people eating, mostly in pairs or groups of fours, and on out to a patio where Rosie's mom and dad and sister are at a big round table next to a glowing fire pit.

Mr. Coulter stands to shake my hand. I liked him from the beginning, when he passed the "shake the deformed hand" test.

"Glad you could join us, Eddie," he says, smiling. I'd think Rosie got her great smile from him, except he's not her real dad. Rosie says he *is* her real dad, but you know what I mean. Not her sperm dad.

Rosie takes the chair next to Mr. Coulter, and I sit next to her, with Zoe on the other side.

Even though it's a chilly evening, between the warmth from the fire pit and the large outdoor heater nearby, it's comfortable out here. But, boy, it's a good thing Max made me change clothes. Everybody's all dressed up. I'm happy to see that Mr. Coulter isn't wearing a tie, though. I don't think anyone wears ties anymore except politicians, and school administrators, and Cameron.

A waiter comes with wine for Rosie's parents and three more wineglasses with something that turns out to be Sprite for Rosie, Zoe, and me.

"A toast," Mr. Coulter says, raising his glass. "To Rosie and her exciting new life at University of the Foothills."

Everyone raises their glasses except Zoe, who sits slumped and pouting between me and her mom.

"Zoe? A toast? To Rosie's new life at college?" Rosie's mom says.

Zoe slumps lower and deepens the frown on her pouty face. "I don't want Rosie to go away to some stupid old college! She's s'posed to stay home with me!"

Mrs. Coulter moves the wine glass beyond Zoe's reach. "No toast, no Sprite," she says.

Zoe reaches for her glass. Mrs. Coulter slides it over. Mr. Coulter again raises his glass, "To Rosie and her new life at UOF," and we all click glasses and take our first sips.

Really, I'm with Zoe on this one. I don't want Rosie to go away to college, either. I'm happy she's got her smile back, but it's hard to imagine that she'll be moving away in September. Or will it be August? Whenever, it'll be sooner than I want it to be.

There's a lot of chatter about college, and UOF, and dormitory arrangements.

Mrs. Coulter turns to Rosie. "I'm so proud of you—so glad you're doing things the right way, not in that roundabout way like I did." She gets that teary-eyed mom look, and Rosie looks down at her Sprite-filled wine glass. I guess that stuff embarrasses her, too.

Mr. Coulter's watching Rosie's mom. He raises his glass again. "And here's to Emmy, for the strength and courage to make the roundabout way work."

We all raise our glasses to that, too. I guess the "roundabout" way he's talking about has to do with Mrs. Coulter getting pregnant in high school, and going to college with Baby Rosie and with hardly any money or family support.

After more talk of college life and the Music Therapy program, and Zoe slumping back down with her pouty face, Mr. Coulter turns to me, "Where will you be going next year, Eddie? Do you know yet?"

"I'm not going to college," I say.

"Taking a gap year, are you?"

"I'll be working with my stepdad in his painting business—studying for my painting contractor's license."

"Not going to college?"

"No. Going to work."

Mr. Coulter pauses, like he doesn't know what else to say. Zoe perks up. "You do that, Rosie! You can paint!"

"But I want to be a music therapist, remember?"

Zoe slumps back down.

Rosie's dad says, "Well. You can always change your mind, go to Hamilton Heights Community College."

I nod. This is how all conversations with non-family adults have gone since the beginning of my senior year: I'm not going to college. I'm going to work with William. You can always go to community college. It's a broken record.

After an awkward silence, Rosie's mom picks up her menu. "Let's see what we're going to eat. I'm starving."

There's stuff on this menu I've never even heard of. Pickled fennel, smoked chickpeas, wild arugula and forbidden black rice, something called a Toy Box tomato. And the prices! $32 for a pork chop? And $26 for the chef's pasta. There's a beef filet for $46???? For one person?

Mr. Coulter tells us to order anything we want, it's a special celebration. He beams at Rosie, then turns his attention to the menu. What to order? I like salmon, but $33.45? I keep my eyes on the menu, as if studying it, and listen to what the others are considering. Mr. Coulter decides to have the Seared Maple Leaf Duck Breast, with blackberry gastrique, whatever that is. Mrs. Coulter's going for the Honshimeji Mushroom & Spring Vegetable Risotto. Pizza's on the menu. Fancy pizza. "Artisanal" pizza cooked in an 800-degree oven. I'd order pizza, but maybe that seems too everyday for this place?

"What're you going to have?" I half-whisper to Rosie.

"Ummm," she says, checking the menu. "Either the risotto, or a Caesar salad with chicken."

So, okay, the Caesar salad's a good choice, but I'll have mine with grilled shrimp instead of chicken so I won't be a total copycat.

When it's Zoe's turn to order, she says, still slumped down, "Plain pizza." Mrs. Coulter asks if they can get a pizza with only tomato sauce and mozzarella, and the waiter writes what seems a lengthy note on his order pad.

"Hey, Eddie," Rosie says, "Tell Zoe a joke so she can stop being such a grouch."

Zoe sits up a little straighter. "Yeah, Eddie."

Everyone at the table's looking at me. "I can't think of a joke right now."

"C'mon, Eddie!" Zoe says.

"Just tell her any old joke," Rosie whispers.

"Well, okay...What happens when it rains cats and dogs?"

"What?" Zoe says.

"You have to guess."

"Just tell me!" Zoe says.

"Nope. You have to guess. What happens when it rains cats and dogs?"

"Ummm. You could get hit on the head?"

"Nooooo. You might step in a poodle."

Zoe dissolves in laughter, which gets everyone else laughing. "Another one!" she says, pulling at my sleeve.

"Okay, but that's it."

"And one with dessert!"

"Zoe. Stop pestering Eddie," Mrs. Coulter says. "You've got to eat your dinner before you even think about dessert."

"Tell me an elephant joke!" Zoe says.

The pest has been begging for dog jokes lately, so it takes me a minute to pull an elephant joke out of my memory. "Okay. What time is it when an elephant sits on your watch?"

"What time?" Zoe says.

I shake my head.

"Ummm. Is it lunchtime?"

"No. It's time to get a new watch."

Another round of laughter. Zoe laughs at my joke. The rest of us laugh at Zoe laughing at my joke. There's more college talk, and some talk about the raid on those Patriot places. I wasn't the one who brought *that* subject up.

"It's hard to believe all that was going on a few miles away from where we're sitting right now!" Mr. Coulter says.

"I haven't seen any of those Patriot guys at school since the raid," Rosie says. She glances my way, but I'm concentrating on drinking my Sprite. I know she's dying to tell what she's heard from me, but I've sworn her to secrecy.

Mrs. Coulter asks what I'm reading now.

"I finished *The Grapes of Wrath*. Now I'm starting that book you loaned me a while back, *Thunderstruck*. I'm sorry it's taken me so long to get around to it. Do you need it back?"

Mrs. Coulter laughs. "I'd forgotten I'd even loaned it to you.

"I didn't think I'd read it. It's a lot longer than most of the books I read."

"But after the first page?" Mr. Coulter says.

"I kept reading."

"It's compelling, isn't it?" Mrs. Coulter says. "There's so much history in it, but it reads like a novel."

Rosie says, "Starting on the last day of high school, I'm gonna read a book a week. Every week until I go to UOF. Anything I want. I can read anything I want!"

Mrs. Coulter laughs. "That warms a librarian's heart."

"It's been a long time since I read *The Grapes of Wrath*," Mr. Coulter says. "But I still remember how Tom Joad—Tom, right?"

I nod.

"How Tom Joad's mother was so afraid he'd be killed, like the preacher who was killed standing up for the poor people and getting them to stand up for themselves. And then Tom's going to do the same thing. Right? And that idea that we don't have separate souls, we're all part of one big soul. So, even if Tom gets killed, his soul would be everywhere. Right?"

"Yeah, I know the part you're talking about," I say.

"Well, I like that idea, that all of humanity is one big soul instead of a lot of separate, competing souls," he says.

I start to say how I like that idea, too, when the food arrives. And then all we're doing is eating. Which is fine with me because this is the best Caesar salad I've ever tasted in my whole life.

I rest my free hand, under the table, against Rosie's upper leg. She runs a finger down my forearm to the tip of my hand and back again. I move my hand to the inside of her thigh, only the silk of her dress separating skin from skin.

"Another joke!" Zoe calls.

"Let's get our dessert order in first," Mrs. Coulter says.

Rosie takes my hand and moves it from her upper thigh back to a resting place on the table. We sit there, holding hands, as if that's all there is to it. But I know there's more.

"Chocolate soup!" Zoe says.

"Chocolate soup for me, too," Rosie says. "That's what you should have, too," she tells me, "gain more weight back."

We all order chocolate soup, which turns out to be a heavy chocolate sauce served in a soup bowl, with a scoop of "house made" vanilla ice cream floating on top.

With dessert comes one more corny joke, not worth repeating, and a little more talk about what a life-changing experience college will be for Rosie.

When Mr. Coulter looks at the check, he says to Rosie, "I'm sorry, Honey. We just spent your first year's tuition."

Rosie smacks him on the arm. "Not funny, Dad."

After dinner, I drive me and Rosie around for a while, giving the rest of them a chance to settle in with "Modern Family" before we go back to Tilly. Not that Tilly's off bounds or anything, just…awkward.

I take us past William's mom's house to show Rosie where we've been painting.

"It's kind of a creepy neighborhood," she says. "All that graffiti and so much trash in the lot across the street. Isn't his mom afraid she'll get robbed, or mugged, or something?"

"She says she wouldn't want to live anywhere else. People look out for each other."

"It still feels creepy to me."

I drive us over to the San Marino house which Rosie likes better. Then I drive us to a place in Hamilton Heights that we painted last year. I don't know why it's taking me so long to get us back to Rosie's. I've been wanting so much to get into Tilly with Rosie again. Between my slow recovery, and Rosie's study schedule, it's been a while. Now? Maybe I'm kind of nervous? But when Rosie runs her hand from my knee to the top of my thigh, and says she hears Tilly calling to us, well...I get us back there in a hurry.

As much as I'd rather Rosie not go away to college, it's cool how free-spirited she is now that she's been accepted to UOF. Honestly, I'd secretly hoped she *wouldn't* get in, and she'd end up at HHCC, and things could stay the same with us. But the acceptance brought her easy laugh back, and her broad smile, and her warmth, so I get that it's as important for her to go off to college as it is for me to stay here and work.

CHAPTER TWENTY-SEVEN

Transitions

Once Rosie was accepted to UOF and the pressure was off, we spent almost all of our spare time together. After work with William, or after I'd cleaned Joe's studio, or after Rosie's soccer practice or game, we'd get together. Sometimes she'd walk Peppy and Buddy with me, or sometimes we'd hang out with Brent and Brianna at the park. Or we'd play cornhole at Brent's. Usually Meghan and Cameron came for cornhole, too.

Meghan got to be so good at cornhole we started teasing her about getting a cornhole scholarship to M.I.T. She was about as interested in M.I.T. as Brent was, though. She's going to some fashion design school in September. She falls for a guy who wears Toughskins and a tie, and she's going into fashion? Another of the mysteries of Cameron's appeal. But one of Meghan's major interests is Islamic fashion—she says it's the fastest growing fashion market in the U.S. She's not Muslim, but it's a big market.

We did all of the high school senior things—prom, all night party, senior picnic, big graduation ceremony. There were 822 graduates, and the ceremony was on a Friday afternoon in the Hamilton Heights Civic Auditorium. Cameron and the other seniors in the band were already up front, but the rest of us slow-walked down the long aisle to the band playing "Pomp and Circumstance," the way we'd practiced the day before.

After everyone got where they were supposed to be, Mr. Hockney did the welcoming thing—a great occasion, proud day for graduates, also for those who offered love and guidance along the way, etc. Already I was starting to sweat in my polyester cap and gown.

Hockney said that since the beginning, Hamilton High has been a safe and welcoming place to students of diverse ethnic, racial, and religious backgrounds. But, as he was sure we all knew, there'd been some troubling "incidents" over the course of the past school year in which a small group of students were claiming to be the "real Americans," and had bullied others who didn't fit their "real Americans" category.

He went on, "And now, as our graduates prepare to take their next steps in the broader world, and as we all go about our daily lives, the choir seniors, with your help, will honor the real Americans. Please remain standing after the national anthem."

Mr. Taggerty motioned choir members to the front, asked us to stand, and started the band, choir, and audience on "The Star-Spangled Banner."

With "Gave proof to the night," the screen came down from the top of the stage and a huge world map labeled WHERE CHOIR MEMBERS CAME FROM was projected onto it. A bunch of black dots were scattered across Eastern and Western Europe, and a bunch more across the Middle East, Mexico, Central America, Southeast Asia, Africa, China, and Australia. The words to another song came on the screen, in red, over the map. "Please join us," Taggerty said. Sofia played a chord on the piano and the choir started, "This land is your land, this land is my land."

By the end of the first line, everyone was singing along about how the redwoods and rivers, desert and mountains, oceans and wheat fields, all belong to all of us. Pictures of people from all over the world and in all possible colors flashed in front of us, then the dotted map came up again with the last verse of "This land was made for you and me!"

As the choir came back to their seats, the crowd stood clapping and stomping. Hockney smiled, waiting for people to calm down, then introduced Anh Tranh, the Valedictorian.

I don't remember much about what Anh said because during her talk I sat looking at the dots on the map behind her, thinking about my dot in Mexico, and Anh and Phong's dots in Vietnam, Imani's in Africa and Olivia's in Mexico, Rosie's double dots in Mexico and Western Europe, Sofia's in Iran. I'm pretty sure Brent and Cameron's dots would be somewhere in Western Europe.

I like the idea that this land was made for everyone. But if I've learned anything during my senior year, it's that some people really don't like the idea of this land being made for all of us. If they had their way, the only dots on the map would be in the Western Europe section. Sofia's learned that this year, too, though maybe she already knew it. Olivia knows it now. What about the Joad family in "The Grapes of Wrath"? Their dot would have probably been in Western Europe, but they were a different kind of immigrant. Outsiders, even after generations in this country. And that poor trans kid Mario told me about? It didn't matter where that dot would have been. Same with the gay guy the Patriots beat up last year. Still, like Max and I talk about whenever we have one of our sweetness-of-life ice cream times, the world is full of good people. And judging by the crowd's reaction to the song, there are a lot more of us who want this land for all of us than there are who want it only for people like themselves.

I rubbed my thumb over my WWCCD bracelet. One of Cesar Chavez's famous sayings is "Together, all things are possible." Maybe that's what people were clapping and shouting for. Not that this country is for all of us, but that it could be.

The applause for Anh and whatever she'd said brought me back to the now of graduation. Then, after too many pictures and lots of hugs with relatives and friends, and after we'd turned in our hot rented caps and sweaty gowns, we made our way to the parking lot where a caravan of buses waited to drive us to Universal Studios. It took a long time to load the buses because everyone had to be searched before they got in. I bet the security guys ended up with plenty of beer and booze in case they wanted to have their own party.

Universal Studios was fun. I liked seeing the tricks they use for special effects, and the Wizarding World of Harry Potter made Space Mountain at Disneyland look like a kiddie ride. Phong was obsessed with "The Walking Dead" place because he's experimenting with putting zombies into his "Vernon the Cowardly Vampire" stories.

Rosie and I saw everything we could and ate everything we could and walked all over the place. I think the only people who were awake on the way back to Hamilton Heights were the bus drivers. At least, I think they must have been awake because we got back to campus safe. At three in the morning. The best part of grad night, though, was going back to Tilly with Rosie, and sleeping wrapped up with her, and waking up with her when the sun shone through the tiny window. It was the first time we'd ever spent the whole night together, and I'm happy to say, it wasn't the last.

* * * * *

Once school was out, I started working full time with William. Rosie volunteered at a day camp for kids with "special needs." I was happy painting houses and offices, something new every day. Rosie loved what she was doing with the kids. We both had money in our pockets. We went to a couple of concerts, and to the beach almost every Saturday. A few times we took Zoe and Imani to a movie, or Rosie brought Zoe over to play "Frozen" with Imani, which was good, because Imani for sure missed Olivia. The worry of getting deported and being separated from their kids was too much for Carla and Arsenio, so they all went back to Mexico. William keeps complaining that he can't find a good mechanic like Arsenio to do all of the needed repairs on the old pick-up we use for work.

Anyways, Rosie and I had a great summer together. We didn't exactly say this, but I think we made it count because we knew we'd soon be separated by hundreds of miles. But at least until September, when college started, we were together and free and happy. I think most of us after graduation from Hamilton High felt a new sense of freedom. Not Brent, though. Mr. Bruno kept pushing him to try harder for engineering. Because of his position in the engineering company, he could give Brent the step up he never had when he was getting started. "Give Britney my step up," Brent told his dad.

Something happened when Brent won the cornhole tournament and got a taste of life without math pressure, and he was never going back to the old way. The pressure from his dad, though, was so extreme that Brent was miserable. His mom was miserable, too, seeing the misery of her husband and son. So Brent decided everyone would be better off if he made his *Into the Wild* fantasy a reality. He was going to pack up and live in the wilderness, away from everything—not Alaska, but some "River of No Return" place in Idaho.

Cameron and I both tried to talk him out of it, but he wouldn't budge. He'd take a Greyhound to somewhere in Idaho, then hitchhike into the interior, Christopher McCandless style. It was all mapped out. But the evening before his early morning departure plan, his mom came to his room to see if he wanted to add anything to a laundry load. She looked in right as he was zipping up his duffel bag. When she realized what he was doing, she totally freaked.

Mrs. B. called a family meeting. Told the dad she loved him, was so grateful that he loved his work, and that his brains and talent enabled him to make such a good living for all of them, but he *had* to stop trying to turn Brent into an image of himself. She said everyone had a right to find their own path and if he didn't let up on Brent, she wasn't going to stay around to watch him make a mess of things. The three sisters who were home for the weekend cheered and clapped. The dad walked out. Brent unpacked his duffel bag.

Mr. B. stayed away for three days—stayed quiet for another three days after he came back home, then he lightened up. Everybody lightened up. So now, Brent's a happy liberal arts guy on his way to some small college up in Oregon. He'll decide on a major later.

As for Cameron, he left town the day after graduation. He's taking a gap year with another guy from the band. They're backpacking, staying in youth hostels. I got a postcard from him yesterday. They were in Barcelona. Next stop—Portugal.

* * * * *

On Sunday of Labor Day weekend, Rosie and I went up to Lake Gregory. She was leaving for college on Wednesday, and we wanted to make the most of the time we had left. It'd been exactly a year since we started to get acquainted at this lake, a year since we first knew we were interested. So that's the time we count anniversaries from. For a while, Rosie had this thing about what was our *real* anniversary date? Maybe it wasn't the lake day. Maybe we should be counting from our first kiss. Or from when we first said "I love you" to each other? Or, you know, from our first Tilly? But we decided to stay with the lake date because that's when it all started.

Just like a year ago, it was dry and hot, and the lake was a cool relief. We swam straight to our buoy. Rosie reached for it and let it hold her afloat while she scissor-kicked. I treaded water.

"Tell me a joke," she said. "Like, do you remember that corny elephant joke from last year?"

"Why did the elephant take a roll of toilet paper to the party?"

"Because he was a party pooper." She could hardly get the answer out before laughter got the best of her. She was laughing her free laugh, the one that came back to her after she got the acceptance letter from UOF. She was laughing her full out loud musical laugh. I was just laughing and snorting. It wasn't that funny but the laughter stayed for a while. This time, though, there was no Brent to swim out and interrupt us. It was just me and Rosie and a bunch of people we didn't know.

I moved in closer to Rosie, sharing the buoy with her. Then she got all serious.

"It seems like such a long time ago, doesn't it? Sort of like we were still little kids back then, and we're not anymore."

"Yeah, I guess. Maybe because we've been through a lot this year."

Rosie looked away, wiping at her eyes, trying to hide that she was crying but not doing a very good job of it.

"Rosie...Hey...Rosie?"

"It's...I'm scared. I'm scared to go away. I'm scared you'll stop loving me. I'm scared of college. What if I'm not smart enough?"

I wiped her tears away with my hand, which left her cheeks even wetter. "You don't have to go away if you don't want to," I said, getting my hopes up.

She shook her head. We got out and sat side by side on our towels, not talking for a while.

"I won't stop loving you," I tell her. "That'll never happen."

She nodded her head. "I don't know why I'm so scared," she said. "It's what I've always wanted."

"Don't go," I told her.

She shook her head again. "I have to," she said.

"I know," I said, putting my arm around her and pulling her close. And I did know it was right for her to go to UOF, and I also knew I was going to miss her like crazy.

* * * * *

She's been at UOF for three weeks now. We text back and forth a lot. Love texts, and heart texts, and miss you texts. Rosie's probably sent at least a hundred pictures since she's been gone—the creek that runs past their dorms, the room she's sharing with Brianna, the picture of me tacked to the wall over her dresser, the music room, the giant oak tree in the middle of campus, a skinny stray kitten they've taken in and are fattening up. They've named the kitten Simba. I like that. Most days we Facetime, but…not the same.

Hamilton Heights is like a different place with so many of the people I've been around all through high school gone. I know things feel different for Imani, too. Max keeps saying how wrong it was that Carla and Arsenio were forced out of the only home their kids have ever known. They're having a hard time finding a replacement for Carla at Dr. White's office, too. Max says no one can replace Carla. So, I guess we're all missing people right now, but I'm pretty sure nobody's missing anyone as much as I miss Rosie.

Jason's not anyone I miss, but I do sometimes wonder what happened to him. Mario says the FBI gave him a whole new identity—birth certificate, Social Security number, school records, the works. He had surgery on his throat so his voice won't be so squeaky. One of the FBI guys told Mario Jason's voice was like that because back when he was seven or eight, one of his mom's boyfriends got irritated with him and gave him a quick karate chop to the throat. No wonder he rolled up in a ball that day I chopped his throat.

Mario doesn't know where, but Jason's living somewhere in the Midwest with a foster family who doesn't know anything about his Patriot past. Besides the FBI, there's only one other person who knows Jason's past—some social worker or something. How weird would that be?

Not being in school anymore is strange. Like, almost all of my life, the parts that I can remember, I've been in school. And now I'm not. I like working, accomplishing something real, not sitting in bullshit classes pretending to listen to boring stuff. I like putting money in savings and still having plenty left over to spend, but I miss friends.

These days, if there's a patio where we're working, William and I eat our lunch there. If not, we take it to whatever park is closest. We never eat inside on the job because, you know, paint fumes. Usually we talk about the job, or the next job coming up, or maybe some family stuff. Sometimes, though, we just read. I've passed *Thunderstruck* on to William, which was fine with Rosie's mom. It's about Guglielmo Marconi and the invention of the telegraph, and it's also got the story of a murder in it. Honestly, I never thought much about the importance of the telegraph, but it was a really big deal at the time and, really, except for some of the details that I skimmed about conduction and induction and short waves and long waves, it was a real page turner. William probably won't skim.

I'm reading *Just Mercy,* which Vincent passed on to William, and after he read it, William gave to me. It's by this guy, Bryan Stevenson, a lawyer, who works to help death row inmates—almost all are poor, black men. From growing up around Vincent and hearing his stories of trying to help poor people, mostly Mexicans, get fair treatment, I figured out early on that justice isn't exactly equal. And I know that rich people get away with a lot more than poor people, and that black and brown people get stopped by cops a lot more often than white people do. But the cases Stevenson writes about are way beyond anything I might have imagined. Cops tampering with evidence to convict an innocent black man and let the guilty white man go free. Racist district attorneys bribing witnesses to testify against black suspects, and on and on.

"Soul numbing," William said when he handed *Just Mercy* to me. That about says it. On the other hand, though, I know our system of justice works sometimes. The guy who molested me is in prison. Thirty-two Patriots are in prison.

Anyways, lunchtime with William is hella different than lunch on the quad at HH. It's quiet. And clean. And nobody's ragging on me about what I'm eating. Sometimes I miss the noise, though, and the crowd of kids, and Cameron and Brent. Especially Cameron and Brent. Don't get me wrong. I don't want to be back in high school. Maybe I'm still just getting used to my changed life.

As for friends, Phong and I hang out together sometimes. We're turning "Vernon the Cowardly Vampire meets Simba the Courageous Cat" story into a real comic book. It was a big hit in the WriteLight book, and the pest keeps pushing us for the next installment, so maybe it's not too bad.

Phong's going to HHCC—says his parents can't afford to pay for a four-year college, and he's not smart enough for a scholarship. He may transfer after he finishes HHCC. Or maybe two years of college will be enough. He's taking graphic design and advertising and he's already doing some web design work for a couple of small businesses. We might get an apartment together if he gets more work. Or if our comic book turns into a best seller.

As for the White Supremacist shit, hardly anyone showed up for a "White Lives Matter" rally in the park last month, and there hasn't been much hate sign trash since the Patriots were shut down. But then, over the weekend, a bunch of "Protect White America" flyers bordered with "14 Words" were tacked to trees and pinned on bulletin boards at HHCC. Students rushed to tear the signs down and replace them with "Love Not Hate" fliers, but it sucks that the hate signs went up in the first place.

According to Mario, things have mellowed some in Redville. He gets a bigger picture, though, because of his work on the hate crime unit—he says, in the whole country, hate crimes have increased by 17% since the election. How sick is that! But, speaking of the election, I turned eighteen on May 22nd and the next day I registered to vote. Until this past year, I didn't pay much attention to politics. Sure, I liked the previous president, that he talked about hope and everyone working together, but I'd never given much thought to how the person in office has such a great effect on our lives—how they can make things a lot better, or, like now, they can make things a lot worse. It still gets to me that the guy who's president now got 2.8 million votes less than the woman who *should* have been president. That's just wrong. When I vote, I'll be sure to vote for candidates who say they'll fight to change the electoral college system.

In the meantime, William's teaching me how to estimate the costs of a job, materials and labor, and how to write a contract for customers. In another year, I'll have enough experience to apply for a painting contractor's license. I'll need to study a lot if I'm going to pass the test, but I don't mind studying when it has a real-life purpose.

And, speaking of studying, I've signed up for a yoga instructor training class that'll start next month. Tuesday and Thursday nights for six months. I've been leading a class in Joe's studio on Wednesday evenings, but it'll be better to have an official certificate. Joe says I'm a natural. I don't know about that, but I've been doing yoga for half my life now, so it feels natural enough.

What else? Something shifted in me after that attack. I don't think I was *that* close to dying, but it felt like I wasn't that far away, either. Whatever. It's hard to explain, but it's like I appreciate life more now. Not just mine, other people's lives, too. Not just people I care about, either, just … everybody. Like maybe we *are* all part of the same big soul, like Tom Joad said. Like we're all connected. But, then, does that mean I'm connected to the Patriots? Never mind. It's not just hard to explain. It's impossible. Maybe it's just that I'm more grown up? Anyway, it's a good shift. That much I know.

Here's something else that's good. In three-weeks-feels-like-three-years, I'm driving up to UOF for an overnight with Rosie. Brianna's coming home that weekend, and we can have their room to ourselves. Yesterday, Rosie texted a picture of eight six-packs of lubricated condoms that her mom stuffed into the narrow drawer of Rosie's bedside table.

The picture caption was "Can't wait!" with lots of heart emojis.

Sometimes I get scared, like our lives are going in different directions, and what if Rosie stops loving me? And then I look back over our texts and do that thing that I learned to do a long time ago. I stay in the now. The now where Rosie loves me.

ABOUT THE AUTHOR

Marilyn Reynolds is the author of eleven books in the popular and award-winning realistic teen fiction True-to-Life Series from Hamilton High. She has also written a book for educators, *I Won't Read and You Can't Make Me: Reaching Reluctant Teen Readers*. She has a variety of published personal essays to her credit and was nominated for an Emmy for the teleplay of *Too Soon for Jeff.*

Ms. Reynolds worked with reluctant learners and teens in crises at a southern California alternative high school for more than two decades. She remains actively involved in education through author presentations to middle and high school students ranging from struggling readers to highly motivated writers who are interested in developing work for possible publication. She also presents staff development workshops for educators and is often a guest speaker for programs and organizations that serve teens, parents, teachers, and writers.

She lives in Sacramento where she enjoys neighborhood walks, visits with friends and family, movies and dinner out, and the luxury of reading at odd hours of the day and night.